THE ETERNAL STRUGGLE

TWO WORLDS ONE WAR

JAMES ROURKE

Open Books
PRESS

Published by Open Books Press, USA
www.openbookspress.com

An imprint of Pen & Publish, Inc.
Bloomington, Indiana
(812) 837-9226
info@PenandPublish.com

www.PenandPublish.com

ISBN: 978-0-9846359-2-4

This book is printed on acid free paper.

Printed in the USA

This book is dedicated to my wife, Shannon Rourke,
who lovingly supports me in all that I do.
I love you, Shan.
Thanks for everything.

Acknowledgements

There are many people who lent their time and talents to the creation of this book. My agent, Andy Whelchel, deserves praise for his perseverance and patience. He never stopped working to get this book to print and managed my "writer's neurosis" with great care and skill.

Jesse Coull, Sandra Donovan-Driscoll, Jay Driscoll, Phil Marchesseault and Linda Lamothe all offered insightful reflection and editorial aid during various stages of the writing process. That these English teachers took the time to do this despite their workloads is greatly appreciated. Lorraine Dooley and Karen Davenport-Diaz routinely offered their perspectives as history teachers and lent their support when the road to publication became rocky.

My mother, Virginia Rourke, and brother, Timothy Rourke, also offered valuable insight. I truly appreciate Tim's help as he struggles on the road to publication himself. I look forward to holding one of his books in the near future.

Special thanks go to Alysha Carmody who teaches in the Norwich Free Academy's visual arts department. Her students participated in a contest to create the book's cover. I would like to congratulate the three finalists Leoness Leon, Dan Cellucci, and Matt Vocatura. Leoness Leon's submission was used as the basis of the cover. Congratulations, Leoness!

I would like to thank Kristie Leonard, the director of Norwich Free Academy's Land Library, for all her support and ideas regarding the book's promotion.

One former student in particular was instrumental in the editing of the manuscript. Abby Larkin read the manuscript as a high school student granting me a valuable teenage point of view on the story.

And lastly, very special thanks to my wife, Shannon, who had a ring side seat from which she witnessed the seven-year struggle to publication. Many rejection letters were received over that time and Shan refused to let me give up or to give up on me.

Prologue

From the journal of Niccolo Bontecelli:

Sometimes I find it odd that I still write my thoughts down as I did on Earth. I suppose the routine brings me comfort, not that I suffer much here in Limbo. Although, to be honest, the length of my stay continues to cause me some concern. So many souls visit this place and move quickly to Heaven, while I stay behind. As I look in on Earth, I see the year is 2072, making it over five centuries since my bodily death. Five hundred years at the edge of paradise, but never allowed in. I should be angrier I suppose, but I only feel a faint sadness.

Perhaps my current melancholy has been brought on by the recent ascension of one of my charges: the 136th soul I can honestly claim to have personally aided to paradise. Every departure brings me joy yet I wonder why can I not help myself? Is the joy I feel for my students somehow keeping me here? Do I enjoy my role in Limbo too much? Do I even enjoy my role here or is it merely familiar and, therefore, safer than leaping to the unknown that I may not be ready for or worthy of? Such questions may be difficult to answer, but they certainly can never be answered unless uttered or written.

Alas, these puzzles will have to wait. Danielle and Dylan are due to orient a new group of souls soon and I must be there to evaluate them. Dylan is close to completing his task; today could well be his last in Limbo. Will his exodus bring me closer to my own?

Chapter 1
Welcome to your Afterlife

"Welcome to Limbo. My Name is Dylan." The speaker was a bearded man who seemed to be in his mid sixties. He stood on a stage looking up at an audience seated in a tiered lecture hall. The faces before him, which numbered well into the hundreds, wore a mix of complete bewilderment and apprehension. Their clothes were all reminiscent of their previous life, the sparse garb of a Papua New Guinea Huli tribesman on full display alongside the pressed suit of the Wall Street broker. It was a sight that, despite all his years in Limbo, brought a gentle smile to Dylan's face as he began his presentation.

"All of you are newborns recently conceived when your bodies, the physical shell that so many of you thought was the end all of life, broke down. Do not concern yourself with how you came to be here, but rather what to do now that you are here. It is my pleasure to explain your options to you." As Dylan spoke his smile faded, but his voice was inviting and placid. His soothing tone reduced the shock many newcomers to Limbo felt more effectively than his carefully selected words. His eyes scanned the crowed before him adding to the effect that his words were spoken to each distinct individual. This was not merely a presentation for group consumption.

"The good news, barring any unsightly accidents, is that Heaven awaits you all—in due time, of course. Some past errors, bad habits and poor judgments must be amended."

Dylan stopped speaking for the sole purpose of checking the spectators' mood. New arrivals' reactions to Limbo ran the gamut from quietly curious to complete bewilderment. In Dylan's experience bewilderment was never good, for it often prevented the audience from not only hearing necessary information but also reduced the ability to understand even the most basic concepts. The two seconds he hesitated was enough time to determine that paralyzing disorientation was not an issue with this group. All eyes were focused on the stage. Some eyes were wider than other. Some lips were being sucked in as the listener strained to integrate their unexpected arrival in this mysterious place. Some individuals leaned back in their chairs, attempting and failing to appear at ease, while others were leaning forward in their seats. All shared one common trait; their eyes were trained on Dylan. "Quietly curious," Dylan thought as he resumed his orientation duties.

"There are two methods available to perform this task. The first is to exit through the doors in the back of the auditorium. They lead to, what can be considered, the reincarnation center, where you will be sent back to Earth and inhabit a new body. Please understand…" the turning of heads and muffled conversation caught Dylan's attention. He changed his focus without breaking his cadence or tone "…that I am trying to explain some important information and it would be easier without the commotion in the back of the room. Do we have a question?"

A mumbled conversation in the back of the auditorium ended and the embarrassed participants hastily elected a spokesman.

"I…ah…well, that is…I am an atheist and how can this…?"

Another man leapt to his feet and interjected, "and I am a Christian and I am very uncomfortable, why…?"

With a look that combined exasperation and yet a complete lack of surprise, Dylan raised his hands as if stopping traffic. It was obvious that this was not the first time he had to quell some discomfort brought about by his explanation.

"Please allow me a second to address that common, but very important, concern. I am well aware of the dogma all new souls cling to upon arrival. Let me be the first to apologize to all atheists for the fact that, yes, there is an afterlife—sorry to let you down." The sarcastic barb was softened by the playful glint in Dylan's eye and the wry smile that appeared on his face. A handful of audience members, taking themselves far too seriously, maintained an air if indignation. A vast majority of the room took the witticism for what it was. A few particularly inquisitive souls sensed the concealed self-deprecation in Dylan's remark. Eyes still alight, Dylan continued.

"In addition, for my Christian friends, I apologize for reincarnation and the lack of pearly gates. To the Buddhist, there is, and you are in fact, a soul—yet you were indeed no soul while your host body functioned. To the strict, orthodox Muslim there will be no dancing virgins and to the Hindu there is the decision, your personal choice, not to be reincarnated. Your karma has brought you here but it does not dictate your path from this room. There are no debates to be had—

limbo is what it is, your theories not withstanding. It takes most new souls one to three earthly years to merely accept limbo for what it is. The sooner you truly accept this place, the sooner you can begin the necessary work to leave. Your final detoxification starts with acceptance."

The souls in the room were almost uniform in their body language, leaning forward, not daring to miss a word. Dylan took note of their attentiveness and continued.

"The first item new souls struggle to accept is the fact that no world religion has ever been completely right or wrong. The originator, who is currently using the name Rovac Zaypoq, wants to be known, but finite minds have great difficulty grasping the infinite. Rovac reveals himself in glimpses, restraining himself so as not to destroy the psyche of those who sense his presence. People receive these small bits of information and interpret the best they can. The depth of Rovac's being seems too great for one reality, so some cultures dichotomized him into watered down pantheons, hence your Greek or Nordic religions. During the Roman Empire, a small group of people felt the divine presence and embraced what their mentor called the Holy Spirit while other followers embraced the Father. Centuries before this, in China, a man named Lao-Tzu felt the divine spirit and called it the Tao, while in the same breathe pointing out no Earthly name could truly describe the force he felt. Regardless, he dedicated his life to understanding what he experienced and embraced the calming ebb and flow of the Tao. Buddha touched the great unborn and Confucius, at the age of fifty, recognized its unmistakable pull. Atheists often feel the great gap between creator and created, but fail to sense the divine presence in the nothingness and embrace non-existence rather than sacred emptiness. Many believers never have the courage to enter that void. Therefore many atheists stand, unknowingly, on the brink of an encounter with an aspect of Rovac, closer to eternity than many 'believers'."

The information Dylan provided caused small conversations to spontaneously begin throughout the room. Some of these conversations were quite intense while others were subdued. People shared moments of personal insights with complete strangers while others sat undisturbed in personal contemplation.

Dylan patiently allowed the buzz in the room to linger; knowing any attempt to quell its rise too early would be ineffective. As more and more eyes turned back to him he continued, strongly projecting his voice at first and, as more and more minds turned his way, resuming his more casual tone.

"On Earth, people feel compelled to adopt one doctrine or another, clinging to the need to belong to the right group or the need to project certainty rather than the desire to understand. The necessity to accept that you know nothing and grow as a spiritual being is anathema to many earth bound souls and even limits your growth in Limbo. As you are new here, it is expected that you still cling to some Earthly limitations—the very limitations that make limbo necessary."

Hands shot up and small conversations erupted throughout the hall before the last words were even spoken. Dylan pinched his nose and let out a small breath, "The inevitable," he whispered more to himself than anyone, "has occurred."

Raising his hands Dylan quieted everyone without speaking a word. Despite his humble appearance and easy manners he had full command of the room. The last conversation came to a mumbling halt and Dylan spoke. "You obviously have questions. Please raise your hands and I will answer them all. All right…from the front please." Dylan pointed at a woman who stood and spoke.

"Who is Rovac Zaypoq? Is that…?"

"Yes," Dylan answered. "That is the being, the force, the divine essence that you call God is currently using. He, for lack of more effective vocabulary, loves the names various world cultures throughout history have assigned him and changes his name occasionally paying homage to the creativity of people. His current name, which he has been using for approximately four centuries, was created by the shortening of his previous name Re Olorun Vishnu Allah Conticciviracocha Zeus Amaterasu YahwehPangu Odin Quetzalcoatl."

Dylan looked around the room as he was speaking. His explanation of Rovac Zaypoq's name caused the withdrawal of a number of hands. A look of satisfaction crossed his face, but did not make a home there. After scanning the room Dylan called upon an elderly man to his right. The gentleman stood and adjusted his worn, tweed suit. Once he completed his adjustments he voiced his sincere question.

"Why, if I am in fact a soul…why do I feel no different than I did on Earth?"

Dylan's initial response was a subtle nod; a silent sign that he felt the question was a good one and a positive step away from explaining dogmatic beliefs and labels.

"I could answer that question, but if you look to my left you see a door. On the other side of that door is another theater where another presenter will speak to you. He or she is required to give you information pertinent to the question you just asked. I have no desire to detract from their presentation so I ask you to be patient—your question will be answered in due time."

"Thank you," the questioner said as he gave his jacket a final tug and sat. Dylan offered a sincere smile in response as he searched the room for the next question.

"The angry looking man in the middle row—your question please."

"Sorry if I look angry but how can you call Christianity a limitation?"

"When did I do that?" inquired Dylan, fighting the urge to roll his eyes.

"Earlier you said…"

"Earlier I said Earthly limitations. You took my words and twisted them into what you wanted to hear—allowing yourself to feel persecuted and indignant. It will behoove you, and greatly reduce the duration of your stay, if you improve your auditory skills and focus on having an open mind instead of a suspicious or easily offended one."

Dylan's strong and unapologetic tone caught some audience members off guard. Despite their ages, they were all new to Limbo and Dylan reminded himself of this reality. A quick glance to the floor, almost undetectable as he turned to his right was enough time for Dylan to recompose himself and continue in a cordial tone.

"By Earthly limitations I also meant human limitations. Humanity is limited, by time, circumstances and a myriad of events and forces that fill your days. Almost all souls leave Earth traumatized by the experience of being trapped in a mortal shell. Limbo, in its simplest sense, is a detox center for souls. Some stay to be 'detoxed' while some souls, not just Hindus and Buddhists by the way, use the reincarnation center in the back…if I may continue my planned comments?"

The silence and complete lack of raised hands in the hall was answer enough.

"As I was saying, the doors in the back lead to the reincarnation center. Souls seeking to prepare for Heaven, but still craving the tension of humanity may depart for Earth via that door." Some people started to rise as he quickly added, "-after I am done providing you the information you need." The impatient participants quickly sat and Dylan, mildly perturbed, resumed his discourse.

"Before leaving for Earth you will choose three talents to bestow on your new host; hence some people seem 'naturally gifted' at certain activities. Of course, free will dictates the host can reject the gifts you attempt to confer—resulting in unfulfilled potential. Also know this: when your new host dies, the soul you currently are will be changed and resemble the new host much more than you, the gift giver. The soul sitting before me will be unpredictably altered and, in many ways, unknown despite continued existence. You will, however, experience the highs and lows of mortal life, and provide gentle guidance from within; intuition and gut feelings have an origin after all."

Heads bobbed and a chorus of 'ahhhs' rained down on the stage as the entire audience connected with the concept of intuition. No hands were raised, however, so Dylan completed his lecture.

"This concludes my presentation; those seeking reincarnation please exit via the back door. Those seeking to stay in Limbo use the door to my left. Once you leave this room, your destination cannot change. Limbo or reincarnation—choose now."

"But," a soul that appeared no more than seventeen shouted, "shouldn't we know more about Limbo before deciding?"

Dylan tensed up for a second as he glanced at another man taking the stage. The new figure laughed and raised a single finger—mouthing the words "so close" at Dylan. Dylan smirked and shook his head at the newcomer while answering the question, "Free will is quite a burden. Decide please."

Dylan shook hands with the next speaker, Robert. He offered no more direction to the new souls for it was time for them to make, and live with, their first choice in Limbo. Dylan, ignoring a small group of souls gathered at the stage, engaged Robert in quiet conversation. Little did the departing souls suspect the unusual circumstances that kept Dylan in Limbo. Dylan, like Robert, was a former college professor—who blamed every unproductive class session on his students, never realizing his own inability to communicate clearly with the prepared students; choosing to focus on the ineptitude of the slothful and disorganized.

As his Earthly years passed, Dylan grew increasingly arrogant and distant from his charges. There were no longer any diamonds in the rough for Dylan, only the rough. Upon retirement he was much less a teacher than an unfulfilled curmudgeon—lamenting the lack of quality students he had rather than the lack of quality he brought to the students.

Dylan's goal, and the key to his passage to Heaven, was to introduce a group to Limbo with enough clarity that the audience would not need to ask more than five questions. He had been working this room for almost five years and today he had the assemblage discharged in the requisite time, until the sixth question was shouted after he dismissed them.

Robert and Dylan shared a quiet laugh as the students left, recalling Dylan's first effort that produced 187 questions. They also recalled in amazement the story of how Socrates required only three weeks to move from his role as presenter in Limbo to liberated soul in Heaven. Robert, who had been hearing 8-12 question for nearly a year prepared for the next assembly. Dylan watched the sixth questioner leave the room, oblivious to the ramifications of his query.

"I could use a drink or two," groaned Dylan. "I almost had it."

"You need more than two," Robert agreed, then he launched one last barb on his friend, "I would say you need six."

Dylan let out a strong laugh and left the stage as the last souls in the room departed the hall, more choosing reincarnation over the uncertainty of Limbo.

Chapter 2
Initial Revelations

Of the 750 souls who listened to Dylan's presentation, 327 entered the next theater. As before, they sat facing a stage, only two people prepared to address them this time.

"Hello everyone, I am Danielle," the energetic woman on stage said as she waved the group to the front rows. "This presentation is very important so please come to the front so you can hear everything. I need your attention and you need to know this information. All right?"

Some individuals looked at the Danielle as they sat midway between the curved wall of the room and the stage. Few people sat in the front rows. Most seemed unmoved by Danielle's attempts to usher them closer, which consisted of hollow praise for those who ventured into the vacant seats.

"Good for you," she said to a lone individual seated directly in front of her.

"The more interested people always sit up front," she called out to no one in particular. "We could also move a little faster."

The souls hurried to their seats, most not noticing the second figure on stage. He was slowly shaking his head with disappointment. Danielle's greetings and invitations left him cold. Her manner and word choice made it clear that she and her presentation were of prime importance, not the new souls. This need, to be the most important person in the room was Danielle's fatal flaw and overcoming it would allow her final passage into Heaven. The five years she had spent in Limbo saw improvement, but not enough—her stay could be longer than originally anticipated. It was almost sad that, although, she held a leadership position in life, she was no leader—at least not one people would choose to follow; rather they had to because of circumstances. Until Danielle accepted this shortcoming and improved it, she would find the passage to eternal bliss blocked: arrogance and pretense have no home eternal.

"Congratulations on making the choice to remain in Limbo—Heaven awaits all of you!" Danielle looked around the room, hoping her positive exclamation would receive more of a response than it did. She hid her disappointment, almost effectively, behind a well-rehearsed spontaneous smile and continued.

"Here in Limbo we all have certain faults and bad habits that must be broken in order to gain residence in Heaven. The method of doing so varies from person to person. For example, Dylan, in the last hall, was never a great communicator and blamed others, particularly his students, for not understanding him. When misunderstood, he grew angry and disenchanted with his audience. He opted to improve this skill here in Limbo and, once it is refined, he will move on to Heaven."

Jonathan, the soul whose final question lengthened Dylan's stay, spoke up, "I think he did a great job and must be close to achieving his goal. He couldn't have been much clearer."

Danielle, who was already aware of the impact this young man had on Dylan's after-life smiled, and said, "I will pass that on to Dylan—I am sure it will please him to know you felt that way. Now, there are countless methods to 'detox', as Dylan puts it, here in Limbo. Over the next couple of weeks, you will learn of them and, eventually, choose one. Some will choose before others for, as long as you think this is some sort of dream or somehow an amazingly elaborate hallucination, you can not begin your work."

Some souls, who personified the mindset Danielle described, bristled under the reality of her words. She noticed, but did not acknowledge the distress her statement caused until a beleaguered individual asked, or rather, pleaded for a clarification. "I understand I am a soul," pointed out the middle-aged man, "but why do I feel so—normal. Shouldn't I be able to fly or something?"

The elderly gentleman who originally asked this question of Dylan leaned forward, anticipating the answer. He also wished Dylan had provided one, as he found Dylan's manner and tone much more palatable than Danielle's.

Danielle looked at the face of the worried individual with a compassion that bordered on comforting before she returned to her usual position as the purveyor of special knowledge, not a human among equals.

"Here in Limbo souls act very much as they did when intertwined with their mortal shells, only without the interference of Hell bound individuals, or the manipulation of augmenters—which will be explained later. The lack of these wicked forces, combined with the presence of outstanding individuals, allows for potentially rapid growth and quick transition to Heaven. The average stay in Limbo is thirty years—which when compared to infinity is the blink of an eye. You still can eat and drink—for those activities brought your soul pleasure on Earth, although you do not actually need any nutrients. Also weight gain and intoxication is impossible here, which I suppose is both a blessing and curse."

The weight gain comment was meant to draw laughter and it well could have if Danielle had delivered the line correctly. Instead of laughter an uncomfortable silence fell over the room as the audience awaited, and expected, only information, not entertainment from Danielle. Disturbed, but undaunted, she continued her presentation.

"You will also feel fatigue, sorrow and disappointment in Limbo. As for flying, that is not a skill we have developed here in Limbo. In Limbo, souls travel from here to there by walking or using ships. The longer you stay, however, the more talents you will develop."

Danielle almost nodded and added, "O.K.?" to her statement, but held it back, which pleased her co-worker. Those one-word questions added to the end of statements are reminiscent of how a parent speaks to a petulant child, not how adults ought to communicate.

A middle aged woman suddenly blurted out another question. "Has Limbo always existed or did Go…I mean, Rovac, create it?"

"Rovac undoubtedly began the process which created the universe and Earth. How you may ask? No one is one hundred percent sure because he was the only one there—although he has let on that some theories are close to accurate. Regardless, people inhabit the Earth and souls inhabit people. Rovac creates but will not control. The choices you make shape your destiny and the course of history much more so than a Heavenly plan. Rovac is surely many things, but definitely not a micro-manager. He grants you potential and yearns for you to find purpose, find the treasures already held and to make sound decisions. No Heavenly hosts, however, interfere with free will—it is forbidden; even Lucifer respects this rule."

The unexpected revelation that Lucifer exists caused various levels of distress in the audience. Uneasy mumbling and glances abounded. On some faces looks of fear or shock appeared. Anxious chatter rippled across the room. Pockets of individuals stood to shout their thoughts to strangers sitting many rows behind them. Danielle realized mentioning Lucifer's name so early in the presentation was a mistake, but she continued, soothing the room as she did. As she spoke souls returned to their seats and refocused their attention on the stage.

"Lucifer does indeed exist and he was cast from Heaven, never to return. The time of Lucifer's banishment coincided with the creation of Limbo. Earth's history rolled forward as expected, dinosaurs, ice ages, and the appearance of man taking place. Humans developed quicker than expected. In fact, people were doing so well that around the time of the European Renaissance Lucifer grew worried. You see, when people obtain the highest level of spiritual development possible, the experiment known as humanity will be deemed a success and all worthy souls will reside in paradise and the Earth will no longer be necessary. Earth, Hell, and consequently Lucifer, will cease to exist."

The audience now appeared more perplexed than concerned; the information Danielle offered creating more bewilderment than enlightenment. Souls shouted questions in the hopes of instant answers.

"Humanity is an experiment?"

"Successful people will bring about the end of the Earth?"

"Lucifer doesn't want the world to end?"

The second figure on the stage caught Danielle's attention and, eyes wide with displeasure, signaled her to continue. Danielle nodded and turned back to the crowd, which was still shouting questions. The litany of voices created a single incomprehensible din.

Danielle took a deep breath and addressed the increasingly anxious crowd.

"Rovac created the Earth, Heaven and humanity. Human history has unfolded over the centuries with people occupying almost every continent on the globe." Danielle stopped speaking for a moment to glare down a hand she suspected was going to interject a fact about Antarctica. As the hand sank to its youthful owner's side she continued.

"As people spread there was concern their differences would overwhelm their similarities and humanity would drift further and further from the higher callings of the eternal. When the human spirit reunites willingly with the eternal spirits, humankind will reach its pinnacle—Earth will no longer be necessary and all will live in paradise. That is not truly an experiment. I suppose it is destiny, the only destiny that actually exists."

Danielle paused for just a moment, startled by the thought she had just given voice to. She glanced over her shoulder at the second individual on the stage, still standing unobtrusively behind her. She allowed herself to be momentarily distracted, as he appeared to jot a note on a piece of paper. Danielle refocused herself and spoke.

"Lucifer desperately wants to prevent this from happening, but knows he cannot—therefore he seeks the next best alternative, delaying the reunification of humanity and spirituality insuring his prolonged malignant existence. As Lucifer feared, people progressed at an alarming rate. Before the year 1500 most cultures not only embraced, but had a clear articulation of how to form at least some level of spiritual connection—whether the great traditions of China, the use of mediums in Great Zimbabwe or the overwhelming respect for nature and the great spirits we see in the natives of North America. Great works of literature blessed Europe. The Heian age in Japan saw a respect for the intellectual and artistic skills of women that the world rarely experienced to that point, perhaps since. China's technology was incredibly advanced. Africa supplied more gold and salt to the world than any other continent—who would have suspected these respected traders would eventually become traded themselves as slaves. The golden age of the world was occurring—the experiment was close to over—just two or three more millenniums were needed."

A startled voice called out, "Two or three millenniums constitutes almost over?"

"The timetable of infinity moves differently than the finite schedules you are used to on Earth. The thought of the end being 'near' filled Lucifer with dread so he launched a new plan, designed to extend his existence indefinitely. To discuss this I present to you the man who holds the dubious distinction of being the longest current resident of Limbo—Niccolo Bontecelli."

Niccolo stepped forward, a powerful presence in this and, one would think, any environment. His eyes carried a strength that seemed transcendent, even to those who would be his peers. It was difficult to tell if his feet actually touched the ground as he moved to the front of the stage. His voice filled the room with uncommon power.

"Lucifer's desperation caused him to embrace an audacious strategy. In approximately the year 1550—he liberated 20,000 select souls from Hell with a specific mission; conquer as much of Limbo as possible and maintain a Hellish foothold in the realm. The damned overran two of Limbo's nine plains before our forces rallied and halted there spread."

As he spoke, Niccolo clapped his hands above his head and brought them slowly to his side, causing a blinding flash to illuminate the room. When the audience's power of sight returned they witnessed the spread of the damned into the regions of Tolmace, since renamed Nafarhel, and Galiktus. A narrators voice accompanied the hologram, speaking to their minds, not their ears:

The souls in Nafarhel were conducting their normal business—running the taverns, orientating new souls, performing construction and the numerous other tasks used to prepare souls for eternity. None expected the fissure that suddenly ripped open in the ground or the aggressive attack that followed.

The souls of Limbo, caught completely unprepared for this unprecedented attack fell before the invaders without great resistance. Captives were taken to the hastily constructed detention center, named the Hall of the Impaler. The hall was so-named to honor one of the generals who led the invasion Vlad the Impaler, also know as Vlad Dracula, the Romania prince who became the inspiration for the Dracula legends. Alexander the Great, Christopher Columbus, Ch'in Shi Huang-ti and Genghis Khan were amongst the other generals. All of these men of violence and conquest revealed in the carnage they brought to Nafarhel and their freedom from the malevolent depths from whence they came. The frightful horde quickly subjugated the area. Souls cannot die, but they can be detained and the captured residents of Limbo were used as slave labor, forced to reshape the landscape into the image of the generals choosing. Grim castles rose and military barracks completed.

The residents of Limbo grew fearful because of the attack, uncertain what the invaders next action would be. A collection of heroes, those who had been freedom fighters in life became the challengers of darkness in death. Men like William Wallace of Scotland, the Celtic warrior Veringetorix, the Roman Emperor Octavian, Sundiata of the Mali kingdom in Africa and the great shogun Minamoto Yoritomo united to confront the invaders. They quickly learned that the spiritual energy used to create solid light rakes, shovels and pulleys, the mechanisms of creation, could also be used to makes spears, sword and shield, weapons of war.

While Limbo prepared for battle, the plains of Galiktus

were evacuated, allowing the invaders to claim two of the Limbo's nine geographic locations. The invaders' success predictably bolstered the monstrous egos of Alexander the Great and Genghis Kahn, and the two conspired to invade Troothgnase, the next available target. Vlad the Impaler, to his credit, counseled his allies against the invasion, for they had already achieved their objective, to gain for Lucifer a foothold in Limbo. Ego and arrogance have often conspired against sound judgment and the armies of Octavian counted on this. He conscripted Leonidas, Spartan general and tragic hero of Thermopylae, to aid Sundiata in the defense of Troothgnase. The forces of Limbo stood victorious, and each felled opponent was dragged back to Hell by black tentacles and talons.

Veringetorix and Minamoto then performed a feint into Galiktus, hoping not to reclaim the territory, but rather draw the troops of Vlad the Impaler and Huang-ti from Nefaral, providing the opportunity for William Wallace to steal into the Hall of the Impaler and free the captured souls, for no soul destined for Heaven deserved to be trapped indefinitely in that sorrowful place. The plan worked well, until Columbus in his floating ship, *Twilight*, intercepted Wallace and almost captured him.

Columbus was distracted in his attempt to apprehend the Scotsman by a former subordinate, Niccolo Bontecelli, who had accompanied Columbus on his second voyage to the new world. Niccolo and Columbus engaged in an aerial battle as Wallace withdrew from Galiktus, leading the prisoners to freedom. Unfortunately, Niccolo's skill and vessel did not match his courage and Columbus forced his one-man ship aground, taking his former crewman captive. Niccolo languished in the Hall of the Impaler for 270 years, freed thanks to the wit and guile of a newcomer to Limbo, George Washington.

After Wallace's escape, the forces of Limbo held the line along the border of Galiktus, preventing further encroachment. With this foothold in Limbo, Lucifer launched his underhanded scheme to prevent the development of humankind, therefore preventing the ultimate victory of good over evil.

The holograms ceased and the narrator's voice silenced. Niccolo spoke to the astonished audience.

"Lucifer sends new souls to the lands of Nafarhel and Galiktus on a regular basis. You see Limbo has a direct connection to Earth, something both Heaven and Hell lack—it is the conduit from the spiritual to the temporal world. Ancient beings, angels for example, can reach Earth without Limbo, but souls need Limbo to make contact. The souls of the damned, whom we have dubbed augmenters, endeavor to distract humans from the higher callings of free will and focus on the baser elements of the human condition. The more successful these individuals the more time they stay out of Hell, free from torture and misery. To become, and remain, an augmenter is the goal of many residents of Hell. The better their performance, the more time they are rewarded with time out of the abyss and the more centuries they affix to Lucifer's life. Rumor has it when they fail, Lucifer tortures them in ways unprecedented in the annals of eternity."

Niccolo paused for a moment, as the audience grew increasingly tense. An image had formed above Niccolo, demons ripping their talons into chained human bodies. Entrails, limbs and organs littered the floor at the demons clawed feet. "A struggle without casualties is no struggle," Niccolo whispered as, almost wistfully, he watched the gruesome carnage until it faded from view. He continued, cognizant of how shocking the images that accompanied his stories could be to new comers, and yet generally indifferent to how those in the room were responding.

"What these augmenters do, specifically, is single out individual humans, pinpoint their weakness and magnify it so the weakness becomes the person's dominant trait. Distrust, pride, intolerance, prejudice, fear and self-centeredness are but some of the characteristics the augmenters attack. Worse, all the individuals inflicted with the inflated trait often influence other humans in a negative manner, becoming unwitting augmenters on their own accord. Animosity replaced forgiveness in some people. Power became more important in some individuals, even in entire cultures than cooperation. Deceit replaced honesty. The need to appear correct or important replaced the need to actually act with nobility. All the while lengthening Lucifer's life."

A hand rose in the audience and Niccolo stopped his lesson for the question. "Didn't God...I mean... Rovac take some sort of action? Isn't Lucifer cheating by doing this?"

"That question," Niccolo answered, "like all the others in your minds, will be answered tomorrow when we reconvene in the morning here at Martin Luther's hall in the center of the city of Tecktoral. You have heard much today—time to relax and acquaint yourselves with something other than a lecture hall. Leave through the doors to my left and return tomorrow with your questions. If you fear forgetting your question, just write it down."

"Excuse me," a middle-aged woman called tentatively; "write it on what—we have no paper."

"Very true," said Niccolo, somewhat amused by his own over-sight. "Actually you all have paper, if you want it. Watch and listen. As stated in the presentation, spiritual energy can take the form of solid light and form almost anything you can visualize—paper for ex-ample."

Niccolo put his hand together and slowly separated them a sheet of shimmering light filled the space between his hands. He then snatched the "paper" from the air and held it aloft for all to see. He then took his finger and, in large letters, wrote his name on the paper, as if ink were flowing from his fingertips.

"This is my favorite part," he stated as he slapped the paper be-tween his hands causing it to disappear. Closing his eyes to concen-trate for a second Niccolo snapped the fingers of his right hand and the paper, with his name still on it, appeared in his hand. "Go now, tour Tecktoral and practice your light manipulation—it is a skill you will need to develop regardless of the method of 'detox' you choose."

The souls left the hall tentatively, unsure what to expect, but posi-tive they wanted to learn more.

Chapter 3
Presidential Problems
and Earthly Concerns

If Maxwell Grahm had learned one thing serving as President Blaylock's chief of staff the past three and a half years, it was you never knew what to expect when entering the Oval Office on a Monday morning. This fact was magnified now that it was July and it was anyone's guess who would win the election of 2072.

"Good Morning, Mr. President," Maxwell said with formality as he entered the Oval Office.

"It is the morning, Max—but hardly what I would classify as 'good', or even average," replied the weary President.

"Been up awhile, sir?" Max asked the question already knowing the answer.

"Four a.m. Great sunrise today. Hope it is not the high point of my day."

Max smiled in what he hoped to be a reassuring manner, "I am sure it won't be—we have no global disasters planned for today."

"Saints be praised; now if we could just find a way to do something about these numbers," President Blaylock slapped a copy of the *New York Times* onto his desk as he completed his sentence.

Maxwell picked up the paper and read the banner *Third Party, First President?* The headline confirmed the administration's worst fears; throughout the past month, the Self-Determination Party's candidate, Drew McClure, had been surging in the polls. Over the weekend McClure became the front-runner in the polls: 38% of Americans surveyed said they would vote for the independent candidate, 35% for the President and 25 % for Democratic candidate William Casey.

"I will not be the first incumbent President to lose the office to a...an upstart third party! Particularly when the standard bearer of that party is an arrogant, condescending ass hole! Better to lose to that moronic clown William Casey—at least he represents a powerful party, even if he is not a strong man. And you know the worst part? All those indecisive fence sitters out there will vote for McClure because of his lead in the polls. Heaven forbid they think for themselves. A choice exists—a leader with an established record, a preening clown, or a sniveling moron and the undecided will vote for clown because he is the frontrunner! They will vote that way just so they can say they backed the winner!"

The point that the electorate was being exceptionally discerning and not accepting the inevitable victory for one of the two major parties, or bowing completely out of the political process, seemed somehow lost on both men in the room. In reality, President Blaylock, like most politicians, loved unthinking sheep—provided they belong to the right party. The "indecisive fence sitters" did not upset the President; it was the perception Drew McClure "stole" both conservative and liberal voters. If only liberals jumped to the Self-Determination Party, Blaylock could embrace the party as a testament to American work ethic and perseverance.

Blaylock, if not engaged in the fight for his professional life and legacy, might have acknowledged the Self-Determination Party as a true political phenomenon. The S.D.P was a grass roots movement started in 2024 and had worked for fifty years to become the longest lived and most legitimate third party in the history of the United States. Their candidate in the election 2068 was the first third party candidate since Theodore Roosevelt to win electoral votes. Still, the party was seen as an unwanted nuisance, not a true threat. At least not until Drew McClure, an obscure New Jersey representative, burst into the national spotlight in 2069 when he fearlessly questioned President Blaylock's educational platform and foreign policy with the fledgling nation of Klobazkha, carved out of the southeast corner of Russia.

"Perhaps not sir," Maxwell stated calmly. "People being excited by a candidate does not equate into undecided and unregistered individuals voting. Furthermore, the 18-30 year olds love McClure and his shoot from the hip antics, but they traditionally do not vote in large numbers—early 21st century history aside. And even then it was for an established party guy. On Election Day parties vote and third party cheerleaders stay home. We will be alright."

"I don't know Max," the President said as he rubbed his hand along his chin, his political mind overriding his anger. "McClure is not like the last S.D.P candidate—what was his name—Jacobsen? No, I believe McClure will motivate voters in a way we have not seen this century, why do you think both parties have courted Drew in the past three years? No, voters will emerge in record numbers for this election."

President Blaylock looked around the oval office for a moment, gathering his thoughts. When he spoke next his intensity was injected in every word. "The race will be tight until the final polls close in November. I…we are going to have to fight…extremely hard…to achieve victory."

He turned his back to Maxwell for a moment glaring out the window at the beautifully manicured White House grounds. He turned back quickly, fist raised then crashing to his desk three times as he continued. "We will maintain our hold on this room!" A coffee mug fell to the floor, but Maxwell did not move to pick it up. He learned not to interrupt the President's rants with either word or action during their campaigning days. "The alternative is unacceptable! Completely unacceptable! Fucking McClure! We should have crushed the S.D.P when we had the chance! No…we are in for a fight."

Maxwell knew he needed to redirect the President's energy. "Mr. President, the polls now mean nothing—you have the Middle East summit coming in August. A solid resolution for Israel and the bolstering of Iraq's struggling democratic regime will enhance our numbers substantially."

"You're right Max, I know you are; but haven't Presidents been trying to achieve those two goals for years?"

"But you're the President now and we are in a position to succeed where others have failed. Stay the course, we will be fine." Maxwell Grahm almost believed his own words as he left the nervous President alone in the Oval Office. There was one certainty; it would be a campaign season like no other.

The Eternal Struggle

Chapter 4
Independent Challenger

Drew McClure felt invigorated as the press gathered at the hastily assembled Monday morning press conference. The weekend poll that saw McClure as the front-runner in the campaign sent shockwaves through the national media and they converged on the headquarters of the Self-Determination Party, doggedly chasing the story of the century.

Drew looked out a window at the converging masses and allowed a brief, sardonic smile—one noticed by campaign manager Brian Murphy.

"Drew, this is a great opportunity, don't get too playful out there," advised Brian.

"Brian, Brian, Brian—you should know me better. I may be completely dismissive of what those vultures write, but I know my opponents hang on their every word, especially Casey. Hell, William probably checks opinion polls when deciding what time to go to sleep. Those cretins out there love a story, but they would hate to see me elected because their influence on this nation will slip dramatically when we hold the Oval Office—they will be relegated to reporting events again, not shaping them."

"Perhaps, Drew, but today they can be helpful and you don't want the media to be your enemy." Brian's view of the media was considerably more realistic and respectful than that of the candidate he was trying to help. Brian had been arguing with Drew for years, noting with growing bewilderment, the complete abandonment of Drew's normal policy of focusing on the best representatives of that profession instead of the worst. Brian did not completely understand why this was the case, but he knew the undeniable truth that maintaining a positive relationship with the press was infinitely superior to an antagonistic one.

"Of course not my enemy—just an entity that watches the moves of decision makers. Most of those cowards want to shape policy without the sacrifices necessary to truly participate in decision-making at the highest level. Most of them are contemptible. That being said, I will play nice today—if only to delay your first heart attack."

Brian sighed as he led Drew toward the door to the garden where the press corps awaited. He quickly noted the most admirable quality Drew possessed was, at times, the biggest difficulty with promoting the candidate. Drew overcame alcohol and drug addiction twenty years earlier. This victory, described in Drew's own words, was the greatest and most eye-opening experience of a lifetime. The victory, achieved without AA or any other organizations aid, just the guidance of a small number of close friends, and a mountain of literature, granted Drew a perspective far different from most politicians.

No printed word, no veiled threats, no expert's cynicism affected Drew. Secure in the competency of the people chosen to advise him from within his inner circle, Drew was immune to the storms of a campaign, perhaps because there was no storm acknowledged. Nothing, Drew maintained, could ever be more harmful to body, heart, mind and soul than addiction. What are the words of skeptics compared to the complete dissolution of spirit one feels when one is at rock bottom? Drew's slow climb from rock bottom, aided by the goodwill of his friends, made him a firm believer in the innate goodness of people and faith in the process of life.

While this outlook was refreshing, it could also be maddening. Brian often wondered what the future held for him if Drew failed to become president. Neither of the two major parties would accept him and, whether Drew admitted it or not, this was the S.D.P's best chance to claim the White House. If Drew did not succeed, the Self-Determination Party could well go the way of all previous third parties. Drew saw this as destiny; if the party was meant to survive it will. If not, so be it—life will go on. Brian, conversely, did not want life to go on if he was forever banished from the political arena because of his decision to aid the maverick representative from New Jersey.

Brian paused before opening the door to the garden and whispered final words of encouragement and advice. Drew shook Brian's hand and whispered, "I know Brian, and, as always, thanks." It was times like these when Brian realized the power of the man who would be president, but did not have to be in order to feel fulfilled. Perhaps therein lay Drew's greatest strength.

Cameras clicked and television cameras blinked to life as the press pushed forward to greet the candidate. Drew stood and looked over the crowd, as if forgetting why they were there. He looked over the crowd, drawing a deep breath as the sunlight washed over his face. A monarch butterfly rose out of the garden and Drew watched its haphazard flight with tranquil interest. He had the look of a man preparing for a relaxing walk, not a news conference. The media actually paused with him for a moment rather than immediately asking questions.

"Drew, how do you feel being the first third party candidate to ever show a lead in the polls?" The first question was spoken in a tentative tone, an unspoken apology for breaking the sublime silence.

"Great, of course, but being ahead in polls in July does not guarantee anything come November—so it is great, but almost inconsequential as well."

"Inconsequential? Are you saying pollsters are irrelevant?"

"No one is irrelevant, anywhere in the world regardless of occupation—we would all do well to remember that. As for polls, they have value but as I understand it a majority of people polled were under forty. It stands to reason I would do well in that demographic."

Drew paused and held back the next line, which was to ask the reporter if he represented the pollsters of America and felt a need to defend them. Or if he was merely caught in the thrall of political correctness, constantly looking to force politeness into conversations, even when the exchange was good-natured and there was no ill intent. Thank Heaven for this white knight in the media, protector of decency and good taste; guardian of the offended and insulted, and if you do not feel insulted he will tell you why you should. Drew glanced back at Brian, who exhaled a thankful sigh for both the audible answer and the comments he was sure Drew withheld.

"To what do you attribute the remarkable popularity of the Self-Determination Party and your candidacy?"

"Well, for those who love numbers we hardly have achieved 'remarkable popularity'—60% do not approve of us. Those who do embrace the Self-Determination Party probably do so because they recognize, and look unfavorably upon, the trend in American politics, the replacing of partisan politics some thirty years ago with zealot politics. Democrats and Republicans care more about defeating each other than helping the country. They spend so much time accusing each other of being closed-minded that they ignore the rather obvious fact that they both suffer from a horrible tunnel vision that serves only power and leads to the degradation of people. People only have value as voters to the two traditional parties, nothing more or less— just votes. The S.D.P, by the way, has stolen no voters from either party; rather, intelligent people have abandoned the demagogues for the deliverers. Anyone can nod their head unthinkingly for the major parties; it spares the hard liners, loyalists and apologists the heavy lifting of actual thought. If the major parties want to be angry, they should be irritated at themselves for driving voters away, not at us for giving them a place to run to."

"Wouldn't it stand to reason Casey would have done better too, instead of running third? He tends to be more popular with the younger voters than the President."

"William Casey, perhaps, is your actual story then, not me...or maybe you should find out why the under forty crowd is more fond of President Blaylock than Mr. Casey. Regardless, it is a long way to November. This poll is not the prize any of us wants to claim."

"President Blaylock leaves for the Middle East soon, are you worried that if he does well his numbers will spike?"

"I am worried if he does not do well the amount of violence and discord in that region will spike. That's the important issue."

"Would you say that if your poll numbers weren't so good?" The question had a definite edge to it and the speaker, a young member of the new media attempted to hold Drew's eyes as he spoke. Drew, having abandoned interest in staring contest long ago, offered an intentionally dismissive answer.

"Check the record...my comments now mirror my comments when I first announced my candidacy and the polls and experts discounted me. My motivators are slightly more powerful than public opinion polls." Many of the assembled nodded, some begrudgingly, in agreement. While Drew had a temperamental relationship with the press his statement rang as unequivocally accurate.

"What's next for you and your campaign?"

"Actually, we are headed to the Middle East in about two weeks. We plan to meet with the Saudis to outline the Self-Determination Party's Middle East Policy and how we can work together to improve relations, not wealth. Before we leave, however, we plan to meet with the teacher's union and the N.A.A.C.P—neither has endorsed a candidate yet and I am curious why these long standing supporters of the Democratic Party are dragging their heels." Drew almost ended the answer, but smirked and added, " any theories?" Brian grimaced as he made a mental note and prepared for yet another conversation that might lead nowhere but had to happen anyway.

A voice called, "Last question," from behind Drew.

"If you do not win, will you run for office again?"

"Looking for the next Eugene V. Debs are you?" Drew's question was greeted by blank stares and total incomprehension. No one recognized the name of the socialist candidate who ran for the presidency repeatedly in the early twentieth century. That a group of professionals dedicated to political commentary were confounded left Drew amused. He thought to ask about their educational backgrounds and reading habits, but decided against it.

"Actually, even if I win I do not plan to run for office again." This comment created a stir in the crowd. "Let me explain, I plan on acting in my first term, if I have one, as if it were my second. Most first term presidents instantly start focusing on re-election. Me, I plan on acting as if I can't be re-elected and letting the people decide if I deserve another four years. Every minute an incumbent campaigns, is a minute a job is not getting doing. If I have to spend money to keep my job, I probably don't deserve it. Better that money go elsewhere. I will be President for four years, not a bizarre mix of President and candidate. I am sure you people will keep my name in the public conscience, which will be campaign enough. That is a promise I will make and keep, that and it would be a four years like no other!" With that Drew turned and walked into the S.D.P's foyer, leaving the amassed media shouting questions.

Drew looked back, "I wonder how they feel chasing important people instead of doing something important? Maybe I'll ask them." Brian grabbed Drew's arm and spun them both in the opposite direction.

"Not going to run again, pretty big news…" Brian did not bother completing the thought, for he understood Drew knew where it was going.

"Don't worry Brian, you will be very busy as my chief of staff." Brian's eyes widened as Drew winked and walked off. "Hurry Brian, we have a plane to catch and a future to discuss. It'll all work out, my friend, you'll see."

Brian followed behind the exuberant candidate, wondering for the thousandth time what he had gotten himself into. Whatever it was, the line Drew used when recruiting Brian rang true. It was like nothing he had experienced before.

Chapter 5
Traditional Party, Desperate Times

The Monday morning news could not have been worse for William Casey. He was sure President Blaylock was horrified to think he could lose the White House to an independent candidate—how much worse to be the party leader the first time the Democratic Party came in third? *Candidate Casey presides over the Death of a Party* read the *Washington Post*. A bit dramatic, perhaps, but what if ultimately accurate? How long would it take the party to recover from a third place finish in a presidential campaign? What did his future hold if such a finish occurred, perpetual fame as the answer to a trivia question? Questions like these had haunted William Casey's mind for hours and he desperately wanted to re-focus, but focus on what?

Casey reflected upon his own political career, almost registering to the Self-Determination Party when he was eighteen, but at that young age he assumed the third party would die out, killing his own political aspirations. No, William Casey carefully evaluated his political beliefs and found they mirrored the Democrats more than the Republicans, even if in a centrist manner. How different his life might have been had he followed the courage of his convictions at eighteen. Or if, at thirty-three, he had accepted the invitation of Self-Determination Party who attempted to pull the passionate representative to their party. Casey decided loyalty to the party more important than the yearning of his own heart and mind, which admired the grit shown by the small, but resilient independent party.

The poet Robert Frost once wrote, "I took the one less traveled by / And that has made all the difference." Casey now mused how different his life was from what he hoped it would be because he chose the more traveled route. Winning the presidency and breaking the Republicans' twelve-year hold on the office, was supposed to be the reward for his loyalty. Now it seemed the humiliation of a third place finish would be the compensation for his lack of conviction.

He could focus on the painful truth written in the pages of *The Washington Post, The New York Times* and every other major newspaper in the past two years. McClure's popularity, and that of the Self-Determination Party, was based on the fact that they did offer a legitimate alternative to the traditional parties. Republicans exude an air of arrogance secure, not only in their stranglehold on the White House, but on the world as stewards of the only true superpower. The newspapers identified the Democrats as the apologist party. They accepted the United States' role as world super power, but exhibited guilt regarding past actions taken to claim this position. "Forgive us for our power… but since we have it we may as well use it," could be the Democrats' mantra. Neither depiction was entirely true, but the characterization of the parties was based on minor, not major, distortions of reality.

In domestic affairs, the Democrats had increasingly become enraptured by a subtle arrogance. They knew better than anyone what was needed to bring about positive results. Oblivious to their smug self-importance they never understood why many people saw them as much more capable of speaking in tones of condescension rather than camaraderie. Republicans, perhaps because they were completely unashamed of offending anyone became the party of "honesty," even if the "truths" spoken were ultimately slanted and twisted to effectively accommodate the Republican doctrine. The Democrats, conversely, wanted to appear magnanimous to their fellow Americans, but succeeded instead at being secretive and filled with disdain for those not smart enough to realize what's good for them. Into this mix came the Self-Determination Party and their standard bearer Drew McClure.

Drew openly admitted to shortcomings and flaws, enduring months of what Casey thought would have been humiliating stories of debauchery due to alcohol and drug binges in which a marriage ended because addiction meant more than a spouse. Instead, Drew openly confessed to the validity of the stories, leaving the press almost stunned by his candor, "Yes, I did that and no explanation can change it, or improve that young person now," was a typical McClure answer.

Drew turned the stories of weakness into stories of triumph and good will. Having conquered inner demons the time had come, in Drew's estimation, for America to do the same. Time to come to grips with past inequalities to build true equality. A perceived lack of success did not always mean a lack of progress; it merely signified slow evolution.

"America, a nation in transition," was one of Drew's pet phrases. He vigorously fought to dispel the anger generated by both the real and perceived slights of the past and accept a position of responsibility in the creation of a better life. As he had done for his own soul he now sought the same for his nation, mainly to replace blame with forgiveness. The violence and decisions that created a superpower should be placed on the funereal pyre of history so the nation could exist as a dependable, not guilty nor belligerent, world leader.

The worst pit bulls of the press were often disarmed by Drew's approach. How do you attack someone not playing by the normal rules of engagement, someone not ashamed of their past, but at peace with it? Political strategists struggled to cast doubt on the candidate who seemed to dispel darkness merely by walking into it. The only hope would be that McClure's passivity played as haughtiness, McClure the Monarchist, was one label, but to this point, the electorate liked what they saw. Secretly, so did Casey, but he could not break from his party now, he had to play out his role. William decided the time to follow the wisdom he found in Robert Frost's words had passed. His duty was clear and he would fulfill it.

While William was contemplating his place in the political world his campaign press secretary burst unannounced into the room, jumping quickly into the day's itinerary. "Slow down, John," William interrupted. "Shouldn't we address the headlines?"

"Of course, but not wallow in them—which by the look on your face is what you've been doing. We are scheduled to meet the press in an hour—let's get you ready."

John Tensler was right, but still William wanted a little more time to think before moving on with the day. "Ten minutes, John—I just need…"

"I've given you fifteen extra already, time to go to work."

William rose up and followed John from the room. The uncertainty of the future clung to him like a funereal shroud; only the dead don't have worries like William's.

Chapter 6
Slowly Expanding Horizons

Niccolo and Danielle exited the Martin Luther Hall discussing the various groups they initiated. Niccolo, in fact, was evaluating the performance of various presenters and he was particularly critical of Danielle and her inability, perhaps even the unwillingness, to look upon the audience as equals.

Danielle, a school administrator in life, was well respected by her peer group, but failed to impress or inspire the teachers she worked with. Niccolo, who had become fascinated with the teachings of various philosophers during his stay in Limbo, paraphrased the great Chinese teacher Confucius in an attempt to counsel Danielle.

"Without self-restraint," he sternly stated, "courtesy becomes oppressive and in your case, Danielle, your insincerity is equally oppressive. It is undoubtedly the same attitude that plagued you in life. I wonder if you ever influenced anyone—or if your subordinates just nodded to a title."

Danielle looked away from Niccolo for a moment, her eyes ablaze with anger. Her opened her mouth to speak, but paused as the Italian sailor continued his critique.

"You have yet to orient a group and not have them leave, in overwhelming numbers, finding you are arrogant and condescending. Sometimes informative, but arrogant. Helpful, but patronizing. Never just helpful alone. One and a half years we've worked together and you still make the same impression you made the first week you chose this task. A task you chose, ironically, because with your background you assumed quick passage to Heaven. The greatest paradox of this is the reality that at least half the people in that room, the people you look down upon, will accept their fatal flaw far quicker than you, confront and battle it, overcome and move to Heaven while you continue to deny your shortcomings."

"Now hold on," Danielle snapped as she stopped walking. Her fists on her hips and her jaw tightened as if ready to receive a punch.

"My word choice is better, and I am more patient and accommodating of questions, I don't see how you can say I am arrogant!"

"Word choice, other than saying 'I' not 'we', is not your problem. You are well schooled in vocabulary, but completely lacking when it comes to people. Not all your words hide the facial expressions, the nauseatingly disingenuous smile you use. Do you honestly think you can cover those things up with language skills? Hell, even that pompous ass Robert has made greater strides than you. Even your face now reveals much—Who do I think I am to lecture you? That is your question. If I were so smart, I would not be in Limbo for over 500 years. That would be your next comment. Those are legitimate and expected questions coming from you, for then I am the entity in need of change and not you. Your intelligence becomes a hindrance as your formal schooling only enables you to see a sailor from a bygone era, incapable of understanding the complexities of a modern soul."

Danielle recoiled at Niccolo's words, but did not respond; primarily because she knew, deep in her heart, his words were accurate. She had earned two PhD's in life and taught at an Ivy League school. She proceeded to become headmaster at a prestigious private high school. She was well versed in all things academic and the necessary networking skills needed to maintain the integrity of a reputable institution. These skills served her well, but also distanced her from the middle and lower rungs of society. Perhaps she was like many people, speaking at length of the necessity to aid others, while rarely associating with the needy.

Now her direct supervisor was a sailor, a man without a formal education who died penniless. The type of person whom, in life she both pitied and despised, but never deigned worthy enough to discover if she should do either. Education is wonderful Niccolo once told her, but should it rob you of the ability to walk the streets? Perhaps for the first time in over a year she listened, and learned, from the man whose centuries of life in Limbo taught him more than she had ever considered pursuing.

Niccolo took silent note of Danielle's silence, for it was not her normal reaction. She always had a response, but the pensive look on her face told him all he needed to know; more words were not necessary. Rather time for contemplation was of the essence. Danielle was about to depart, whispering a haphazard goodbye when Jonathan stumbled upon them calling an enthusiastic hello followed by an expectant question, "You guys gotta minute?"

"In my experience, 'gotta minute' often means you want more than that, but I do have some time," Niccolo extended his hand as he greeted the young man. "I would like to have a name, however."

"Oh sure, sorry. I'm Jonathan Styles, but friends call me Jon—I am just...I don't know where to go or what to do. I can't even do that light trick thing. This is all sorta overwhelming."

Niccolo smiled, even though this was hardly the first time he had witnessed a disoriented newcomer. Somehow the unrestrained anxiety of a teen amused him much more than confused adults, who tended to mask their uncertainty behind carefully constructed veneers of collectedness. Little did such people suspect that the mirage of control extended the duration of a stay in Limbo, whereas the courage to ask for aid hastened the voyage to Heaven. While Niccolo mused in silence, Danielle stepped forward to greet, and calm, Jonathan.

"Hello, Jon," Danielle said, her tone regressing to the formalized speech she always used with young people. What may have been a smile flashed across her face as she looked to the ground and then at Jon. She shook hands with the young soul and gently placed a hand on his shoulder. The simple and sincere gesture seemed to draw away some of Jon's anxiety. Despite herself Danielle smiled again as she spoke. "I am afraid Niccolo has just given me some... homework...as well. See you tomorrow in the lecture hall. I leave you in capable, if not always gentle, hands."

Jon watched Danielle depart and turned to Niccolo, who was looking around, seemingly distracted by unseen events. Niccolo's eyes darted, a hunter seeking an undetected prey. Inexplicably, a small smile stretched across his face and he nodded, obviously pleased with some event beyond Jon's reckoning. Jon stood and fidgeted. The silence and his surroundings made him increasingly uncomfortable. Niccolo grew aware of Jon's discomfort and spoke in an easy tone.

"Maybe asking a question will ease your mind," Niccolo offered as advice.

"Yea, right," Jon felt increasingly foolish. "Hey, is it dusk or dawn? The sky is so overcast I can't tell."

"Neither," Niccolo answered. "The sky in Limbo is perpetually gray. There is no day or night, just constant gray skies."

"Isn't that a bit depressing? How are people supposed to feel hope in such...um...bleak surroundings?"

"Bleak surroundings? That is a state of mind young man," Niccolo started to walk the cobblestone path in front of the lecture hall. Jon followed and listened intently to Niccolo's words.

"You are standing outside a hall dedicated to a man who through great internal struggle overcame doubt, found a purpose in life and a connection to the eternal. You are being told this by a man who sailed with Christopher Columbus while standing in the center of a city of almost endless possibility—and you are saddened by the sky? Perhaps you should look within, not up."

Jon nodded, halfheartedly and rambled into his next thought, "I guess you're right. I don't know. To be honest I have a million questions, but, like, right now I just want to relax."

Niccolo continued walking as he spoke. "Your questions can be answered tomorrow. As for relaxation, tell me what you find relaxing and I will see what we can do to help you."

"I like music and I used to play basketball—I was pretty good, too. I was a starter my junior year and was looking forward to my senior season, at least I was until the accident," Jon looked down, saddened by the thought of the car accident that ended his life on Earth.

"Let's not dwell on the… accident… that brought you here, rather let me show you either the basketball courts or the concert hall we have in the city. Both are nearby. The concert hall is off to our right. I believe a fellow named Johnny Cash is entertaining people today. I can bring you to the hall if you like."

"Ah…maybe some other time," Jon said. He did not recognize the name Johnny Cash and assumed it was music he just wouldn't want to hear.

"Well," Niccolo continued, "the basketball courts are on the way to the Rising Soul's Bar and Grill where I am meeting some friends. I will bring you to the park and move on to the Rising Soul's, which is only four blocks from where I will leave you. If you wish to join me, feel free. If not, I will see you in class tomorrow."

"Can I play at the courts or just watch?"

"There are twenty courts, each occupied by players of various skill. I am not sure of the ground rules. I have learned many new games since I have been here and I like baseball far more than basketball. Regardless, we are here. Why don't you…"

"Holy Shit!" Jon exclaimed, interrupting Niccolo. "Do you see who is playing out there!? That's Larry Bird! And Michael Jordan! I mean, I think I'll just watch for now…Rising Soul's, right?"

Niccolo tilted his head slightly and smirked. It was good to see Jon enthused about something. The sooner one feels at home in Limbo, Niccolo observed over his prolonged stay, the sooner they leave for Heaven.

Jon pushed into the crowd gathered to watch the game unfolding on what had to be the main or 'A' court. It was mind-boggling, a team comprised of Larry Bird, Bill Walton, Michael Jordan, Walt Frazier and Nate Thurmond squared off against Jerry West, Charles Barkley, John Stockton, Wilt Chamberlain and Dominique Wilkins. The action was furious and intense as competitive athletes squared off with all the vitality of their youth. Charles Barkley posted up Bird, taking advantage of his strength and quickness to easily get off a shot. The ball never came close to the rim, as Bill Walton and Nate Thurmond converged on the shot, one blocking it the other plucking it from the air.

Jon cheered, not out of loyalty to any team, but because the exceptional level of play simply demanded it. His astonished look made it obvious he was new to this experience. A bystander next to him shouted, "Hey new guy, bet you didn't expect to see this type of show!"

"No way," Jon answered. "Any big guy I ever played against just kinda lumbered around. Who are these guys?"

"The guy who blocked the shot was Bill Walton. He was hurt a lot on Earth, but here everyone is always healthy and playing at their peak. The other fella is Nate Thurmond—great rebounder and shot blocker. His name is sometimes overlooked by casual fans, but he is a real difference maker."

Jon raised his eyebrows in agreement and continued to watch the game. Larry Bird caught a pass on the wing and looked at the rim. The mere upward glance combined with a minor lifting of the ball was enough to entice Barkley to jump. Bird dribbled by and pulled up for a short jumper as Wilt Chamberlain leapt at him. Bird's jumper had an impossible arch as it floated over Wilt's hand and nestled into the basket. As Bird back peddled to defense, he let out, in his Hoosier twang, "Shit Wilt, that shot was a sonovabitch, wasn't it?"

Wilt glared at Bird and set himself purposefully in the post. Walton and Thurmond double him to no avail as the Big Dipper overpowered both seven footers for a rim-rattling dunk. "Ten—Ten. Game point," Jerry West hollered as the team ran back on defense. "We need a stop!"

The next basket would win the game and Bird's team had an enviable dilemma; who takes the game winning shot Jordan or Bird? Bill Walton flashed to the high post and caught a pass from Frazier. He signaled at both Bird and Jordan, who scissor cut the high post, looking to lose their defenders. Jerry West lost Jordan for an instant in the mass of bodies at the right elbow, and Walton hit him for a short jumper. Amazingly Dominique Wilkins was able to call upon his great athleticism to come from nowhere and contest, if not thwart the game winning shot. As the ball still hung in the air, Michael Jordan shouted, "Next!" As it settled into the net, a frustrated Jerry West slapped his hands together in disgust. A new team, led by Magic Johnson and Clyde Drexler took the court. Jon sat and watched; maybe he would take in a couple more games before catching up to Niccolo.

Chapter 7
Old Friends

The Rising Soul's Bar and Grill was Niccolo's preferred haunt. It had not always been such, for he had frequented many establishments in his time at Limbo. The Rising Soul became a favorite in the past twenty years primarily because of the addition of a new bartender. The man's stories and enthusiasm were very appealing to Niccolo and he spent many a day exchanging tales with the bald host.

The overweight barkeep smiled when he saw Niccolo and walked toward him. As he approached he stopped to share a quick story with another patron of the bar. His volume and grandiloquence revealed he still had to learn a thing or two about humility, a trait with which he was somewhat unfamiliar. Regardless of this flaw, Niccolo always enjoyed the stories that came his way, even though sharing them might add months to his friend's stay.

"Good evening, Winston," Niccolo smiled as he enthusiastically shook hands.

"Ah, Niccolo…it would be a good evening but your insufferable Irish comrade is seated waiting for you. Befriending him ought to grant you quick passage to Heaven."

"Alas, it has not worked out thusly, Winston. Perhaps it is your destiny to befriend Seamus and gain release from your current profession."

"Oh, I fear I will wash mugs for all eternity if that is my destiny!" Winston Churchill laughed as he pointed Niccolo to the table currently occupied by Seamus O'Malley. "Tell your Irish companion, 'God save the Queen!'"

Niccolo laughed as he made his way towards a small round table at the back of the room. A lone individual, whose eyes moved gently around the room, resting occasionally to communicate a silent hello with a friend or acquaintance, occupied it.

"Good evening, Seamus," Niccolo said as he sat across from his friend.

"Top o' the mornin' to you too," answered Seamus, "but there is really no morn' or evenin' now is there?"

"True enough, Seamus," Niccolo was not entirely in the mood to exchange philosophical witticisms with the spirited Irishman. He looked back towards the door, but did not see what he wanted.

"What are ye lookin' fer, laddie?" Seamus inquired. "We have a seat waitin' fer ole Abraham when he shows and an extra seat awaiting whomever, as you like to have it. It's not like ye to look over yuir shoulder."

"Sorry, Seamus. I met a young boy today and told him I would be here if he needed further direction. I am half hoping he arrives. He was dumbfounded, but curious and not all the youth who arrive nowadays do so with an air of inquisitiveness about them. It is always nice to greet a youth not completely ashamed to admit they need assistance."

Seamus rolled his eyes, "Well if ye wanted the lad 'ere why didnja just invite 'em? Not every little thing 'as to be left to chance, ye know. I know ye like playin' the cool, detached observer, but even the oldest soul in Limbo can be guilty of over thinkin' some scenarios. An' by the way, yuir in a bar fer Christ's sake...ye can turn off yuir advisor voice."

Niccolo feigned annoyance at Seamus' comments. In reality, the Irishman's carefree attitude did, from time to time, infuriate the sailor. Not more than the Italian seaman's preoccupied demeanor and intense brooding exasperated Seamus. Perhaps this is what made them good friends; they learned much from each other even when they didn't want to.

"For your information Seamus, I did not invite the lad because he was captivated by the basketball park. I left him there and told him where I would be, surrounded by good people and confounding Irishmen."

"Niccolo, was that an attempt at humor? Careful now, yuir reputation may be at stake."

"Seamus, the only thing I am worried about ruining is..."

"Hold that thought, Niccolo. I seem to have found someone seeking your company." The voice came from behind Niccolo, startling him momentarily. He turned to see Abraham Lincoln, wearing a tan button down shirt and blue jeans, standing behind him with Jon. "May we join you?"

"Of course...sir, of course." Lincoln's expression made it clear he wanted his identity kept anonymous for as long as possible. He seemed slightly amused and obviously wanted to let Niccolo and Seamus in on the joke. Jon, bursting with enthusiasm, did not notice the exchange of glances.

"Niccolo, those courts were great! What unbelievable games! Anyway, I got a little lost and this guy helped me find you. I can't believe how much he looks like Abraham Lincoln, can you?"

Seamus was the first to chime in, "Yuir right laddie. He does indeed bear an uncanny resemblance to that famous man."

"I thought so, too. Man all you need is a tall black hat and suit and you would be all set—the perfect look alike!"

"Jon," Niccolo instructed, "take a good look at this man."

Jon did so and smiled, mouthing the words, "He's a perfect copy."

Seamus laughed uncontrollably as Niccolo slowly stated, "Look again and remember where you are."

Jon looked at Lincoln again and the smile faded from his face, replaced by shock, awe and embarrassment. "Ohmigod…you are Abraham Lincoln…but the hat and suit…where…."

"A man guides a nation through a civil war and his legacy two hundred years later is tied up in his wardrobe. Alas, a truly humbling experience," Lincoln pretended to be dismayed as he spoke, his head bowed and his hand clutching his chest. "It's alright son, you are not the first soul thrown off by my lack of a stove pipe hat."

"Amazing how that ole hat never caught on as a fashion statement, though," Seamus interjected. "Ye would think some Lincoln fans may have donned them for a little while, only to stop when they got beat up at school."

The group laughed, except for Jon who was shocked at the cavalier attitude Seamus exhibited in front of Lincoln. Despite his age and the fact Abraham Lincoln never meant more to him than a name to memorize for a test, Jon was, inexplicably, personally offended that someone would be so inconsiderate in front of such a great and prominent man.

"Hey, shouldn't you be more respectful. I mean that's…."

Lincoln stopped Jon mid-sentence, "That's a man enjoying the company of friends, not a picture staring at you somberly from a book. In case no one taught you this, people from history were and are real and enjoy a good laugh as much as anyone, but thanks for defending me from Seamus' unprovoked attack."

"Perhaps he should have been at the Ford's Theater," Niccolo mumbled quietly, but loud enough for the table to hear.

"Careful, Niccolo. Ye may be accused of havin' a sense of humor!" Seamus shouted with delight. Winston Churchill looked over from the bar and shook his head, not entirely certain how Niccolo tolerated Seamus' presence.

Jon waited for the laughter at the table to die down before speaking again.

"I'm sorry. I'm still adjusting to all this." Jon shook his hands in front of his face, emphasizing the word 'this' as he spoke. "I know we are supposed to have questions answered tomorrow, but can I have some answered now? I mean I don't even know how I am supposed to know when tomorrow is since there is no day or night."

Niccolo tilted his head to one side, contemplating Jon's question.

"The concept of changing days is not a bad place to begin. We have town criers who inform souls of important events, including class times for new souls. The use of the word tomorrow is more of a habit and comfort than actual necessity.

"And," Seamus threw in. "It is also easier than saying, 'return when the town crier calls.'"

"That makes sense. I guess a part of me wonders why I am here. I am only seventeen. Shouldn't I be good enough for Heaven? I've done nothing seriously wrong."

"Aye lad, ye have done nothing, seriously wrong—which means you should get to Heaven quickly enough, but don' think ye've don nothin' wrong either. In fact, we may have some things in common. My name is Seamus O'Malley, former member of the I.R.A., Irish Republican Army. The Brits were bad and we were good. Life is so easy when everything is black and white. Ye lived the same way, without the physical violence, but the hurtful verbal assaults aimed at geeks, Goths, preps and others who could be your friend if only they just dressed and thought the "right way." Ye spent so much time labeling everyone; ye barely got to know anybody. What was it like, laddie, to call the wealthy students in yuir school snobs when ye never held a conversation wit'em and at the same time ye longed to be one of 'em? Or yuir own snobbery when ye looked at the poor, did ye not recognize yuir own flaws; or do ye jus' hide 'em hopin' na a soul shines a light into yuir shadows? Did the contempt ye felt for both groups eventually cause some self-loathing? Hate is funny that way, the more you give out the more it infects yuir being. Shades of gray, laddie, like the skies of Limbo, that's the place to live; where the real living, learning and thinking occurs. Only by wading into the mists can ye find the final, unifying light. I believe ye died, young Jonathan, before ye even knew what ye were or what ye stood fer."

Jon felt wounded by Seamus' evaluation but was hesitant to respond. Abraham fathomed that Jon, perhaps, did not want to lose his temper in his presence, so he stood and excused himself.

"I am going to order some drinks from Winston. I'm sure that will include at least ten minutes of story telling."

"Maybe fifteen," Niccolo said with a quick wink.

Lincoln smiled and left, a single wave to Seamus preceded his departure. Seamus made a small hand gesture and continued to stare at Jon. He recognized the fact that the boy had words for him, but he did not know if Jon had the courage to voice his anger.

Jon finally spoke; an almost inarticulate grumble inquiring what Seamus thought he was looking at.

"A typical, twenty-first century imbecile," was Seamus' response. "Yuir capable of running a computer, but incapable of actual thought. Tell me, is ignorance truly bliss?"

Jon unconsciously checked how far Lincoln was from the table as he hissed, "Who the Hell do you think you are?! You're nothing but an old, used up asshole. You can't talk to me…"

"On the contrary, boyo, I can an' just did. You donae like my words, there is nothin' keepin' ye here, now is there?"

Seamus' response disarmed Jon. He was used to Earth where when a teen said certain things to adults they forced their authority on him. He was thrown out of classes plenty of times on Earth, but only when he wanted to leave. Jon always laughed when a teacher regained control of a class by doing exactly what Jon wanted. Seamus' calm demeanor left him stunned and uncertain—and it showed.

"What's the matter, Jon-boy—disappointed I'm nae up in arms over yuir outburst? Ye think yuir the first person to ever swear at me? If so ye must be daft, e'en stupider than I thought."

Jon flinched, but was not sure what to say. The tension he felt immobilizing his tongue. Seamus, after pausing just long enough so Jon knew he lost an opportunity to speak, continued.

"On Earth there would be those who would say I was too insensitive to a youth like yuirself, but you stay because in life many adults tiptoed around ye, bein' sensitive, perhaps speakin' in euphemisms— more worried 'bout bein' sued or coverin' their asses than providin' actual guidance. Aye, ye meet many adults full of words, but few and far between were actually honest with ye. Strange time ye lived in, the façade of carin' has so replaced actual concern few could e'en tell the difference—and those who could, especially the young—thought it smarter to be a wise ass than a leader. Tell me I'm wrong, boyo."

Seamus looked over his shoulder and caught Lincoln's eye and the former president gave Winston Churchill a knowing glance and returned to the table. Jon sat in silence, mulling over Seamus' words, but never contemplating leaving the company of these men. As Lincoln sat and handed drinks to everyone Niccolo leaned closer to Jon.

"Jon, the real fault, perhaps the worst flaw of all, is to have faults and not try to amend them. If Seamus' words hurt you then evaluate your anger, for he wasn't attacking you."

"Actually…" Seamus began, but Niccolo halted him with a sharp glare. The Italian continued, his gaze lingering on Seamus for an extra moment. The Irishman merely smiled, amused by his unshared thought.

"Look into your own life and figure out why the words were upsetting. I suspect a truth was revealed that you would have preferred stayed hidden. That, unfortunately, is what occurs in Limbo—and is the way to Heaven. Seamus is not an adversary, rather he is acting as a guide, if you choose to follow him."

While Jon sat weighing Niccolo's words Lincoln added to the discussion, "Very wise words Niccolo, but I am curious about the 'real fault is to have faults' phrase you used—are you still Limbo's leading expert on Confucius? I swear I heard a fellow use a similar phrase the other day…and he attributed it to his honored teacher"

"I never miss his lectures," Niccolo confessed. "Once a month he comes from Heaven to conduct classes and attempts to help souls find the path to Heaven quicker. I always attend. Sometimes he comes alone, sometimes with other great thinkers. Regardless of who he travels with, his words move me, and inspire me, greater than any other words I have read or heard all these years."

"I just don't see," Jon rejoined the conversation, "how my need for independence could cause such problems. So what if I choose not to befriend wealthy kids or poor ones. I have a right to choose my friends."

Lincoln responded to Jon's inquiry. "Choose friends, yes –but what type of friendship is built on a foundation of insults and the belittling of others? And who says individuality must exist in isolation or surrounded by only like thinking people? The true sign of a strong individual is the ability to maintain a sense of self amidst those of differing opinion. This, coupled with the ability to grow and change, shows strength, not weakness."

Niccolo pointed at Jon and began speaking with great vigor, "You, in fact we all, would do well to heed the words of Abraham. In fact, he is a fine example of what we are discussing. The voices in his own party heeded caution when dealing with slavery during the civil war. Abraham himself attempted to bury his personal wish to end slavery in exchange for fulfilling his official duty of saving the Union. This inner struggle played out in the war, an indecisive president leading an indecisive army; the wrong generals in charge at the wrong moments. But one voice, whether in speeches, print or personal visits kept pulling at the president, appealing to the highest calling of his nature."

Lincoln raised his glass, "Frederick Douglass." The other two men, well aware of the near reverence in which Lincoln held Douglass, respectfully raised their glasses as well. Jon, while unaware of the enormity of the man they spoke, was well aware of the obvious need for silent admiration, a choice the men at the tabled noticed with high regard.

"Niccolo, before you continue to embarrass me with your well meaning history lessons let me just remind you, I still contend events controlled me much more readily than I controlled them."

"I wouldn't mind hearing a little something about Frederick Douglass," Jon said with great sincerity.

"He was very important," Lincoln confirmed. "A man of great intellect, integrity and pride. He acted as a most trusted guide to me in dark times and was, in many ways, the conscience of the nation throughout his life. During the Civil War he also had no formal title. Earthly societies often honor titles too readily instead of people. His story from slave to owner of a newspaper to international speaker and beyond is quite amazing."

"I can't say with honesty, and I am not brave enough to lie in front of Abraham Lincoln, that I always paid attention in school as effectively as I could have." Jon's confession was met with small laughter from all at the table and a sense of relief.

Seamus dropped a hand on Jon's shoulder and said through a broad grin, "Ye don' 'ave to feel bad about tellin' lies in front of ole Abe, I do it all the time."

"I do have one question," Jon continued as Seamus removed his hand. "I hope it's not too personal." The three men looked at each other and seemed undaunted by the prospect of Jon's query. "Niccolo, you've been here for over 500 years and, Mr. Lincoln, you died over 200 years ago—why have you been here so long?"

"Because they are two stubborn pains in the ass, that's why!" Seamus hollered before the other men could get out a word. "Ye both should ha' been out of Limbo at least fifty years ago, but hold onto yuir culpability for events beyond yuir control like some sort of prize of honor. This lad should nae have even met the likes of you two stubborn ole fools!"

Lincoln and Niccolo, the two targets of Seamus' outburst, had distinctly different reactions to their friend's admonishment. Lincoln seemed genuinely unfazed. Seamus was entitled to his opinion, even if it were incorrect, or more accurately, incomplete. Niccolo was noticeably upset. He had engaged Seamus in this discussion before, believing his point was clear and should be accepted and respected by his companion. The fact it was not disturbed Niccolo. He was prepared to delve into the issue again, but Lincoln absentmindedly patted Niccolo's forearm, calming him down. He then looked at Jon who was taken aback by the sudden shift in mood.

"I don't understand what just hap…"

"Ye will, laddie, ye will, but nae now. Tis nae the right time for this discussion as I do 'ave some of my own duties to attend. Any last questions before I take my leave?"

Jon, eager to change the subject, quickly spoke. "Only one, actually. Why is everyone speaking English here—is that the universal language or something?"

"And here I thought we all spoke Italian," Niccolo offered as a somewhat unhelpful answer.

"It is very simple, Jon," Lincoln began, giving Niccolo a discontented look as he spoke. Niccolo shrugged his shoulders and smiled as Seamus quietly applauded Niccolo's answer. Unfazed by the antics surrounding him Lincoln continued, "You hear everyone in the tongue you speak most effectively. Niccolo is in fact speaking Italian, but you hear English. When I speak, Niccolo hears Italian. When Seamus speaks we usually hear inane babble and so forth."

"Inane babble, aye? Maybe I will try to be more profound. Perhaps, 'Four score and seven years ago' will win me fans."

"Or foes, don't forget all my foes," Lincoln replied as he stood and shook Seamus' hand. "I too must take my leave, Winston and I have some business to discuss. Niccolo, please take care to let our young friend relax a little—he has been challenged enough for one night."

Jon and Niccolo sat together for roughly an hour discussing history, Limbo, and the fact that basketball was a far superior game to baseball. In the course of the conversation, Jon was reminded how much he liked learning and wondered why he was less resistant to that fact now that he was dead.

Chapter 8
The Summons

"Everyone is present, I assume," Niccolo said loudly, calling the lecture hall to order. The town criers had been announcing the reconvening of classes for almost a half hour, more than enough time to be where one belonged. As Niccolo prepared to continue two souls hastily ran into the hall, apologizing for being late.

"No problem," Niccolo replied. "In Limbo we have nothing but time. Go enjoy some free time on me—be on time tomorrow."

One of the individuals looked as if he were going to debate the issue, but Niccolo sent a glower that revealed half a millennium of conviction, and the recipient wilted before the intensity of his ancient strength. The two procrastinators left the room grumbling, but both would arrive early the next day.

Niccolo greeted his audience again and reminded them of where they had ceased their last session. He reviewed the information about augmenters and how they manipulate the traits in people, causing them to focus on the worst, not the best in themselves. "One of you thought this was cheating. It isn't because…." Niccolo dragged out the last word, looking for the audience to complete it. He was not disappointed.

"Because of free will," an attentive individual stated. "The augmenter never tampers with free will, so the target can choose to resist them."

"True," stated Niccolo. "Unfortunately, the augmenter's attack is undetectable, very powerful and not unaided by most societies' tendency to focus on the negative anyway. Furthermore, they will stay with an individual for years until the characteristic they are attempting to make dominant overrides all others in the person's personality. Unaugmented people succumb to temptation and doubt every day. Those with increased negative traits find resistance that much more difficult."

The crowd started to murmur, most wondering if they had ever been manipulated in such a manner. A single word form Niccolo recaptured their attention.

"Now," Niccolo said loudly, "Rovac became aware of these augmenters the moment they started their work and was content to observe
the ramifications of this most devious plan. Rovac was impressed by
Lucifer's cunning and content to examine the impact this new breed
of souls had on Earth. He saw it as a test of free will. In a short time,
one hundred years, he realized the need to use Limbo to balance the
scales for humanity, creating both aid for people and a new avenue to
Heaven for the souls of Limbo. I have chosen this path; I am a hunter,
currently inactive. We hunt augmenters, engage them in spiritual combat, and vanquish them to Hell where they belong. You may choose to
be a hunter as well with each defeated augmenter bringing you closer
to Heaven. Every time we defeat an augmenter we liberate a human
from the direct influence of these wicked manipulators. That human is
then allowed five seconds of clarity—freedom from focusing on that
which the augmenter trained his or her eyes on. These five seconds do
not reduce the inflated negative trait the person now has, but reminds
them of the multitude of possibilities that exist if they can change
perspective. Often in the five seconds, the person feels the need to
call an old friend or mentor, reread a book with new eyes or recap-
tures an interest long discarded as hopeless. These new thoughts do
not fade when the five seconds are over and free will allows the person
to return to focusing on the augmented trait or pursuing the new path.
In the end, the person chooses their path, for that is how lives and history are made."

Niccolo pointed at a raised hand as he seated himself on a chair
he summoned with his own spiritual energy. Niccolo's casual creating
of a chair created great nervousness in the would-be speaker, who had
spent the better part of their time in Limbo unsuccessfully creating
paper. The flustered individual stumbled into their question, 'I was...
that is...I can't even make pap...Anyway, what risks does a hunter
face and how does this spiritual conflict take place?"

"The good news," Niccolo said humorlessly, "is you are dead—
so you won't risk your life, but you can risk your soul and freedom.
Remember I languished in a prison for 270 years. Such can be the fate
of a defeated hunter. The weapons are a matter of your will power,
experience, confidence and the personality of the hunter. Some shoot
beams of spiritual force. Some make spiritual swords. I prefer a self
loading crossbow pistol...though I have used other weapons in the
past"

Niccolo extended his hand menacingly and the shimmering
weapon appeared. When he opened his hand, it disappeared as quickly

as it materialized. As his audience gawked in awe Niccolo continued his comments.

"A veteran hunter can easily defeat a neophyte augmenter, and visa-versa. The more closely matched the combatants, the more uncertain the outcome. Every time a soul is struck by a spiritual weapon they are damaged more so by the will of the bearer than the choice of armament. Upon receiving a requisite amount of damage, an augmenter returns to Hell, or a hunter becomes a captive. These battles tend to take place in the nothingness that exists between Limbo and Earth. There are crevices in the ground throughout Limbo. By entering these fissures, augmenters can touch Earth and manipulate humans. Hunters pass into the same crevices, seek, and banish the loathsome manipulators. In recent times, very recent times, the most powerful augmenters have developed the ability to touch Earth from Limbo itself, making themselves more difficult to stop and more dangerous to Earth."

The crowd began to raise hands and voices, but an uncompromising glare from Niccolo silenced them all, only the bravest left their hands raised. As Niccolo called on the first questioner, a new soul strolled onto the stage. The group recognized Dylan, who wore a grave expression and seemed oblivious to the presence of any soul in the room but Niccolo. Dylan snapped his fingers and a slip of paper appeared. He handed the paper to the Italian, speaking solemnly. Niccolo read the message and quickly departed, his mind instantly focused on the uncertain future the note foretold. Obviously recent rumors about the past three decades in Lucifer's Limbo were, as feared, far more accurate than Niccolo would have liked.

Chapter 9
Past Events, Present Danger

Thirty years ago Lucifer surveyed the landscape of Limbo, setting in motion the chain of events that currently threatened all of Limbo. At that point in time, Lucifer decided a new administration needed to supervise the activities of Limbo.

Vlad the Impaler remained in Limbo after the first war ravaged the realm. Over the centuries, he formed an alliance with Jefferson Davis and the two men ruled Nafarhel. Andrew Jackson, Benedict Arnold and Francisco Pizarro oversaw the daily organization of Tecktoral. There rule was unchallenged and, as such, complacency had replaced tenacity.

Augmenters in the regions were diligent in their attempts to manipulate humans, but worked in a manner Lucifer viewed as uninspired. The augmenters made daily forays into the fissures of Limbo, influencing people, battling hunters and, occasionally, retreating to Nafarhel or Tecktoral when battles went poorly. A veteran augmenter was a valuable commodity; therefore, Jefferson Davis suggested a policy of strategic withdrawal over pushing a bad position. The others readily agreed, for they hated training neophyte replacements. If the timetable for the war stretched over millenniums, perhaps to eternity, there was no need to push for unlikely victories.

This lackadaisical approach to war against goodness infuriated Lucifer and he sent Adolf Hitler to Tecktoral and Joseph Stalin to Nafarhel. Lucifer's plan was simplicity in itself; place two men with insatiable appetites for power in subordinate roles and wait for their natures to take command. He assumed it would only be so long before the two twentieth century dictators desired control of Lucifer's holdings, if not more of Limbo itself.

Stalin and Hitler wasted little time differentiating themselves from the rule of Vlad and his cohorts. Retreat, hence failure, was unacceptable to Hitler and Stalin. Without the dread of punishment, what motivation did augmenters have to extend their capabilities? Augmenters should fear returning home in defeat more than the power of the hunt-ers as this would make them fight harder.

To institute these tenets Hitler and Stalin carved out small king-doms, which they ruled without consulting the entrenched leadership. Retreating augmenters were greeted with disdain, and, whenever pos-sible, banishment to Hell. Some augmenters fought back against the spiteful duo, but Stalin's iron will and the inconceivably malicious force that was Hitler's soul was undeniable. They viciously swept aside all challengers. Some residents of Nafarhel privately wondered if Lucifer himself had come in disguise.

Vlad Dracula realized, as did the other leaders, that the two tyrants were blatantly ignoring their power and policies, but were ineffective in their efforts to bring Hitler and Stalin into the fold. Civil War could not be far away.

For twenty years, the unremitting twosome practiced the craft of being augmenters. They also built alliances amongst themselves and with new souls Lucifer sent into the powder keg he created. The two decades proved ample time for Hitler and Stalin to build confi-dence, and they decided to seize control of Nafarhel and Galiktus; Stalin would claim Nafarhel while Hitler would assert his authority over Galiktus.

Stalin challenged Vlad the Impaler and Jefferson Davis to spiritual combat within the confines of Vlad's own hall. The more experienced men accepted, for they knew an attack was imminent and believed they could combine forces to overcome the upstart rogue from the Soviet Union.

Their assault was fierce, Vlad Dracula firing huge spears at his adversary. The spears struck with terrible force, each one more than powerful enough to end a conflict with most souls, but Stalin was like no other. The man whose orders claimed some thirty million lives would not be felled like some simple murderer or amoral lawyer. The blasts of energy Stalin issued forth rolled with the cold of a Siberian winter, creating a chill even in souls. Remarkably, Stalin was able to emit these cold blasts while generating shields that blunted Dracula's assault. Those spears that did blast through Stalin's defenses did no telling damage.

Terror grew in the heart of Vlad Dracula, for he felt no certainty that he could overcome Stalin's might. He looked to Jefferson Davis for aid just as the Confederate president fired beams of black light from his hands. Stalin casually watched the beams approach. When they struck, Stalin was unfazed; his body absorbed the assault in a manner reminiscent of the ocean accepting a thrown stone. Davis stood in stunned silence, never had he seen his greatest weapon so ineffective. Had Davis truly understood Stalin he would have not been surprised in the least. Hate fueled Davis' spiritual assaults. To use hate against Stalin was to use gasoline to douse an inferno.

Stalin glanced over his shoulder as Vlad Dracula fell to his knees, pummeled by the relentless winter gale. Vlad wondered where his top generals, Nathan Forrest, Champ Ferguson, and Sumanguru were, for he desperately needed their aid.

The souls who entered the room were the answer to his unspoken question. Rasputin, Catherine the Great, Lavrenti Beria, and Mao Zedong strode towards Stalin's side. They wore sadistic smiles, having turned Dracula's fortress into their personal killing field. What forces the Impaler had left were fleeing the Mongolian horsemen and the secret police of Ivan III, whom Beria had recruited to aid with the assault. The success of the foot soldiers freed Stalin's top lieutenants to join him in the final victory over Dracula and Davis.

Dracula did not recognize these individuals though he knew instantly whom they did and did not support. Jefferson Davis turned his attention to the new combatants but was helpless before their combined might. Mao and Beria were barely able to act before Catherine entwined Davis in a combination of webs and barbed wire. Rasputin created a murky, cannonball-sized sphere, which tore a hole through the Confederate president's chest. Davis looked down, not at his wound, but at the ground opening up below him. His enemies saw ominous talons and tentacles pulling Davis' to Hell, but his mind's eye saw his worst nightmare: black soldiers come to capture him while he had nowhere to hide. Too terrified to even scream, Davis slunk into the pit, the tentacles effortlessly pulling the defeated, despondent soul down to an eternity of suffering.

Stalin did not witness the demise of Davis. The fierce Romanian demanded his full attention. Dracula struggled mightily but could not force Stalin to even take a backward step.

"So you fail on your knees like a wounded dog," Stalin spoke brusquely. "Hell is too good for you."

With that, Stalin focused the windstorm of his fury tightly into Vlad's eyes and nose, tearing the spiritual beams deep into the soul of the impaler. The scream Vlad let loose did nothing but stir Stalin's desire to press the advantage. Stalin began to destroy Vlad from within, threatening to rip the soul asunder, completely disintegrating all that was ever the Prince of Wallachia.

The ground opened up for Hell to claim the defeated combatant and, amazingly, Stalin unleashed a cold blast that caused the minions of Hell pause. Beria placed a hand on Stalin's shoulder, shouting, "Enough, Iosif! You have won. Do not do that which you are considering! Even Lucifer dares not destroy souls!"

Stalin looked at Beria, discontinuing the bludgeoning of his defeated foe. "Perhaps I am more horrible than he," was Stalin's answer, delivered in a blood-chilling tone. The tentacles of Hell, for what could be the first time in eternity's record, gently lowered a soul to the abyss. All was not right with this kill.

Stalin assessed the room, announcing, "Let none doubt who is the boss here." The souls understood their cue, and turned on Mao. Stalin felt Mao's might was necessary to infiltrate the castle and achieve victory. However, he also believed Mao's ambition would lead to an inevitable showdown. Better it happen at the time of Stalin's choosing. Mao fell quickly before the surprising assault, and Stalin exited the room even before the Chinamen fell, wondering if Hitler's attack in Galiktus was equally successful.

Had Stalin taken the time to consider his fears he would have quickly concluded they were unfounded; no force in Galiktus could withstand the well planned and focused assault Hitler unleashed on that territory. Two images easily associated to Hitler's life were the wolf and fire. At least two of his headquarters were named after wolves and his S.S. was affectionately referred to as a "pack of wolves." Fire was an omnipresent force, from the Reichstag fire that led to the passage of the Enabling Act, to the furnaces in the death camps, to Hitler's own suicide, when his final orders before he took his own life was to incinerate his body and bunker. Fire was always attached to the man whose perverse visions became a nightmare revealed.

These dual images became the weapons unleashed on Galiktus, as Hitler's twisted mind conjured spiritual wolves for he and his men to ride into battle. The fire-breathing wolves announced the arrival of Hitler's host. One could almost feel pity for the damned souls as Hitler and his rampant hordes redefined the word evil for them.

The army of annihilation razed the towns and villages of Galiktus. All they encountered were sent to Hell. New imports would quickly repopulate the region, no need for stragglers who might feel loyalty despite their wicked disposition, to the old regime. As Hitler and his most trusted aides approached the fortress of Andrew Jackson, they found the entrance on the opposite side of a great chasm too broad to leap, even with the aid of phantom wolves. The floating ship, *Twilight,* approached them and the men looked up with apprehension, until Christopher Columbus tossed Benedict Arnold, bound in chains, over the bow.

Arnold crashed to the ground, his face revealing a mix of fear and anger. Without a word, Christopher Columbus hurled two knives into Arnold; enough to drive the failed hero back to Hell. As the knives struck Arnold, ladders descended from *Twilight* and brought Hitler and his three companions, whose mere presence caused Columbus discomfort, onto the deck. No one even bothered to watch as the forces of Hell dragged Benedict Arnold to his eternal home.

As *Twilight* soared over the walls of the fortress towards the central keep, Andrew Jackson and Francisco Pizarro prepared their final stand. Columbus readied to disembark, but Hitler waved him off. He wished to win this final battle for Galiktus accompanied by only his three Nazi companions; Heinrich Himmler, Reinhard Heydrich and Josef Mengele, high ranking Nazi's, all of whom shared Hitler gruesome outlook in life as well as death.

The four horrific souls entered the unprotected keep as if it was already their possession and, in reality, it was. Himmler, the supreme commander of the entire Nazi police force, including the dreaded Gestapo was, in life, intimately involved in all aspect of the Holocaust. Heydrich was answerable to only Hitler and Himmler in life; in death, the same was true. Mengele was a Nazi doctor, callously conducting experiments on Jews at Auschwitz and selecting individuals destined for labor or gas chambers. To these men, the opportunity to assert their dominance over Limbo seemed natural, their time in Hell well worth the possibility of creating a new Reich in Limbo.

Himmler, Heydrich and Mengele descended on Pizarro as remorseless as a plague. Pizarro, the man who led an undermanned force to victory over the Incas, now found himself helpless before the powerful triumvirate whose might quickly banished him from Limbo.

The fall of the conquistador held no interest to Hitler, for he already turned his attention to Andrew Jackson. The infernal force of Hitler's presence filled the room, terrifying the former president. Never had he felt so insignificant. As Hitler approached Jackson, spirit wolves came forth, breathing hot flames and driving Jackson's back to the wall of the keep. Jackson lashed out with darts of energy, but they were impervious to his attack. The wolves howled as they surrounded Jackson, keeping him immobile for the final denouncement.

Hitler looked, almost pityingly, at his victim, as he approached. He felt a strange kinship with Jackson, as both men orchestrated the systematic removal of unwanted people from their lands. In some ways Jackson had created a blue print Hitler could well have followed as he unleashed his final solution in Europe. Now he shared his vision with Jackson.

Hitler grabbed Andrew Jackson's head, pouring into his mind all the horrors of the Holocaust in the span of three seconds. Jackson's body convulsed at the gruesome images he beheld, be they gas chambers, starvation or the burning of homes, and the devastating knowledge that his own actions were an inspiration to the evil soul standing before him. Jackson would have an eternity to contemplate how, for all his achievements; no one admired or understood him more than the Nazi dictator. As Hell opened its maw and pulled Jackson down, he wondered if any suffered more in the abyss than he had in the last two minutes of his existence in Limbo.

Hitler cared little for what Jackson thought as he turned to his men. Heydrich and Mengele would stay behind and begin the rebuilding of Galiktus, with a keen eye focused on leveling their opponents home and building a fortress fitting the Fuhrer. Hitler and Himmler flew with Columbus to Nafarhel to meet with Stalin and plan the future.

Stalin and Hitler decided their mutual survival required cooperation, if not an actual alliance. Events from their time on Earth left the two men incapable of trusting the other, but present circumstances demanded some agreement. The two decided that, for the time being, rebuilding the regions they now controlled and putting into practice their own unique rule was of prime importance.

The forces of Limbo, they concluded, would never raise arms against them, for they had long ago learned to co-exist with wicked neighbors. The forces of light would, undoubtedly, choose to increase the amount of might gathered in Valdor and Hodvold, the two territories which bordered Galiktus exclusively, while paying special attention to the defenses of Troothgnase. The cold war had come to Limbo, lasting ten years until Hitler violated the peace and invaded his neighbor, Troothgnase.

Chapter 10
Show of Force

An eventful week on Earth had little impact on the race for the White House, which was rapidly becoming a two-way contest between the Republicans and the Self-Determination Party. The Democrats seemed assigned to the ignobility of a third place finish. Regardless of this situation all three candidates had to address the events that unfolded at the Middle East Peace Summit. Events scripted and implemented by President Blaylock. The various headlines and reports, predictably, followed the philosophy of the news outlets.

"...New technology shocks and stuns the world..."
"...President's announcement mixed with arrogance leads to negative reviews, both at home and abroad..."
"...President well within his rights to limit access to American discovery..."
"...America, thanks to Republican leadership, a technological leader again..."
"...Fantastic technology, unspectacular unveiling..."

While meeting with the assembled leaders of the Middle East, an annual summit always fraught with peril and possible disaster, the President unveiled the newest technology created by the U.S. military. The new invention, a transportation chip, was nicknamed "Theve Technology" after the primary inventor, Steve Theve. The transportation chips had been used by the U.S. military for approximately four years and was deemed safe enough to be introduced to the general public.

Each chip, which could be held in a pocket or attached like a pin to an article of clothing, was programmed to interact with specific computer programs and discs. The chip, along with up to 500 pounds of weight, both human and inanimate, could be teleported from one set of co-ordinates to another. Only one chip could be used per person, therefore to transport twenty-five men required twenty- five teleportation chips. The announcement explained how the United States was able to enjoy some improbable and sudden successes in the never-ending battle with terrorists.

The President then made a controversial decision, arranging for ten fully equipped Marines to appear as he announced the existence of the transportation technology, enabling those with a limited imagination a concrete example of the potential benefits and hazards of the technology. Each Marine appeared, brandishing knives, and disappeared within two seconds, ample time to do extensive damage had they been wielding more threatening weapons. One Marine appeared directly behind the President of Iran, the knife held menacingly over his head. This action was viewed as either over kill, unnecessarily hostile or appropriately dramatic depending on the station reporting the meeting. Perhaps even more contentious were the statements made by President Blaylock following the unveiling of this technology.

President Blaylock announced that for the foreseeable future the "Theve Technology" would remain only in American hands and would not be exported at any price. The possible abuses of this technology, especially if terrorists possessed it, were too frightening to consider. The U.S. government would continue to perfect the transportation chips and they would be released, in due time, to the American public. Like all new inventions, its impact would be small at first, but eventually Theve travel would replace cars and planes as everyday modes of transportation. The need for gas and oil would drop accordingly. Projections pointed to the probability that, in twenty years, the United States would use oil and gas in such quantities that domestic production would be more than enough to cover the demands; dramatically and irrevocably altering the relationship between the United States and certain nations.

The remainder of the summit, whether it were promises made to the democracy of Iraq or a new wave of resolutions between Israel and Palestine, was overshadowed by the president's proclamation and the manner of its delivery. Maxwell Grahm, who had spoken to the President immediately after he, like the rest of the world, witnessed the demonstration of the Theve Technology, prepared to enter the Oval Office for the traditional Monday meeting with the President. He had been in his office since 4 a.m., occasionally leaving his desk to pensively pace the halls only to return to stare holes into the walls. He pulled his suit taut and adjusted his tie for the hundredth time as he entered, reminding himself that he was entering the Oval Office.

"Good Morning," Maxwell began before reigniting a conversation that President Blaylock had not allowed to take place on the phone. Standing in the center of the Oval Office and struggling to maintain a courteous tone Maxwell continued. "I thought we agreed not to demonstrate the effectiveness of the 'Theve Technology' at the Summit. We were only going to make the announcement."

"Good Morning to you too," President Blaylock responded, looking up from a report he was scanning. "As for your question, you discussed at great length your misgivings at such a demonstration, I never agreed not to hold one. I am sorry if we did not communicate clearly with each other."

"Communicating with me is the least of our worries, don't you see what you've done?" Clarity not formality, Maxwell realized, was of the essence. The President who had an answer for the posed rhetorical question, however, cut off the chief of staff.

"What I've done?! All I've done is strike fear into our enemies. America has been seen as little more than a paper tiger in that part of the world since I've been alive. The time is right for others to tremble at our position as a world leader again. A super power is nothing if their power is not respected, and even dreaded. Those Marines appearing and disappearing showed our edge to those gathered and to the rest of the world watching. Everyone now knows how inescapable our reach is. Add to that the devaluation of their greatest natural resource and my announcement reminding them of America's preeminence is all the more devastating. And you would have me withhold that moment? For who, our European 'allies'? For countries that constantly promise aid in the apprehension and disruption of terrorists, only to always fail us? For nations long on strong talk, but completely lacking fortitude? We will not wait for the indecisive to discover courage, besides they can't find what they are not looking for! They deserve to feel shock, surprise and fear. Maybe they will realize terrorists can't be talked into submission!"

"I hope you enjoyed your moment, it may cost the election," was Maxwell's terse response.

"Or," President Blaylock said in unrepentant tones, "it might win it."

Televisions, newspapers and the never-ending stream of internet outlets echoed the concerns of President Blaylock's long time confidant.

"...Drew McClure views Presidents actions as unpresidential..."
"...William Casey believes President "made U.S a bigger target than ever..."
"...Forceful President may have gone too far at Mid-East summit..."
"...European leader stunned by callous President..."
"...What is leadership...?"

Drew McClure and William Casey were quick to denounce the approach used by President Blaylock in unveiling the 'Theve Technology'. On CNN, MSNBC and Fox the candidates consistently reiterated joy at the technology's existence, but bewilderment at the manner and timing of the announcement. Drew believed the announcement all but negated any possible positives achieved at the summit. All the delegates could focus on was the way the 'Theve' would change the future, lost at the summit was the very real need for solutions in Iraq, Israel and Palestine. "The entire conference," McClure noted on CNN, "became an opportunity for President Blaylock to beat his chest like some sort of enraged gorilla. Hardly the behavior we need from a head of state, and much less than the American people deserve."

William Casey also voiced dismay with the President's action, pointing out that such a show of force could well escalate anti-American feelings. "Such feelings," William Casey explained, "rarely disappear because of fear. Fear may, and that is a big if, stop action, but not thoughts. President Blaylock's conduct was appropriate for an immature teenager showing off their latest gadget, not the chief executive of the United States. If President Blaylock wants to be so dramatic, let him take up acting and star in an action movie. We need better from the President."

Post-summit polls reflected McClure's and Casey's words. Almost all information pointed to Blaylock falling farther behind McClure, with the gap between Casey and the President shortened. McClure stressed to Fox News the Mid-East summit was undoubtedly the wrong forum for releasing the information about the Theve Technology. "Everyone at the meeting was shortchanged; it became, at the least, a pep rally for American ingenuity, not a problem solving session as originally planned. A meeting designed to build hope, became a vehicle to spread fear and contentiousness. The reverberations of the failed summit will be felt for far too long."

This statement brought predictable anti-America wolves to Drew's door, but they had no impact on the position the Self-Determination candidate chose, in fact; they seemed to strengthen it. Drew enjoyed the philosophical discussions held on the network shows and continued to speak freely, convinced voters would flock to the S.D.P because honesty without animosity has an appeal all its own.

The Democrats in the media and capital hill also denounced the President's methodology, but their criticisms carried a century of deep-seeded enmity, hence they were fiercer and more belligerent than Drew's and the S.D.P.'s. William Casey recognized this as one of Drew's greatest strengths, combined with the position the S.D.P. enjoyed as a true underdog; which carried an appeal neither major party could touch. The Democrats, due to their inability to claim the White House in recent years tried to paint themselves as underdogs, the party of the common man and little guy, but it was a shallow attempt, for they had a long history as a major political party. No, the Democrats often, and unfortunately, came across as angry and shrill, "vote for us because we are not Republicans" seemed to permeate every word a Democrat said, an undercurrent of anger made visible by the analytical voice of Drew McClure, whose greatest enemies, addiction and loss, existed in the candidate's own soul, not in the Republican or Democratic party.

The S.D.P had no axe to grind, no century of harsh political battles to fuel a seething anger. All they had was an underdog's hope and the vision of their standard bearer. As hard as William tried to stay above the fray, he failed to obtain the rare ground occupied naturally by Drew McClure.

Such matters were inconsequential to Drew, whose eyes were trained on the future. It was essential that an upcoming interview on the popular show *People and Politics* goes well, giving the S.D.P momentum as they departed for Saudi Arabia. Most candidates would not take such trips, wisely spending their time campaigning in the States. Drew wanted to remind the public this was not your ordinary race, and this candidate could appear presidential even without the title.

Chapter 11
War Room Consultation

Niccolo hurried out of the Martin Luther center into the streets of Tecktoral. He walked purposefully down the street, passing the Raphael Art Museum as he hastened to the library in the center of town. The library was easily the largest single structure in Tecktoral, filled with over 1,000,000 titles, classrooms and lecture halls. Niccolo often visited the library for two to three hours a day, often reading the works of philosophers throughout the ages as well as poets and an occasional novel to relax.

The lecture halls usually featured speakers visiting from Heaven who offered insights and new perspectives to age-old questions. A message board in front of the library advertised the expected arrival of Rene Descartes and Immanuel Kant. Niccolo mused he would like to hear the two men speak, but knew he would likely not have the time. The note Dylan handed him was a summons to the seldom used war room in the basement of the library; a room which was only used to discuss dire situations.

As Niccolo entered the hallway leading to the war room he knew only one thing, the ten years of tension between Troothgnase and her neighbor must have erupted in some manner. He also knew, given the nature of these neighbors that the breach was almost certainly a military attack. When madmen tethered the dogs of war hell often followed in their wake.

The tension in the room as Niccolo pushed through the double doors was high, but not suffocating. A small group of familiar faces sat at the table occupying the center of the room; their faces revealing both a quiet acceptance of danger and a level of confidence in their capacity to over come great obstacles. They also understood an unspoken truth, no matter how terrible a situation may seem, it is probably worse.

Winston Churchill stood at an end of the large, rectangular table. He was chomping on a conjured cigar, chewing on it out of habit, creating no smoke from the unlit spiritual stogie. He appeared anxious to begin the meeting as he waved Niccolo to a seat next to Seamus who smiled a greeting to his friend. To Winston's right sat Abraham Lincoln, still dressed casually, but his eyes smoldered with the intensity that enabled hin to endure the Civil War. Sitting directly across from Lincoln was Leonidas, the Spartan general, and Col. Robert Gould Shaw, the commanding officer of the 54th Massachusetts, the first black company to see action during the Civil War. Three of Shaw's men, all dressed in Union blue, as was Shaw, accompanied him to this meeting.

"Gentlemen," Winston began with the voice and presence that brought hope to England during the darkest hours of World War II, "our worst fears are indeed upon us, the ten year cold war is over and the time for armed conflict has arrived."

Every head nodded in agreement. The desire for peace often means nothing when war is declared. The limitless potential for evil that existed in Galiktus and Nafarhel only intensified this certainty.

"It would seem," Churchill continued, "Mr. Hitler is up to his old tricks. Three days ago a force of Nazis, Vandals, militants and extremists, led by Columbus and Heinrich Himmler attacked the peaceful residents of Troothgnase. They have complete control of the area and there is no reason to believe the capture of one state will satisfy Hitler's greed. He has settled into the area himself, surveying the damage. The ferocity of their assault crushed all defenses and, undoubtedly, will lead Hitler to believe all of Limbo's states can be easily taken."

"I will prove the lie in those words," Leonidas snarled. Churchill, who was no stranger to the need for determination in the face of danger, nodded in agreement.

"You will get your chance, General. We all will. We are to send aid to the city of Tylferling in the Dagduada Forrest. Our small expedition will join a larger force there. As the larger battles rages, a small group must locate and defeat Hitler in combat, for the loss of their general will cause his army of riffraff and cowards to quickly lose heart, for their courage is not their own, but an extension of his audacity."

"Careful wit' those words, Winston," Seamus said sharply. "I seem to recall those 'cowards' having some success in the past, or 'ave ye forgotten? We should ne'er underestimate an opponent. Especially a ferocious one."

Churchill raised his fist and prepared to respond to Seamus only to be interrupted by Abraham Lincoln, who saw no need to be distracted by side arguments.

"What of this Joseph Stalin? What action has he taken?"

"Stalin has not moved from his mountain fortress in Nafarhel. He seems to be carrying on the normal business of that Hellish realm… training augmenters and sending them to do battle in the fissures under threat of cruel punishment. He and Hitler share a frighteningly despicable view of humanity, but share no loyalty to each other. It seems Hitler acted alone, though I suspect Stalin may send him aid if needed."

"Any chance this Hitler will halt his expansion?" Niccolo asked. "The force behind Hitler does not, I am sure, want to risk losing the foothold gained in Limbo."

"I think not, Niccolo. Experience tells me Hitler does not stop. He must be stopped," was Churchill's vigorous response, his fist striking his palm as if smiting Hitler himself. "In fact, it is our hope that a small force can bring Abraham to Hitler's lair, for we believe Abraham holds the key to stopping Mr. Hitler for the final time. The 54th Massachusetts will lend their might to the forces at Tylferling."

Lincoln nodded, knowingly, for Winston and he had begun this discussion the night he met Jon in the Rising Soul's. He was, however, disturbed with the announcement of the 54th's potential involvement. "I understand Leonidas and other Spartans willingly leave Heaven to risk their freedom hunting augmenters and that is his right. From all I have heard the risk of battle is Heaven to a Spartan and I claim no special authority over them. I am opposed to the involvement of Col. Shaw and the 54th. These men have all passed on to Heaven and should remain there. They have fought and died for me during their lives, proving their valor and honor far beyond the call of most men. I would not have them risk their souls for me now. They have done, and suffered, enough. We can find other able-bodied soldiers in Limbo, souls still searching sanctuary in Heaven. We ought not call upon those who have already earned their rest."

"Permission to speak freely, Mr. Lincoln?" Col. Shaw stood at attention before his former commander-in-chief.

"Do you truly think you need ask? Permission humbly granted, under the condition, you understand, that such requests are unnecessary from you to me."

Shaw looked at his men for a second and spoke, "Mr. Lincoln, my men and I were not called upon. The conflagration in Troothgnase was brought to the attention of Leonidas in Heaven, for he and his men are always searching for the opportunity to test their mettle.

He spread word of his intent to other generals and men of war who somehow found Heavenly rest. When we heard we could aid you, we volunteered for duty."

"Mistah Lincoln," one of Shaw's men quickly spoke up, then hesitated, wondering if he was out of line, unworthy perhaps to speak at this gathering. An encouraging look from Lincoln was enough to allay his fears. "Col. Shaw is right. Da' whole 54 wantsta help you git to Heaven. You been in Limbo long enuff. You deserve to leave and we, well, we wants to help is all."

Lincoln, having learned long ago to listen to the messages more than speech patterns, looked upon the proud soldier and smiled. The soldier's lack of formal education did not detract from his sincerity or eloquence, to think otherwise would be the height of arrogance. "You, your Colonel and your comrades have done enough. You stood courageously before Fort Wagner and granted me the gift of faith rewarded." Lincoln paused for a moment, picturing the horrors of that battle. Faith rewarded, he whispered to himself before continuing.

"I cannot ask more of you than that. If my destiny lies in a confrontation with this Hitler, then I will fight that battle. Yours does not and I will not take you with me."

Robert Gould Shaw stood silently for a moment, searching Lincoln's face for a weakness to exploit, a facial tell to direct the Colonel to a more persuasive argument. The man who found himself pinned down by cannon fire at the foot of Fort Wagner, who charged headlong into the teeth of the enemy shouting his last words, "Forward 54!", found Lincoln's face more daunting than the mightiest Confederate fortress. "Very well, Mr. Lincoln," was all the response that Shaw could muster. "Rest assured we will keep an eye on you and wait for the day when we may hold conversation in Heaven."

"I look forward to that day myself," Lincoln responded and the small delegate blinked from sight.

Niccolo was next to speak, pointing out that he had charges under his tutelage and was loathe to leave them all behind.

"I am aware of your responsibilities, Niccolo," Churchill responded. "You may bring two of your pupils with you, for the danger they face, the victory they secure, will undoubtedly hasten their departure from Limbo."

Niccolo considered Churchill's words and quickly produced two postcard-sized rectangles of light. He concentrated for a second, and then flicked his wrist as he snapped his fingers, causing the two cards to disappear. Jon and Danielle would receive invitations to meet Niccolo at his new ship, *Sundiata,* the next time the criers called. If they did not show he would assume they were not interested. Jon, he believed, was going to choose to be a hunter so this mission was, to Niccolo, merely an extension of that duty. Danielle may well welcome a break from the lecture halls where she experienced only limited success.

Seamus O'Malley rocked forward in his seat, uncomfortable not with the chair, but with the planned rendezvous with the armies of Tylferling. "Just a quick point. Ye say Troothgnase 'as fallen', so why won't Hitler attack Hodvold first? Troothgnase and Galiktus can both be used fer launchin' an attack aimed at Hodvold. Could we be headin' to the wrong place?"

"I think not, Seamus," Leonidas replied. "The Skadistine Mountain range, which creates a formidable natural barrier, dominates most of Hodvold. Hitler will take the Dagduada Forest before even contemplating an assault on Hodvold."

"That makes good sense, indeed it does, but then why nae conquer Valdar, it also neighbors Hodvold. It still feels we are merely headin' towards Tylferlin' because they won the coin flip, or perhaps we jus' takin' a fifty-fifty shot in the dark."

Winston Churchill chomped a few extra times on his cigar before answering. He realized the legitimacy of Seamus' questions, but he still preferred someone he viewed as a subordinate to be more trusting when given orders. Still, the only outward sign of displeasure was the delay before answering.

"We have another reason to believe Hitler will order an attack of the Dagduada Forrest, aimed at the destruction of Tylferling, and it lies in his ego and hatred. Hitler has a deep hatred not just of Jews, but of Poles, Slavs and any minority. Two of the most influential residents of Tylferling are Lech Walesa of Poland and Stephen Biko of South Africa. To capture them would bring a moment of warmth to the cold core of Hitler. Ego, narcissistic ego, adds to his need to attack the region. The best military mind in that area is Grigori Zhukov, the Russian entrusted by Stalin with the defense of Moscow when the armies of Hitler threatened to demolish the city. Marshal Zhukov performed his duty well, fiercely defending his homeland, as any man should. The battle hardened soldier eventually found himself in the wolves den, helping the Red Army claim Berlin as a prize of war. Stalin rewarded him with banishment from any and all important post war assignments, jealous of his popularity with the common peasant and suspicious of his relationship with American and British diplomats. Stalin would attempt to erase his name from history, not allowing his name to be mentioned at celebrations commemorating the defense of Moscow. Only Zhukov's great popularity stayed Stalin's hand from claiming his life. Thus does Stalin reward loyalty and service. For Hitler, Zhukov represents defeat and the chance for revenge. Zhukov's soul in chains may be a greater prize to Hitler than all of Limbo itself. Hence, we believe the attack on the Dagduada Forest is imminent."

Seamus was more than satisfied with this answer and appreciative of Churchill's willingness to divulge information. When the Prime Minister finished his explanation Lincoln patted his arm, congratulating him for his patience and eloquence.

Niccolo's thoughts moved to Danielle and her "because I have final say" approach to leadership. She could have learned much from this exchange, Churchill did not have his strategy approved because he ran the meeting or had the most degrees, but rather because it was the product of careful research and its validity was beyond reproach, holding up to the scrutiny of the hard to satisfy Seamus. How many times had Danielle ended discussion by proclaiming her authority, not proving beyond all doubt the value of her plans? Of course, Niccolo mused, one must have a plan that fulfills, or at least considers, everyone's needs in order to defend it properly. Danielle's primary concern was reputation and legacy, and if it helped the greater good; that was a bonus.

"Niccolo," Churchill bellowed. "How soon until your vessel is ready?"

"Convene at Dias' Way at the next crier's call."

Winston slapped his hands together, "Excellent! Then forward for truth, honor and the end of darkness!"

Niccolo and Seamus exchanged a quiet glance, both men more amused than inspired by the bombastic, but animated, outburst. Lincoln stood and quietly departed. Somehow this man who had little love for combat found his entire presidency wrapped around a savage war and now it appeared his soul, which sought only serenity, could only find violence. For a second he wondered if he sent the 54th off for the stated reasons or because he couldn't fathom why one would leave the tranquility of Heaven for the clamor of war.

Chapter 12
Departure

Jon and Danielle approached *Sundiata* as Niccolo and Seamus prepared the ship for departure. Both held the invitation to the dock and both were brimming with excitement and curiosity. Niccolo summarized the nature of their journey, emphasizing that the two novices would only come as close to battle as he wanted them to. They were, after all, unfamiliar with combat.

As Niccolo suspected both agreed to join the expedition. Jon because he planned on becoming a hunter and Danielle was eager to learn from Churchill, Lincoln and any other famous leader they would meet. Niccolo heard the veiled insult without being bothered, for Danielle was still prone to decide whom she could learn from based on standing in history and society rather than the merits of what they say and do. Niccolo wondered how many potential teachers Danielle never noticed because she was rarely willing to be their student.

When Niccolo completed his explanation, Jon asked about the name of the boat, recalling that name was mentioned in the "video" he watched his first day in Limbo. Niccolo expressed admiration that Jon recalled the name and briefly explained the reason Sundiata became the name of his ship.

"Sundiata was a small, weak boy before becoming King of Mali. In fact, his frail appearance saved his life. A ruthless King, Sumanguru killed eleven out of twelve sons of a powerful rival, believing this heinous act would quell all thoughts of rebellion. The twelfth son, Sundiata, was allowed to live because he seemed too weak to ever pose a threat. As Sudiata grew to an adult, he became popular and powerful, his army constantly growing. Eventually his armies defeated those of Sumanguru in bloody battle, enabling Sundiata to become King. To me, the most inspirational aspect of the tale is that, Sundiata could have, and many people would have, allowed his past to make him bitter and angry with the world, but he chose not to. Upon becoming King, Sundiata ruled by his wits and intelligence, his even-tempered rule helped reestablish the prosperous gold-salt train of Africa. His willingness to remember his past, but not be controlled by it is an inspiring lesson. One I struggle with regularly. I hope by naming my ship *Sundiata* I can inherit the best traits of a good man."

Jon, as he had proven already, was an attentive student, provided the lesson did not involve learning about himself. Niccolo thought it wise not to ask Jon what, if anything, he learned from the tale. Time enough for probing questions, for it was a three day "sail" to Tylferling and either he or Seamus were sure to rattle the boy's mind eventually. No need to rush the experience, or deprive Seamus the joy of instigating the discussion.

"Man, I never learned about Sundiata in school, I don't even recognize the name," was all Jon had to say after Niccolo's explanation. Danielle had also been listening with interest, amazed at the depth of Niccolo's knowledge—forgetting, as she often did—that Niccolo had been in Limbo for 500 years, plenty of time for the driven sailor to complete an extensive self-education.

Niccolo, seeing the rest of the group arriving, turned to greet them. With one ear he heard Seamus' response to Jon's statement. "Don't feel bad Jon boy. Most schools 'celebrate diversity' by hangin' posters in February and by havin' their administrators pose for pictures with minority students. Window dressing overtook substance in yuir country well before you were born. Ask Danielle about it." Danielle understood exactly what Seamus meant, and unlike the Italian, was not able to dismiss the insult. She filed it away for future use as ammunition when she confronted Niccolo for allowing such insensitivity and crudeness go unchallenged.

Niccolo greeted his companions warmly and requested they board quickly for their departure was almost at hand. Jon and Danielle had very different reactions to the ensemble; Jon having met Lincoln earlier was not as awe struck in his presence. Lincoln and Winston Churchill's arrival, on the other hand, staggered Danielle and she could barely conceal her amazement. They did share the same reaction to Leonidas, both feeling a sense of dread when as he strode purposefully to greet Niccolo. He gave no indication that he even noticed Jon or Danielle.

As Niccolo showed Seamus a couple of improvements recently made on *Sundiata* Jon called up a question. "Hey, Niccolo! If there is no morning or night here why is there a bright moon in the sky?"

Niccolo looked up and responded quickly, "It's a portal...just... watch."

A bright light shone through the opening, illuminating the dock. As the light bathed the companions their thoughts and beings were overwhelmed by an unearthly serenity. The joy of a wedding day, the elation of watching your first child's staggering attempts at walking, these emotions were but bland memories compared to the rapture the portal's light wrought. Slowly every head, first John and lastly Niccolo, looked down, no longer capable of handling the joy they felt. Only Winston continued to gaze into the sky, which was glowing with the most beautiful of sunrises, not the typical gray of Limbo.

A figure strode from the center of the light, heading towards the travelers. It took little time to recognize the individual, for it was Franklin D. Roosevelt, without his wheelchair and seeming to be in perfect health. Winston Churchill enthusiastically greeted his old friend and ally.

"Franklin," Churchill said the former president's name as if it were a proclamation unto itself. "Have you come to see us off, old friend? What an opportunity, to defeat Hitler again, and to end that Stalin's reign of terror as well. I feel blessed beyond compare."

"The two scoundrels don't stand a chance, especially with the fine companions you have gathered for this mission."

"They are all up to the task, even Seamus, whose keen mind will let no plan proceed unexamined to the last detail. He can exasperate, but his ability to keep men, even the leaders of men, on their toes is invaluable."

"Excellent. Is the company leaving soon?"

"As soon as we board and Niccolo gets her in the air. The hosts of Heaven must be nervous to send an emissary to see us off. Tell them to worry not, Winston is on the case!"

"Winston, with your spirit victory would be too easily secured. I am not here to see the defenders of Limbo leave. No, I am here to take you home."

"Now? You take me now? Not when I was tending bar, but as I prepare to confront evil! Where is the justice in this?"

Franklin placed a hand on Churchill's shoulder and whispered softly, "Can they succeed without you?"

Churchill looked sadly at his companions, envisioning the toils they would soon face and the triumph he believed they would eventually enjoy, even without his services. "Yes, Franklin. I believe they can. They can succeed without me."

"Then let them, Winston. Let us take our leave."

Without another word, or a backwards glance, Franklin Roosevelt and Winston Churchill passed through the glowing portal, which closed instantly behind them. The remaining souls, gathered on *Sundiata's* deck, watched in awe at what they had experienced.

"So that is an ascension," Seamus said to no one in particular as he looked into the sky, searching for the portal and knowing it was gone. "I hav' naer seen one fer myself."

"I have witnessed close to a dozen, the feeling doesn't change. One never tires of even a glimpse of Heaven," Niccolo replied.

"Isn't it rude not to even say goodbye? What kind of manners are those?" Jon asked in an accusatory tone.

Niccolo explained the moment to Jon the best he could.

"A soul ascending to Heaven is aware only of his guide and the portal. The moment Roosevelt appeared we became nothing but shadows to Winston."

Jon shrugged, accepting the answer but also wanting to make light of the situation. He continued in a good-natured tone, "That sounds good and all, but still he could have made a speech or something. I thought Winston Churchill loved showing off at ceremonies?"

"True enough, laddie, but, what manners can ye rightfully expect from an Englishmen?"

"Souls from Heaven can visit Limbo as they like, therefore if Winston decides a more proper goodbye is appropriate he will return to say them." Niccolo paused for a moment, then turned to Jon and continued in a scathing voice.

"I am sure you will be at the top of his list Jon, seeing how you never even met the man and probably slept through the lesson about him in school. It must be nice to consider yourself the center of the universe. Why would any historic figure greet you kindly when all you ever gave them was a puddle of drool as you snored through your classes? We embark on dire business and I bring fools –a stupid, modern, unthinking dolt. I imagine there is truly nothing you have to offer than dull comments intended to be humorous. We haven't left yet and I already regret taking you."

Niccolo's outburst stung Jon for it shot like an arrow dismounting a rider. No mercy, just unerring precision designed to kill. Seamus reached for Niccolo's arm, whispering, "Come now, laddie, the boy was merely…"

"Enough chattering, we are not thoughtless, gossiping children. Best if we depart soon."

With those words, Niccolo proceeded to a chair located on a raised platform at the back of the ship. There were no steering mechanisms or controls near the chair, nor were they necessary, for it was Niccolo's will that drove the vessel, not man made machinery.

As Niccolo silently steered *Sundiata* towards Tylferling he looked around the deck. Jon, whom Seamus had effectively cheered up (Don' let'em worry ye lad, sometime ole Niccolo is jus' fulla shit.), and Danielle were pointing down at the city of Tecktoral, amazed at the expanse of the city. For the briefest of moments, they were tourists on a sightseeing expedition, not rookie combatants preparing to battle evil.

Lincoln sat alone seemingly lost in thought, undoubtedly he was contemplating the myriad of outcomes the coming conflicts presented. Finally, his gaze fell onto Leonidas and Seamus. The Irishman was creating spiritual weapons and firing them at targets created by the Spartan general, who found himself duly impressed by his companion's marksmanship.

Chapter 13
Unexpected Disaster

The mood permeating the private plane carrying Drew McClure back to the United States was dark and uninviting. The few media on board worked as silently as possible, tapping the keyboards of their laptops with a gentleness often reserved for holding a newborn babe. Others whispered into digital recording devises, capturing thoughts to use in later stories. Self-Determination party members sat in silence while Drew agonized in a private chamber in the back of the plane.

Fewer people were returning to America than expected because of a terrorist attack that killed five of Drew's personal bodyguards in a hotel in downtown Riyadh. The Saudi government quickly apologized and denounced the attack. The worst loss, however, was the kidnapping of Drew's eleven-year-old daughter, Erin, whom Drew brought reluctantly, only relenting when both the S.D.P. security and the Saudi government assured safety. There seemed to be no end to the ability of terrorists to shatter guarantees of peace with unexpected actions executed with expert precision. Drew sat and cursed the fool in the mirror who forgot the lessons of the past.

News of the attack and kidnapping dominated the news from the moment it occurred and was unrelenting in its wake. Questions abounded from Drew's carelessness to new, almost paranoid, concerns about travel. What was the proper U.S. response was asked even before anyone knew who was to blame. Dozens of small, seemingly unrelated terrorist groups formed in the past twenty years and any one of them could have organized the kidnapping.

Democrats quickly blamed the Republican president for creating the atmosphere for the attack. Republicans countered, pointing out the eight years Democrats controlled the White House and Congress coincided with the rapid growth of terrorist groups. Democrats believed their endless rhetoric and promises to "get tough" without taking meaningful action was enough to stay the hand of wickedness. This arrogant assumption combined with a lack of military spending clearly made this terrible attack possible.

None of these questions or the ceaseless bickering between the established parties meant anything to Drew McClure. Erin McClure was kidnapped, what else mattered? In an hour or two, Drew would be half a world away from her. Drew felt, for reasons founded in emotion, not logic, that staying in Saudi Arabia would be productive. Brian had convinced Drew to leave, pointing out that milling anxiously about Saudi Arabia's capital served no purpose and would be no help to Erin.

Drew sat alone in the small office, fears dancing about the room like mosquitoes on a summer evening. Drew read a favorite anecdote about the Buddha, hoping to find solace. There was once a man who could not believe the Buddha was as serene as he had heard. No one could be so content to be beyond agitation. This man sought out the Buddha with the intent of causing him to lose his temper. Upon finding the enlightened one, the pilgrim acted as rudely, obnoxiously and arrogantly as humanly possible. For three days the Buddha unwaveringly returned kindness for rudeness, finally causing the visitor to cease his antics and ask why he had not succeeded. The Buddha's simple answer, the man was offering a gift the Buddha did not want to receive. For twenty years Drew had successfully declined unwanted gifts, but the misery the terrorists offered was inescapable. The words of the Buddha never seemed so uninspiring.

While Drew struggled on the edge of despair Niccolo sat in his private quarters in the hull of Sundiata. He was angry with himself for the way he finished his explanation. There was no need to be condescending to Jon, the boy was joking around, not intending any harm or disrespect. His outburst was now viewed as not only unnecessary, but little more than an immature projection. Niccolo realized, alone in his cabin, why he had acted so poorly; he was jealous of Winston's ascension. The sight of the portal gave Niccolo a moment of pause, wondering if his time had finally come. When he realized it hadn't he looked for an opportunity to release some frustration, and he picked the weakest person he could find. How unbefitting a captain on his own vessel. Niccolo pulled some books off the shelves behind him and read some favorite passages. While reading, he began writing an essay longing for the wisdom of the pages to flow into his mind.

Brian Murphy rose from his chair and knocked on the door to Drew's private office. He pushed the door open slowly, not waiting for permission to enter, for he knew what the answer would be. Brian looked at Drew and saw the personification of crest fallen. The sight of his longtime friend so depleted altered the direction Brian planned on taking the conversation. Empathy replaced resolve as Brian began to speak.

"Drew, I don't have the words..."

"Then maybe you shouldn't speak. And who said you should come in?"

"Common sense did," was Brian's quick response. It was obvious sympathy would serve little purpose in this room. The time for support would follow the return of conviction.

"Common sense also says you should..."

"That you should get on your feet and prepare for the media. You think they won't be at the airport for the latest story of the century? You can't present a public image like this, it will crush the campaign."

"Fuck the campaign! My daughter is out there—God knows where—and you want me to worry about a campaign?"

"Yes, because in two weeks she may well be found and what then?"

"Then I apologize for my pride. For foolishly believing I could keep her safe while parading her into harm's way."

"Bullshit! Like it or not a big part of your life has been pursuing the moment we are in right now—a true changing of the guards. Either you never believed a word you said or..."

"Or What! Or I am scared to death for Erin? That's the reality—I am horrified, immobilized, incapable of thought, and...

"And the first step to solving a problem is admitting you have one, right? Of course, you're scared, but she's alive...and so are you. Live your life, be what you promised yourself you would be. Did you really crawl out of a gutter twenty years ago just to allow some cowards to push you back down now? This is a time for faith, and friendship. You won't walk alone, Drew. Have you ever?"

Drew stared at Brian wishing to be angry with him but instead he felt silent admiration, wondering how this loyal friend knew what words to say. Not knowing what words he should speak, Drew sat in silence.

"We arrive in 90 minutes," Brian said in a subdued tone.

Drew looked aimlessly at his watch, his blank expression revealing his thoughts before they found voice.

"Brian, you will address the media. Inform them I plan to continue my campaign and will hold a press conference in forty-eight hours. They won't be happy, but I need time to rest and time to recover some strength."

"Very good, Drew. We will weather this. You'll see."

Brian left the room feeling relieved. Drew's eyes, however, did not see him go, for they sought out the liquor cabinet kept in the office so guests could enjoy a drink. *In the center of Koba, Stalin took a deep breath while he silently raised a glass to his lips.* The liquor cabinet seemed to fill the room. Drew's thoughts quickly left politics and even Erin's well being, to having a single drink. Just a little something to calm overwrought nerves. One sip could possibly bring gentle relief. *Alone in his cabin Niccolo read a favorite passage written by St. Francis of Assisi*

> *...O' Divine Master*
> *Grant that I may not so much seek*
> *To be consoled, as to understand*
> *To be loved, as to love*
> *For it is in giving that we receive...*

And another written by Confucius

> *The man of the highest moral virtue*
> *Wishing to stand firm, must lend firmness to others*
> *Wishing to be illuminated, will illuminate others*

Niccolo sought another book and continued reading, satisfied, for the moment, to reflect on his jealousy and admit his own need to correct some shortcomings.

Drew snapped out of the spell the liquor seemed to cast and paced the room. It had been years since alcohol had called so strongly. Somewhere in Limbo Stalin smiled, for the pieces all seemed to be falling into place.

Chapter 14
Reaction

The news of the Erin McClure kidnapping sent both major parties into frenzied activity. Republicans and Democrats desperately wanted to use the event for political gain while not appearing to do so. President Blaylock and William Casey both assumed the role of sympathetic peer, while party members tossed insults and facts at each other, under the guise of concerned politicians asking the crucial questions in the hopes of improving the nation.

President Blaylock, in no small part due to the spectacle of the Middle East summit, struggled more than William Casey did to strike a compassionate chord. Despite the efforts of the media and his own abrasiveness, President Blaylock's numbers continued to climb. The nation, as was its custom during a crisis, turned their eyes towards the highest office for answers. Maxwell Grahm knew all too well the fickle nature of the public and the necessity of capitalizing on the Republican's current momentum. Despite his determination, Maxwell hesitated when he opened the door to the Oval Office.

"Come in, Maxwell. Thomas just wrapped up his presentation."

Thomas Pierson, the National Security Advisor, closed his binder and thanked the president for his time. As Pierson departed, he stopped to greet Maxwell Grahm in a professional, though far from cordial, manner. The Secretary of State, Gene Grant, and the Secretary of Defense, Alexander Schipp, also took their leave, followed by the C.I.A and F.B.I liaisons. Only Grant took the time, or had the inclination, to wish Grahm a good day. As the room emptied, Maxwell Grahm' eyes were drawn to the huge seal of the President embroidered on the rug in the center of the room. The great bald eagle held arrows in one talon and an olive branch in the other. There wasn't a soul in this early morning meeting, with the exception of Gene Grant, who wouldn't gladly see arrows grasped by both claws.

"No need to enter the room with such trepidation, Max. We were merely discussing the latest intelligence, looking for clues to the location of Erin McClure. We weren't planning a full scale invasion of the Middle East."

"Of course not, Mr. President. What have they come up with?"

"Nothing substantial as of the moment. We suspect she is held in Iran, for more terror cells have made that country their base of operation in the past decade than any other locale. The C.I.A. believes the Fist of Allah is most likely responsible, for they have a reputation of political kidnappings as opposed to plucking random tourists off the streets. They also tend to be hyper-aggressive, believing it spreads fear. Rocket launchers, somewhat dated, but effective weapons, were used to blow up three civilian vehicles on the street as the kidnapping occurred. The Fist of Allah then detonated the small, but potent bomb that destroyed the door to Erin's room and killed two bodyguards. The Soldiers of Allah, as they call themselves, quickly killed the remaining bodyguards and made off with young Ms. McClure. It was a professional, if brutal, job."

"Have they claimed responsibility yet?"

"No...no group has contacted us with demands or just to boast. How are we doing politically?"

"Better than expected. Your speech pledging Erin's safe return played well across the country. The Dems have attempted, with some success, to point out how your sometimes aggressive nature may have inspired the attack, but," Maxwell's eyes widened and hands both raised, palms facing President Blaylock who's brow had furrowed at the mention of the Democrats, "our people have pointed out terrorists need little provocation to spread terror, it is what they do."

"Damn right it is! This is why I loathe Democrats...and why they can't hold this office." The intensity in the President's eyes augmented his words, creating a knot in Maxwell's stomach. President Blaylock continued, not noticing the anger he was emitting.

"Democrats will blame the victim for anything, provided the victim isn't a Democrat! If the victim is a Dem, well, then the attacker just didn't understand the sophisticated humanity of the victim, but rest assured we'll spend billion of dollars to educate, and indoctrinate, them with Democratic rhetoric. Mark my words, Maxwell, no Democrat is taking this office from me."

Blaylock's fierce determination often left two impressions, either the stimulation of activity in subordinates or concerns that he could become a fanatic in the attempt to achieve a goal. His next comment did little to dispel Maxwell Grahm's apprehension.

"We have pulled even with McClure in the polls. If the S.D.P. continues to struggle to find their footing and we find Erin and punish those responsible, our momentum heading into the fall will make victory in November inevitable."

Before continuing Blaylock noticed the look on his chief of staff's face.

"Spare me, Maxwell, I only voiced what you already knew was true. It may sound distasteful, but an incumbent president giving the orders that led to the rescue of a popular rival's child would be played up by the media to an epic degree. You know that's true."

Maxwell Grahm prepared to argue the point, but reluctantly admitted the truth of the President's word. "Fine. You're right. It is undeniably true. We should not, at any time, make it appear, or even allow the perception, that we are banking on that truth."

President Blaylock rubbed a hand over his pursed lips and chin. "Of course not. That was not the impression I meant to make. Thank you, Maxwell. Disturbed and determined is the image we need, not opportunistic and selfish."

Maxwell handed President Blaylock a dossier before departing the office. As he left, Maxwell Grahm asked one more question.

"The image we need or the realization of what we should always be, Mr. President?"

The question hung in the air and President Blaylock offered no answer, not that Grahm expected one. The polls indeed had The S.D.P and Republicans running an even race, but it was the third place Democrats who had the chief of staff's attention. With blood in the water, it was only a matter of time before the Democrats made a serious move.

Even as Maxwell Grahm left the Oval Office, the Democratic leadership was meeting in the living room of William Casey's plush home in Northern Virginia. The manicured lawns, which led to dazzling flower gardens, stood in direct contrast to the anxiety-ridden meeting.

William Casey sat in an old rocking chair, intently listening to the conversation unfold around him. The bedlam of the room almost made it impossible to listen to the cries of his inner voice.

Mike Fuller, William Casey's campaign manager was finishing a recap of the week's turbulent events, "...and Drew McClure has yet to meet the press personally. Brian Murphy issued a two minute statement, taking no questions, and rushed off, presumably to meet up with Drew."

A very professional, middle-aged woman shook her head in agreement. William Casey found himself wondering how she avoided whiplash brought on by the feral violence of her nod. "That's great, Mike," she declared. "We can easily portray the S.D.P as a still fledgling party, not ready for the stage they are on and incapable of handling a true crisis. McClure's inability to lead the S.D.P through this turmoil can be used to legitimately ask if McClure has the resolve to lead the country through a larger, all encompassing disaster."

"Excellent, Sarah!" John Tensler interjected. "We should also call into question McClure's decision making. What kind of parent brings a child to the Middle East? Does America need that type of irresponsibility in the White House?"

Mike Fuller, content with their strategy for the S.D.P., turned the conversation to disrupting the momentum gained by the Republicans. "Blaylock prides himself on creating a world free of terrorism. We take advantage of his own speeches to remind the electorate that al Qaeda's network was ultimately shattered when the Democrats controlled the White House. We juxtapose Democrat success with Republican failure to protect traveling emissaries and we could become the party viewed most capable of ensuring safety."

The excitement in the room was a physical force, at least it felt that way to William Casey, who was more inclined to walk amongst his wife's prized flowers than listen to anymore of this conversation. Michelle Bele, who could well become the Secretary of State should Casey be victorious, foresaw the opposition's parry.

"As much as we hate to admit it, al Qaeda's demise also triggered an alarming growth in small terrorists groups whose activity the Democrats failed to anticipate or contain. The Republicans are sure to use that information the moment we bring up national security. I am surprised they are not using it more as it is."

William was impressed by Michelle's statement, she never failed to place integrity above all else at strategy sessions, a habit that infuriated some but he greatly admired. Looking at his aides, he wondered why honesty like Michelle's seemed to be the exception to the norm among so many people who dominated his party. Open discussion, he reminded himself, has no place in politics. This thought bounced around his mind for a moment, but rather than speak, he stood and walked to the double glass doors which led to the garden as the dialogue continued unabated. He half listened until a joyful declaration forcefully grabbed his undivided attention.

"You could be right, Michelle, but Blaylock's arrogance coupled with McClure's inactivity must be seized upon. This could be the break we've been waiting for!"

"The break we were looking for?" William stopped the discussion abruptly. His face was taut and his eyes revealed a deep bitterness. The room hushed, uncertain what thoughts William was preparing to voice.

"Don't worry," William said to the perplexed faces now looking up at him from the sofas in the room. "I was thinking the same thing. I was thinking, what we need is one of the leading candidates to suffer a horrible personal tragedy that we can exploit for political gain. Maybe McClure's mother could further accommodate us by being diagnosed with cancer!"

"William," John Tensler began, "that is not what we are saying."

"Besides, we already issued a statement expressing our thoughts and prayers are with the McClure's and their friends," Mike managed to state with complete sincerity. Sarah nodded in agreement, plucking an apple slice from a fruit platter on the table in front of her. Only Michelle even attempted to grasp the depths of William's concern.

"Really? Well, everything is just fine then. Don't forget to run more ads depicting the Republicans as angry curmudgeons completely lacking human compassion. Thank God, we are here to offer sincere kindness, not hollow rhetoric. How many lies does it take to convince a liar they are telling the truth? When does hypocrisy become palatable? How many more times must we witness the egregious disingenuousness of a democratic senator yielding the floor graciously to an 'esteemed colleague' when behind closed doors, the same senator feels almost inhuman contempt? When did we become this way?"

William opened the glass doors and strolled into the sea of flowers. Michelle watched him walk until the flowers overtook him. The rest of the Democratic campaign advisors dismissed their candidate's outburst as a sign of the stress he was under and the pressure the entire party felt with their continued third place showings in the polls. It had to be difficult to be the most notable member of a party struggling to maintain their standing. William Casey was fortunate, they decided, to have in his corner stalwart professionals who unflinchingly kept their eyes on the big picture.

Chapter 15
A New Pact

In the center of Hell's Fury, Hitler's capital city in the center of Troothgnase, Wolves Bane Castle stood; a reminder to all of the predator within. On this day, however, Hitler was more interested in diplomacy than dictatorship. He rode out of his fortress on the back of a giant wolf accompanied by the angel of death known as Josef Mengele. They road down the hill on which Hitler's fortress rested and through Hell's Fury, greeted by the familiar, straight armed Nazi salute. Swastikas hung off the front of every residence and dormitory. The creation of a new Reich was underway, as was the elaborate ceremony Hitler demanded in his presence. Augmenters goose-stepped to the fissures, traveling in wolf packs, as Nazi submarines did during World War II. The intensity and effectiveness of Hitler's assault on Troothgnase was eerily reminiscent of the Nazi Blitzkrieg. As his fortress was constructed, Hitler felt the same rush of invincibility that filled him at the onset of World War II.

He also reminded himself that the great disaster of the war was the iron will of Joseph Stalin for only Stalin's odious spirit kept Russia, and the allies, alive during the war. Had Stalin fallen, the world, Hitler knew, would have been his. It had to be that way. England was a fallen world power, incapable of defeating the Nazis. America was even more contemptible. That nation had been seduced by the world Jewish conspiracy and, as such, was greatly diminished from the experience. No nation that befriended the Jew and other undesirables could have defeated him, not even the mighty United States. No, the Reich's power could only be bested by the unbreakable and merciless resolve of another dictator. A nation clinging to its past and a nation willingly mixing its blood with a parasitic people lacked the tenacity for victory. Stalin was the key.

Now, as a new war began, Hitler wanted assurances that Stalin would not decide his fate again. He relented to meet the Russian at a time and place of his bidding, a show of kinship that may receive a reward. Stalin had made clear he planned only to cover Hitler's back, not shoot him in it. Hitler sought more; he desired to persuade the enigmatic revolutionary to join in the campaign to overcome all of Limbo, not merely a section of it.

As the great wolves devoured the miles from Hell's Fury to Koba, Stalin's capital city, Hitler was taken aback by the simplicity in the towns of Nafarhel. The structures Hitler ordered constructed to announce his dominion dwarfed these small huts and dwellings. Augmenters dove into the gaps of Limbo with maniacal intensity, a desperation borne of terror. Guards stood over the holes, forcing the faint hearted back to combat and aiding augmenters who dragged captured hunters back to Nafarhel.

The fervor with which the souls worked fascinated Hitler. The order he demanded in his Nazi ceremonies mirrored by the efficiency displayed by the lowliest of workers in Nafarhel. Hitler understood in that moment, all that mattered to Stalin was the work, the accumulation of power, and the elimination of those who would take either from him. The trappings that so often accompanied power meant nothing, just like the thirty million lives he extinguished to obtain and preserve his absolute authority. Stalin, if he worshipped anything, worshipped power alone, not power and pageantry.

Koba was as nondescript as the outlying towns had been. The perpetually gray skies of Limbo seemed almost bright by comparison. Hitler shook his head and wondered how this simple man brought him such ruin. It mattered little, Hitler reminded himself, for this was the time to strengthen allegiances, not engage in brash treachery.

Eight Mongolian soldiers, men who had terrorized the steppes of Russia with Genghis Kahn, greeted Hitler as he slowly rode through Koba. They requested that Hitler disperse the spirit wolves. The wolves faded like a mist as the horsemen of Genghis Khan led Hitler to a small house, a dwelling one would suspect belonged to a hermit, not a man whose very name made men tremble. Stalin sat on a small wooden chair in the center of the dwelling's only room. Some four feet behind him stood Beria and Catherine the Great. Surrounding the three leaders stood sixteen officers of the Red Army. They stood in a semi-circle, each aiming crossbows at the only entrance of the room. The Mongolians closed the door behind Hitler, barring it to prevent escape.

Hitler's unease was apparent, as was his anger at the outrageous breech of protocol. The only outward sign of Hitler's anger was the sudden appearance of wolves outside the small building. Despite his rage, Hitler spoke in an affable tone.

"I though we agreed to be accompanied by only one aide, you have me outnumbered." A wolf's lonely howl accompanied the words of the Fuhrer.

Stalin stared at the man who proved to be the greatest nemesis of his life and spoke abruptly, "To be honest, I did not trust you. But, as you say, we had an agreement, which I will honor now."

With a wave of his hand, Stalin created a second door in the back of the room. The soldiers escorted Catherine the Great outside and Hitler again recalled his wolves.

"You know why I come, Joseph. Together we could overrun Limbo."

"Such a venture would be suicide. The forces of light would eventually rise up with such strength we would be stopped and sent back to Hell. Such a fate I do not desire."

"Nor do I, but destiny has brought us here together. Think of it, Limbo is the means to influence Earth. If we controlled all of Limbo we would, eventually, control Earth as well. To finally conquer not one world, but two—such an accomplishment is worthy of us."

"I know nothing of destiny, I know survival. You play a dangerous game. I know of your attempts to augment humans from the safety of Wolves Bane's walls. You spread your energy thin engaged in war in Limbo and reaching Earth in such an exhausting manner."

Hitler stared at his ally - his adversary, doubt creeping into his mind. "How would you know of such things? Do you spy on me? Who have you corrupted?"

"Calm yourself, Adolf. I only know this for I too reach out to Earth from this very room. It requires great energy, and no distraction, to reach through the gaps. But to manipulate power on Earth from afar is our greatest weapon. Limbo could remain divided and we could have Earth under our thrall."

"You lack ambition, Joseph. I would have two empires, not partial reign over two. So long as Limbo remains split, we could never have dominion of Earth. You know this."

"Perhaps you lack patience, Adolf. My machinations are in place; they are neither as fast nor as impressive as yours, but will yield the results I crave."

Stalin's immobility was wearing Hitler's limited patience thin. The Fuhrer decided ultimatums might work where requests failed.

"I will bring war to the whole of Limbo, with or without your aid!"

"Then without it will be," Stalin quickly stated, unmoved by Hitler's sudden intensity. "I do promise, however, to guarantee the evil sovereignty of Troothgnase and Galiktus. I have never been fond of enemies on my boarders. Attack, recklessly if you choose. Our holdings will remain…pure as it were."

Hitler regained his composure and attempted to end their discussion in a gracious manner. "Then there is little more to discuss. I wish you luck in your deliberate endeavors. There will be a place for you in the Eternal Reich."

"I wish you well, be sure not to lose that which we gained."

As Hitler left Koba he was content that Stalin would protect his states. Stalin watched Hitler ride off, knowing full well that no other soul in Hell could maintain the buffer between Nafarhel and the gathering forces of munificence as effectively as the man who was the Nazi party. Let Hitler play war, for it reduced the number of hunters his augmenters confronted, provided Troothgnase and Galiktus did not fall prey to his opponents; that was the one event Stalin could not allow to happen.

Chapter 16
Simple Strengths

Brian Murphy entered Drew McClure's two-bedroom apartment in Bethesda, Maryland and did not like what he saw. The pulled shades created midnight at 5 p.m. An uneaten sandwich sat on the coffee table in the living room and newspapers were strewn across the counter that separated the kitchen from the living room. The unkempt apartment was of minor importance to Brian; Drew was far from neat, forever claiming a good mess was the sign of unrealized genius. The true cause of Brian's consternation was the bottle of scotch resting next to the ham on rye. Brian reached for the bottle and was relieved to find it unopened, but the presence of alcohol in Drew's home was, to say the least, disturbing.

As Brian put the bottle down, he heard a sound he couldn't identify coming from the second floor. He quietly crossed the living room and turned to his right, facing the stairs that led to Drew's bedroom, study and bathroom. What if the scotch was reinforcement for whatever was being swilled upstairs? Brian had witness Drew's fall once before and was there for the rising as well. He wondered if he possessed the strength to be that friend again. Of course, an overtaxed mind could be creating a scenario that did not exist.

Brian started up the stairs, pausing only to read the prayer of St. Francis hanging on the wall at the start of the incline. Bedlam was coming from above. Music was blaring while Drew screamed incoherently. Brian forecast a dismal future until he reached the top of the stairs and laughed at what had caused him to envision the end of the entire Self-Determination Party. Bruce Springsteen's song, *Badlands*, was blasting from Drew's stereo and a horrible voice was singing in the shower.

Badlands, you gotta live it everyday
Let the broken hearts stand
As the price you gotta pay
Keep pushin' till it's understood
And these badlands start treatin' us good!

Brian, not being a fan of either Bruce Springsteen's or Drew McClure's singing, retreated to the relative quiet of the living room. When the water stopped running, and the music died down, Brian called upstairs, "Still planning your post political career?"

"Je-sus! You know it will be hard to win this thing if you scare your candidate to death!" Drew was downstairs in about five minutes, wearing jeans and a black t-shirt, a Springsteen inspired look, Brian thought.

"You O.K.?" Brian eyed the scotch as he asked.

"Erin's kidnapped, my ex is, as expected and with obvious reason, pissed. The papers are struggling to be sympathetic, but partisan…and I'm sober. One day at a time, I suppose."

"Why the bottle? Are you tempting fate?"

"No, just testing will. I almost took a drink on the plane. I was suffocating…dying. The only thing tighter than the walls closing about me was the tightness of my throat. I knew one drink would stop that pain. It was the first time in years I even thought about a drink. It was a powerful feeling, too powerful. Almost …." Drew's voice trailed off, leaving the thought incomplete. He wasted no time searching for the lost thought, but continued in another vein. "It occurred to me driving home that, as President, I will be around alcohol almost every time I attend an official function. It will not look good if the head of state is sweating like a pig and cotton mouthed whenever we entertain visiting diplomats and world leaders at the White House. So I bought a bottle of what had been my favorite stuff and brought it home. And nothing. I feel fine. I guess the reality of the moment, the uncertainty of the future got to me."

"So you traded in your readings about Buddha for Bruce? Interesting choice."

"Any port in a storm, my friend. I am a New Jersey native after all. Could you picture Buddha walking the Jersey shore? Maybe bringing enlightenment to the patrons of the Stone Pony."

"Maybe he would. Anyway I just wanted to check on you and let you know we are scheduled to meet the press in two days. Try to rest."

"I will," Drew stated in a quiet tone. "I am tired and the road we are on now will require strength."

Drew picked up the scotch and tossed it to Brian. His voice suddenly exhibiting power rather than timidity, "Strength I won't find in there. See you tomorrow, Brian."

Brian turned to leave but looked nervously at Drew. There exists a fine line between bravado and authentic confidence and it was extremely difficult to ascertain what category Drew was currently residing in. Brian decided Drew had, over the years, earned some benefit of the doubt and offered a good-natured farewell.

"Rest, Drew. We can start your rock n' roll tour after your presidency."

With that the two friends parted company, both secure in their understanding of one simple truth, walking a hard road with a friend is the only way one should undertake such a journey.

Chapter 17
Shared Regrets

Danielle stood on *Sundiata's* deck enjoying the breeze created by the ship's flight. It occurred to her that this was the first breeze she felt since arriving in Limbo, for there was no atmosphere necessary for souls. She had forgotten the peace a gentle wind could bring to a cluttered mind. Danielle struggled with two questions, the first, why had Niccolo asked her to accompany them on a mission of war. She agreed to join because of the excitement she felt when she heard Abraham Lincoln and Winston Churchill would be traveling with them.

Now, Churchill had moved on and the reality of their mission filled her with dread. She was also concerned about Niccolo's treatment of Jon as they left Tecktoral. Someone should talk to him about his behavior and point out the inappropriateness of his actions. Danielle, lost in thoughts of how she would have handled the situation with Jon much better than Niccolo had, did not perceive Abraham Lincoln beside her.

"A little lost in your mind?" Lincoln asked. "I am hardly famous for my ability to sneak up on people."

"Just a bit distracted," Danielle answered in an absent minded tone. As she turned to look at who addressed her she grew flustered. It is one thing to know Lincoln was on board, it was quite another to find oneself engaged in conversation with him. "I'm sorry..I didn't know it was...I mean...."

"You mean, 'Hello shipmate', or whatever we call each other. Let's say I call you Danielle and you call me Abraham, once you regain your capacity to complete sentences."

Danielle laughed nervously at Lincoln's observation; still amazed he was who he was. Lincoln, who had grown accustomed to numerous reactions from the people he met, continued speaking.

"Concerned about our captain's behavior, are you?"

"Yes," Danielle said sharply. "How did you know? And don't you think someone should speak to him?"

"Niccolo informed me you worked with children on Earth, therefore I assumed his treatment of the youth currently in our midst disturbed you. Should someone speak to him? The real question is, does someone want to speak to him?"

"I suppose I do. Niccolo must understand he can't..."

Lincoln raised a single finger, stopping Danielle in mid-sentence, "You think he doesn't understand? You believe a man who has seen 500 years can't decide for himself when he has made an error?"

"Regardless, his actions were completely inappropriate and furthermore..."

"...some parent may call, claiming the incident damaged their child and will sue your school for every book you've got. Therefore it is your job to, what is that saying I've recently learned? Oh, yes...you must cover your ass, confront the imperfect adult who traumatized the defenseless youth and fix the problem in a manner and timetable you deem fitting. Is that about it?"

Danielle folded her arms and stared over the bow. The breeze was no longer soothing. "So what if it is?" was her short response. The characterization of her outlook made it obvious that Niccolo and Lincoln had held discussion about her at some point, a situation she was not altogether pleased with. Lincoln continued, disregarding Danielle's defensive posture.

"There are processes and people that must be trusted. You put little faith in either, however. This problem is already ninety percent worked out anyway, and you haven't raised a finger."

"How can you say that when no action has been taken?"

"Let's look around, shall we? Niccolo has disappeared into his cabin at the center of the ship. He is undoubtedly plotting our route and celebrating his victory over Jon, correct?"

"No," Danielle conceded. "If I know Niccolo he is beating himself up over his short tempered response, a worse beating, by the way, then you or I would give him."

"I agree. But your mind was entertaining the very silly situation I described. On Earth did you do the same; instantly assume the worst of people, even those you had known for some time? Your school must have been a haven of joy."

Danielle stood in silence, not wanting to engage in that conversation further. Lincoln, aware he had Danielle's full attention continued on.

"Now where is Jon, sulking somewhere in dark shadows?

Depressed and crushed by Niccolo's assault? There he is, in the fellowship of friends and companions."

As Lincoln and Danielle looked across the deck, they spotted Jon practicing his light manipulation. Leonidas and Seamus attempted to teach Jon how to form simple objects, paper, chairs and the like. They were experiencing limited success. Seamus found the experience amusing, laughing from his belly as Jon's structures folded in on themselves or were exaggerated to a ridiculous degree. The common mantra used when teaching light manipulation was concentrate and cut off. Jon had mastered concentrate, but found himself so stunned at his creations he often forgot to stop building them. As a simple chair grew to twenty feet in height, Leonidas decided Jon was hopeless and left his training to Seamus.

"Now we have a problem. Seamus is laughing at Jon and stern Leonidas has written him off. We had best have an intervention before he is completely shattered. Oh, what miracles, he seems fine. Niccolo is punishing himself. At some point soon he will emerge from his cabin and offer an apology to Jon of his own accord, bringing us from nearly to complete resolution. Or you could intervene and reveal how well schooled and capable you are of managing a crisis. People do not always need teams and coordinators to solve problems Danielle, often time and trust is all you need."

Lincoln folded his hands behinds his back and began to stroll off, for he had said what he felt was necessary. Danielle thanked Lincoln for his words as the tall man began to walk the deck again. She added she still wanted to speak with Niccolo, but for her peace of mind, not to offer unwanted, or needed, advice. Lincoln suggested speaking to Seamus first, for he did not know how receptive Niccolo was to being disturbed while in the privacy of his cabin. Danielle saw the wisdom in this and approached Seamus, who had managed to focus Jon to such a degree that his chairs were now merely six to eight feet high.

"Top o' the morn', milady," Seamus stated with a smile. "I am afraid ye are a wee small to sit at the tables Jon-boy is makin'."

"He's doing fine, even if Leonidas lost patience."

"Aye, that's a fellow with a single thought—fightin' seems to be all that drives 'im. He's a bit too cheerless fer my taste. Niccolo could teach 'im a thing about humor, and Niccolo is hardly a laugh a minute."

"Actually, I was going to talk to Niccolo. See how he's doing after the dock."

"Why lassie, that would be might neighborly ov ya. You want give'im a talkin' to about the words he wasted on Jon?"

"Actually, no," Danielle said to the amazement of Jon, Seamus and, in no small measure, herself. "I think Niccolo will work that out. I have other questions."

"Good fer you, Danny-girl. I though fer sure ye were Hell bent on reprimandin' the cap'n fer being human—every person who set foot on the Earth loses the ole temper occasionally ye know."

Danielle nodded in agreement, but Jon felt a need to test Seamus' theory.

"Everyone. Seamus? I doubt that. Why if…"

"Oh, here we go. In ev'ry crowd there's on of ye…Were ye goin'ta hit me with some hypothetical Jesus situation, Jon?"

Jon laughed and stated, "Yea and he wouldn't lose his temper."

Seamus looked at Jon and accepted the challenge of proving his point.

"Ye could be right, laddie…but yuir not. Haven't ye ever heard o'the time Jesus lost his temper with the tax collectors? Flipped a table over an' everythin'. Bein' on Earth takes its toll on everyone, make no mistake. However it is a good thin' Jesus did nae perform this act in the 21st century, otherwise Danielle an' her ilk would call a meeting for the man and force him to attend anger management classes."

Danielle and Jon laughed despite themselves, only encouraging Seamus to continue.

"Ye know when I get angry sometimes I shake my fists and yell 'Jesus Christ'. I wonder, when Jesus tossed that table on the unsuspecting taxman, did he shake his fists, stomp his feet and holler, 'Me! Me!'"

The sight of Seamus screaming "Me!" and stomping wildly around the deck was more than Jon could handle and he walked off laughing. Danielle was equally amused, but waited for Seamus to calm himself so she could continue the discussion.

"Do you think it wise to disturb Niccolo in his chamber?"

"He's a bit touchy 'bout bein' bothered when in his little sanctuary. Seein' you would likely set'em off, I doubt he would let ye in. All the more reason for you to see him," Seamus said smiling.

Seamus blew a small light bubble from his mouth, "Take this and pop it after ye knock, it should gain ye entrance, if that's what ye want."

"Thank you, Seamus." A look of wonder flashed across Danielle's face and she sincerely added to her departure, "You are more than you seem."

"Most people are, lassie. Most people are," was Seamus' response as he walked after Jon. "Git over here, boyo. Class is back in session."

Danielle gathered her nerve and proceeded, with the small, iridescent sphere, towards Niccolo's cabin. A grumbled, "What?" was the reply to her knock on the door. She promptly pierced the small bubble and Seamus' voice forcefully stated, "Take yuir tone and shove it, Niccolo. I will not bandy words with ye through a closed door."

"Come in, Seamus," was the exasperated reply.

Danielle entered the small room and saw Niccolo sitting with his back to the door, reading a book. Four shelves ran the length of the wall. Books covered most of the space, but there were also lanterns, outdated navigational tools and small collectibles occupying space on the shelves. On the table in front of Niccolo were papers stuffed in various folders and a journal. These rested on what appeared to be a map of Limbo. Niccolo could easily have filed away the light projected papers, but liked the mess on his table, it reminded him of his time on Earth when his ship cut through the waves, not the sky. "What can I do for," Niccolo dryly stated as he turned to face Danielle. He did not mask his surprise, or displeasure to see Danielle instead of Seamus.

"Did Seamus come with...," Niccolo realized where Seamus' voice came from in mid-sentence. "You used a voice globe. I taught him that trick and he uses it against me!"

"I guess you should have chosen your student more carefully."

"Indeed," Niccolo responded dismissively. He reopened his book and attempted to appear too engrossed to be disturbed.

"Please don't stand and stare at me, give me your reprimand and move along."

"I wasn't going to reprimand you," Danielle said with great sincerity and a complete lack of defensiveness, as if she did not hear Niccolo's dismissive comment. "I just wanted to see how you were. Your anger earlier today seemed a bit disproportionate to the perceived cause."

"And you are the one qualified to aid me in gaining insight to myself?"

" 'The wise man,' I am told, 'does not esteem a person more highly because of what he says, neither does he undervalue what is said because of the person who says it.'"

Niccolo smiled with appreciation, recognizing the words of Confucius that he had once used to drive home a point to Danielle. He was unaware she even listened half the time, let alone committed words to memory.

"So, why was I so ill-tempered earlier?" Niccolo leaned back in his chair as he awaited the answer,

Danielle transmuted a chair of her own and sat in front of Niccolo's table. "Undoubtedly you were hopeful that the portal we saw earlier was to call you to Heaven, not Winston Churchill."

"Of course, but I wish Winston no ill-will. He deserves Heaven, we all do."

"Is that the actual matter we should discuss? Could you, possibly, believe you don't deserve Heaven? Maybe you have convinced yourself your destiny is to be warden of Limbo. Is that why you push others so hard to grow and move on? You fear they may become century long residents like yourself? Is that why you can be unrelenting towards me? Dylan? Even Jon, who, technically, is not your charge. Despair does not become you, Niccolo."

"A momentary lapse of judgment does is not the equivalent of despair," Niccolo firmly stated, clearly communicating whatever ailed him was not to be superficially labeled as 'despair'. Danielle did not respond, nor did she provide any inclination that she was leaving. Niccolo sat in silence, weighing his next words. His first thought was to dismiss Danielle, but the sternness of his face relaxed and he ceased being Niccolo, mentor of souls and allowed Niccolo, seeker of Heaven to speak.

"As for Jon, his presence, more likely his age, calls to mind my greatest failures. In 1493, when Columbus made his second voyage to the New World he brought a Spanish military force some 1300 strong to subdue an area that would have fallen to half that number. Columbus also invited sailors from Italy to join him, wanting to share his victory with men from his own country. I was seventeen at the time, but was already alone, for my father died when I was four, my mother passed away when I was seven. I lived on the docks, apprentice to any who would take me. When Columbus called for countrymen, I answered. He represented all I wanted, title, prestige, success and the freedom to sail the open seas.

"So I joined him and joined in the glory of conquest. We killed, murdered, stole and raped for...honor. As I understand it we set in motion a chain of events that led to the extermination of the entire populace of the island. Genocide occurred because of the choices we made, the actions taken and the path not chosen. All manner of decision made, but never in favor of mercy. I wanted so much to believe the people we demeaned were truly just "savages". What guilt is there in treating an animal as an animal? But, I never believed the lies; I just lacked the courage to act as my heart called me to. I suppose we could blame the society or the time period, but such explanations ring shallow and selfish. Society did not leave a child orphaned, we did. History did not cut off an ear, we…I did. I forgot my free will and gave myself to Columbus'. When he returned to Europe I accompanied him. Upon landing in Spain I made my way back to Italy. For two years I ignored the sea, my hate for what I thought it represented overwhelmed the joy it had once conveyed. Over time, I came to love the sea and hate only myself. More time passed and I came to love the ocean and accept myself. I spent a lifetime sailing the waters of the South Atlantic, allowing the tranquility of the seas to ease my troubled soul, but never again ventured close to the lands where innocence was lost."

Danielle listened intently for in the past five minutes she learned more about Niccolo than in the previous five years. Niccolo sat in silence, starring out the window to his left. He absentmindedly placed *The Once and Future King* on the table, the release of his words made his shield unnecessary.

"You were little more than a boy when all of that happened," Danielle gently stated. "You worshipped all Columbus stood for and longed to walk in his shoes, before you truly understood what that meant. Even as a child you made a quiet stand, departing from Columbus' company rather than continuing to violate your own ethics."

"Small comfort those words bring and I have spoken them to myself enough."

Danielle shook her head, wishing she could just as easily shake such thoughts from Niccolo's mind. When she spoke her voice displayed, for the first time in Niccolo's presence, confidence intertwined with honesty.

"You are far too hard on yourself. People, older people who should know better have broken faith with themselves for far less than basking in the light of their hero."

"And you, sitting in your Ivory Towers, would have personal insight of this?"

Danielle stared at Niccolo, weighing the consequences of her next move. She had entered the room to assure herself all was well with

Niccolo, now she found herself, yet again, on the receiving end of his queries.

"I would," she said in a barely audible whisper. The simple, two-word sentence dismantled all indecisiveness and she continued in a stronger tone. "At the age of fifty-two, after years of service and commitment to my school, I was told the new science building would bear my name. I was so proud my legacy was complete. That same year three veteran teachers broke a new law, ignoring a landmark Supreme Court decision. Schools were not to have the word 'God' uttered in any way; and three teachers hung posters containing Martin Luther King's 'I Have a Dream' speech."

Niccolo exhaled a humorless chuckle, "Free at last! Free at last! Thank GOD almighty we are free at last!"

"Exactly," Danielle continued. "We can't eliminate 'Bitch, Fuck you, or slut' from the hall of a school, but we can protect the innocent from hearing the word 'God' and reading one of the greatest speeches ever made. Regardless of my personal feelings, I had a job to do. I ordered the posters removed, or at least edited. The teachers refused, calling themselves 'conscientious objectors'. In my thoughts, I sided with them, but their protest was calling negative press to the school. The board of trustees wanted the issue resolved quickly and pushed for the dismissal of the teachers. I did not fight for them at all; the trustees decided the formal naming of the new building would be postponed until the situation was resolved. The implication was clear and I let the three teachers go, you can't break the law and continue to teach, after all. In the press, I called them misguided, reactionary and subversive. I slandered their names, ruined any rapport I had left with a majority of my faculty, banished Martin Luther King from my school, couldn't name you thirty graduates and saw my name placed on a building. Some legacy. So, yes, I do know a thing or two about walking down paths you wish you hadn't."

"So, where do we go from here?"

"The only place to go, I suppose, forward," was Danielle's heartfelt response.

"You go forward," Niccolo began as Danielle looked at him quizzically. "I have some mail to attend to and would rather sit still while writing. I'll move forward soon."

"Fair enough," Danielle said as she walked towards the door. She looked back over her shoulder and was surprised by what she saw. For an instant, so brief she was not sure she could trust her eyes, Niccolo appeared much older than she had ever perceived, as if he were centuries older than he actually was. The vision fled quickly, leaving Danielle a sense of sadness and, oddly, accomplishment. In five years of conversations with Niccolo, she had never felt so competent. It was this sense of triumph that emboldened her to shout over her shoulder, in as good of a Seamus' imitation she could muster, "see ye on deck, Cap'n."

Niccolo looked up, slightly amused, "Stay away from Seamus, he is a bad influence on you."

Danielle walked onto the deck; her heart lighter than it had felt in some time. The pace with which *Sundiata* proceeded reflected Niccolo might have dropped a burden as well.

Chapter 18
A Special Delivery

Niccolo emerged from his cabin; surprised by the rate *Sundiata* progressed. He invested very little mental energy to slow her down as he walked toward Seamus and Jon.

"Hello, Cap'n, I was just leavin' to discuss the subtle uses of humor with Leonidas. I hope yuir time in the privacy of yuir haunt was valuable."

Niccolo stared at Seamus for a moment and the Irishman shrugged his shoulders as he wandered towards Leonidas. Jon started to move away as well, but Niccolo placed a hand on his shoulder, causing the teen to stop.

"I believe I gave you some anger you did not deserve, Jon. I would ask for forgiveness."

Jon's face froze into a mask of bewilderment. The number of adults who openly admitted their errors to him on Earth was, predictably, short. "That's alright," he mumbled, halfheartedly.

"Actually, it's not O.K., but thanks for saying so."

Jon was anxious to change the topic. He was also eager to discuss the amazement he felt, standing aboard a flying boat, "I bet this feeling is something you never get used to, huh? I mean its one thing to be on a boat on the water, but flying? It's real cool. Will I ever be able to do something like this?"

"I don't know," Niccolo said sincerely. "I have been in Limbo a long time and have only witnessed three people levitate and guide solid objects."

"Oh," Jon said sadly. "Have you heard stories of others who…"

Jon stopped talking as Niccolo shook his head.

"Well," Jon said through his disappointment, "it's still cool to be flying in a boat."

"I suppose," Niccolo mused. "I miss the water, however. The wonder of the sea."

"Wonder of the sea? It's wet. It splashes. Fish are in it. We're flying here! Man, you need some help."

"Or I just need some sea gulls. I always loved, even looked forward to, seeing the gulls as I left for the open sea." Niccolo looked up, watching the birds soar on the winds of his imagination.

"The gulls float over you, completely disinterested in you and your destination. All they know is that they belong. Its their world, not yours. Yet they look at you, a stranger to their world in a…friendly manner. I always took their gaze to communicate not anger that you are intruding their space, but welcoming you in. Wishing you well. How many people can you say treat you that way?"

Niccolo stared over the side of *Sundiata* thinking back over the centuries. He reminisced about the joy the open sea always brought him. Niccolo never married, for he would have deserted his wife, without remorse, for months on end. He knew this in his heart and knew to treat a woman thusly would have been a betrayal of her love. No, Niccolo could not leave the sea. He was convinced that the gentle waves that rocked him to sleep and the storms that threatened his very life was all the marriage he ever needed.

His brother, Angelo, and he discussed the topic at length, but it was watching Angelo and his commitment to his wife and children that truly set Niccolo's mind. Someday his sailing days would end and he would marry and treat his bride as she deserved, not as a novelty to come home to. Niccolo died at fifty-five, never marrying, despite always knowing whom he wanted to marry. That this relationship had not come to fruition did not alter the fact that he was more loyal to the sea, himself and his small family than most men would dream of being to their chosen life.

Niccolo became aware of the depths of his thoughts when he saw a group of seagulls drift before his eyes. He rubbed them quickly, stunned that he lost himself so completely in a daydream.

"They're out there, Niccolo. You're not hallucinating," Jon joyfully announced. He watched the four light animated gulls he formed with pride. "While you were spacin' out I practiced a little something Seamus taught me. You like them?"

"Indeed I do, Jon. Indeed I do. That is most impressive. What led you and Seamus to practice the formation of birds?"

"Well, I really wasn't getting the whole make a weapon thing. I've never even held a weapon in a fight, or otherwise, so I just couldn't make one that seemed right. It didn't help that the only weapons I am familiar with are the ones I see in movies, guns and things, but Seamus said light cannot be manipulated into modern weapons, only classics, like swords and arrows or just plain beams of light. I thought that was lame."

Jon looked embarrassed by his confession and Niccolo saw no reason for such feelings. "To never wield a weapon in anger is a thing to be happy about, not ashamed. Things that may impress your peer group rarely impress the larger world. You have no reputation to cultivate here, only the truth of your being."

Jon considered Niccolo's words for a moment, wondering how much time he spent, or wasted, protecting an image of himself rather than discovering his individuality. The words of friends, even more so than enemies, taught him how to act and who to be. Jon noticed even when teachers spoke of being true to yourself, their words rung out as shallow lies. So many of them seemed miserable with their profession; how did they expect to convince students to follow their dreams, when they had obviously given up the hunt long ago? *Schools, where dreams go to die,* was one of the last essays Jon wrote before he died, seeking meaning in meaningless parties because he thought that was were such pearls could be found.

"Well anyway, Seamus asked what I really liked and I told him, animals. I wanted to work at a zoo, aquarium anything that would keep me in contact with them. I loved nature shows and things like that on Earth. Not exactly the kinda stuff you brag about and find yourself popular. But Seamus said it was a good place to start. So, I made a cat, then a dog. Guess I've graduated to sea gulls."

"All manner of weapon is used when battling augmenters, why not a lion or hawk? Continue developing this skill, Jon, it will serve you well. Please excuse me, I have to bring *Sundiata* around."

At Niccolo's behest, *Sundiata* turned east and continued at a steady pace. Seamus glanced over his shoulder at Niccolo, curious about the change of course. Niccolo waved Abraham to his side, engaging him in a brief conversation. Seamus considered joining the two men, but assumed Niccolo would offer everyone an explanation at a time he deemed suitable. The Irishman noticed Jon staring thoughtfully over the stern of the boat and strolled toward him.

Jon stared overboard at the sprawling Plains of Pantaea, unaware of how close he was to souls his own age. The Plains, from the vantage point *Sundiata* allowed, resembled the patchwork patterns of the great American mid west. The farms and orchards of Pantaea were worked by souls who devoted most of their lives to the collection of material goods and gadgets, paying little heed to the splendor of nature. Jon avoided the plains due to his love for the kingdoms of animals, instead being transported to the intellectual center of Tecktoral, capital city of Mimirium. Rolling hills rose between Pantaea and Mimirium, and the lights that emanated from the huts dotting their face caught Jon's eye.

"Captivated by Asgard, are ye?" Seamus asked as he stole up to the Jon. In his teeth, he held a polished pipe, willing smoke to rise from it although no tobacco burned.

"Asgard? That's familiar…I can't place it…."

"Home o'the gods according to Norse mythology, Temporary home o'Rovac 'ere in Limbo."

"You mean…He's here?"

"Oh, I do nae know fer sure. What I can say is this; a long time ago the Norseman envision the king o' their gods, Odin, to be a sullen, dour, brooding fellow. And he had 'is reasons, for Odin had knowledge of the end of all things, the death of Heaven and Earth. His own demise and that of 'is kin. He even knew he would try to prevent this ending, the final battle between good an' evil, called Ragnarok, but would ultimately fail."

"Man, no wonder the guy was so down."

"Aye, reasons fer sadness surrounded Odin. Now, legend holds that ole Rovac occasionally has bouts of sadness himself, fer watchin' yuir finest creation be misused and abused by yuir most challenging creation can be a bit maddenin'. Sadness does nae exist in Heaven, the joy o' that realm is overwhelming, but residents of Limbo, we still catch the full gamut of emotion, as does Rovac. Rovac would ne'er trouble souls in paradise wit' is burdens, so from time to time; he visits Asgard and weeps for his children gone astray. The Norsemen may have felt his sadness on some level and Odin was born. Over the centuries, Asgard 'as become a favorite haunt fer the souls in Heaven who want to check in on their family an' friends. It can be happy in those hills as well, fer there is always much on Earth to gaze upon and celebrate if ye look in the right place."

Jon continued to stare at the hills of Asgard, completely unconcerned that *Sundiata* had stopped moving. Seamus, knowing the original plan never mentioned a stop at the Plains of Pantaea, made his way to Niccolo, even as the Italian was looking for him.

"Don't worry, Seamus, I have not lost my navigational skills," Niccolo called to his friend as he waved Danielle and Leonidas to his side.

"We are making a brief stop in Mylganst. I have received an important message from Tylferling. The towns of Ang-Lu and Mashada have fallen to Hitler and captives have been taken. His forces encroach to the foot of the Dagduada Forest. Tylferling, city of poets, has become a military base, preparing a stout defense. The leadership has escorted all those ill suited for combat from the city, evacuating to the sprawling plains that dominate Pantaea. Important guests have taken up residence in Mylganst and I have a package to deliver to them."

"Deliver it swiftly," Leonidas exclaimed. " I would see no more souls stolen by this craven defiler of Limbo." Niccolo heeded Leonidas determined words for they echoed his own thoughts.

"I agree, Leonidas. I will disembark with Danielle, make the delivery and hasten back to the ship. We must not delay here for long."

The completion of Niccolo's sentence coincided with the halting of *Sundiata*. The sight of the hovering, wooden vessel caused many a soul working the countryside to look skyward in amazement. The main sail, which served only the purpose of bringing comfort to Niccolo with its familiarity for there was no wind to catch in Limbo, fell limp while Niccolo released a rope ladder to allow passage to the ground.

Danielle and Niccolo's feet had just touched the ground when four men rushed to greet them. The two groups exchanged no introductions as they raced to the circular amphitheater. Danielle and Niccolo passed through the double doors, which led to the large rounded room, the only room in the entire structure. A podium stood at the center of a winding circle of chairs. To the right of the podium was a small table, flanked by two seats. The sound of fingers snapping preceded the disappearance of every piece of furniture save the lectern.

"Stephen, we have arrived," Niccolo called to the two men standing some fifty yards ahead of him and Danielle.

"Sorry, Niccolo, I did not see you. Lech and I are trying to agree upon the best floor plan for tonight's open meeting."

"Quite alright, Stephen. These are trying times. I will not keep you long from your duties."

"Nor will I keep you from yours."

Niccolo led Danielle towards the men. As they drew near Danielle suddenly realized who Stephen was. She stood before Stephen Biko, the man who died fighting apartheid in South Africa. The man to his left she did not know, until he introduced himself.

"Hello, my name is Lech Walesa. Most visitors know seem to know Stephen better than me, so feel no shame for not recognizing me."

"I know your name if not your face," Danielle responded. "Your struggles against communism in Poland were most heroic."

Lech bowed his head humbly and raised his palms up, while Stephen wafted the group towards the rounded walls. Support beams, spaced fifty feet from each other, curving up to the apex of the building gave the room its character. Thatch walls spread from one beam to the next; every segment of wall was dedicated to a particular philosopher. The thoughts and teachings of the individual, accompanied by depictive artwork, spread from the dirt floor to a point thirty feet above the ground. Stephen Biko stopped at a plaque and read:

The highest form of government
Is what people hardly even realize is there

Next is that of the sage
Who is seen, and loved, and respected

Next down is the dictator
That thrives on oppression and terror

And the last is that of those who lie
And end up despised and rejected
The sage says little-
And does not tie the people down

And the people stay happy
Believing what happens
Happens naturally

-Lao Tzu

"Proud Danielle, which leadership style do you embody?"

Danielle looked at Biko, wondering how he knew her name while she pondered her answer. "I recently left the bottom rung and aspire only to go higher," she said, completely unashamed to admit her perceived lowly status.

"Well said," Lech interjected. "But I know Niccolo must fly to Tylferling swiftly. Let us sit a moment and discuss our business."

Four chairs appeared, three in a row facing a lone chair. Danielle reached for the singular chair with the eagerness one might reach for a blindfold as they prepared to face the firing squad. To her surprise, Niccolo directed her to a seat between Biko and Lech Walesa.

"So, I assume the situation in Tylferling is most dire," Niccolo began.

"No more so than situations we have all survived," Biko stated with optimism.

"True," Lech began. "Most importantly the military leadership of Tylferling is very capable. Marshall Zhukov shares command with Saigo Takamori and Henning von Tresckow. The force they have assembled is most formidable, including Americans who fell at Normandy and in the jungles of Vietnam. They also have a multitude of inspirational field commanders. Leonidas' expertise at battle will aid both the defensive and offensive capacity of Tylferling. We still believe, however, the key to victory is not the defeat of Hitler's forces, but the defeat of Hitler himself."

"Besides," Niccolo said. "Hitler's forces can always be replenished from the endless supply of nefarious men languishing in Hell. Is it still the opinion of your triumvirate that Lincoln is best suited to defeat Hitler?"

"It is," Biko said. "Although there is another in Valdar who may be equally suited if Lincoln should fall."

"Yes," Lech concurred. "As for our Triumvirate, it is down one since von Tresckow wisely remained in Tylferling, for he is the member of our original company most suited for war. I do have faith in your judgment, Niccolo, and accept his chair filled. Stephen, what say you?"

"I was secure the moment we left Lao-Tzu's wall."

Danielle suddenly realized what they spoke of and stood up, "I don't think I am ready to guide a town in Limbo. I feel I have just begun to guide myself."

"Which is why you are ready for this duty," Biko reassured her.

Niccolo stood and addressed the still shocked Danielle. "It is time to allow others the pleasure of your company. You will prosper under the guidance of these leaders, gradually becoming all you ever wanted. Sailors can only teach so much."

Sadness filled Danielle's eyes. She had finally come to understand all that Niccolo had offered her and would no longer be able to benefit from his centuries of experience.

"Why so distressed?" he asked. "I would think being free of me would bring you joy."

"I am not ready for this," Danielle said meekly.

"The greatest weapon the oppressor has is the mind of the oppressed," Lech stated confidently. "Don't be your own oppressor."

"And don't fear walking alone, no one is deserted in Limbo," Biko added. Turning to Lech he continued, "And don't quote me, at least not when I am in the room."

Lech shrugged as he replied, "It is a good quote. If you said less noteworthy things I would be less inclined to repeat them."

"Is my duty here fulfilled?" Niccolo asked.

Biko and Lech turned to Danielle, who stated with as much authority her addled mind could gather, "It is. May the remainder of your mission go as smoothly as the past five minutes. All of Limbo wishes you well."

Niccolo lent a brief smile to Danielle as he turned to leave the room. Danielle would flourish in her new position; she would not remain in Limbo much longer. Her greatest challenges were behind her, whereas Niccolo and his companions would face daunting trials in the Dagduada Forest.

Chapter 19
Return to the Race

Drew McClure walked into the auditorium on the campus of Georgetown University, the beloved Alma Mater of the besieged candidate. A folding table was standing in front of the assembled throng of reporters. No less then two-dozen microphones sat in the center of the table, the antithesis of a decorative centerpiece.

Flashbulbs ignited and digital voice recorders were brandished like swords as Drew approached the table. He looked exhausted, despite the best efforts of the S.D.P's campaign team. Brian Murphy stood ten feet behind the table with a knot in his stomach tight enough to cause physical pain. His rigid stance, which he hoped communicated attentiveness, was the picture of frozen anxiety. Given the events of the past few days the campaign manager planned this press conference to last no more than twenty minutes. Brian worried that twenty minutes wasn't fifteen too long.

"This seat for me?" Drew joked as the press conference began. He glanced over his shoulder at Brian, sharing a joyless smile as a small number of the press laughed nervously at the comment. Drew adjusted the microphones before him and spoke in raspy tones. "Before we begin I just want to thank all the people who have sent me their best wishes and prayers. I appreciate every one of them. I also would like to thank William Casey and President Blaylock for their regards."

"Drew, obviously it has been a difficult week, could you bring us up to date with what you have been going through?"

"What I've been going through?" Drew paused, running a hand over his face. Brian held his breath, not sure where Drew was going. Drew opted for his favorite option when a situation grew tense, honesty.

"I struggle, to be honest, every day. I can't help but worry about Erin and think of her every day, wondering what she is going through and hoping for her safe return."

"If you struggle everyday why not drop out of the race and dedicate your time to finding her?" The reporter was from the left leaning cable news show *Sure Fire*. As Drew prepared to answer, the only fact Brian was sure of was that the questioner would love to see Drew drop out of the race.

"Two good reasons, actually. I am not a special agent or spy. The White House has assured the nation publicly, and me privately, that they are utilizing the full powers of the government to locate and extricate Erin. I should stay out of the professionals way—worried parents, I am sure, rarely are helpful in these situations. Also, I continue to campaign because I will not act in a manner that would cause Erin to be ashamed of me. To allow terrorists to break me would allow Erin to pity me. I must be strong, for her and myself. To collapse to the ground, my spirit broken by degenerate jackals is not the image I would want Erin to see of me. I will be strong, for her and myself. When I feel weak, well, that is why we have friends."

A representative from *Politics and People* fired the next question. "The White House seems to think the Fist of Allah is responsible, yet they have not claimed responsibility. Do you have any information that might lend credence to the theory?"

"The Fist of Allah, as you all know, has become the most efficient terrorist organization since the fall of al Qaeda. They also have a record of kidnapping foreigners, although they tend to contact the media with every success, so for them to remain quiet is unusual. Regardless, my theories probably don't mean much. The White House has people…highly skilled, trained people…working tirelessly on…" Drew didn't finish the sentence, choosing instead to cough back the lump forming in his throat. Somehow, Brian Murphy fought off the impulse to end the conference.

"Do you, therefore, think it wasn't them?"

"I don't know—maybe they found a new way to spread terror. If they said something, I would know Erin was alive. As long as silence remains their policy all I have is a worried parent's overactive imagination…and that is a terrible psychological weapon to use."

"Do you believe President Blaylock's behavior at his recent Middle East summit caused this attack on your family?"

"As far as I can tell terrorists need little provocation to act as they do. To blame President Blaylock would be a misplacement of my anger. I would not attack him because he is a convenient target; the true perpetrators are on the other side of the world. I would not blame the White House for the fanatical behavior of terrorists."

"Aren't you letting the current administration off a little easy? Someone of your…"

"Someone with integrity would not use the kidnapping of their own child to make political gain. If you choose to walk in filth go ahead, but I decline your invitation to walk in a quagmire of angry rhetoric and finger pointing—I leave that to you. Your agenda is not mine."

Heads shook as a small number of aging hands pushed pens across notepads recording notes on the reaction to Drew's provocative statement. Brian stood unfazed; Drew firing barbs at a member of the media was a weekly, if not daily, occurrence. The reemergence of this part of his personality, a trait Brian often attempted to stifle, was welcome. Brian's body even relaxed slightly, though in a way hardly discernable to the casual observer.

Drew was already answering the next question, explaining how the Saudis and his own advisors understood he would be a target as long as he remained in Saudi Arabia. The possibility of Erin being rescued, only to find Drew was in captivity, or worse, led to the decision to come home.

The conference was going better than expected, so Brian retreated to the corner of the room to check the messages on his cell phone. The phone had only been off for forty-five minutes, so he anticipated no messages of consequence. To his surprise, he had a message from Maxwell Grahm. This call demanded immediate attention.

Maxwell's secretary informed Brian his call was expected and pleasantly wished him a good day, requesting her personal best wishes be passed on the Drew. Once Brian agreed he found himself on the phone with the President's Chief of Staff.

"Good Morning, Mr. Murphy."

"Hello, Mr. Grahm, to what do I owe this honor."

"I am watching Drew on television, we appreciate the stance the S.D.P is taking regarding the administration's culpability for the kidnapping."

"That response was all Drew, we have little to do with the thoughts in that head. I am sure you did not call to applaud our answers."

"No, I would like to meet with Drew in my office at 2 o'clock today. I want to share the progress we have made."

"I thought President Blaylock did not want Drew in the White House, the image of the S.D.P candidate walking in could be endlessly manipulated by the media."

"True, but you have effectively occupied the press this morning. The president is flying to Camp David at 1 o'clock and Casey is speaking to the N.E.A at two. Since your arrival is unscheduled, Hell, it is not even confirmed as of right now, there has been no chance for your visit being leaked to the press. I can have you in and out before they know."

Brian's mind raced over the numerous reasons this invitation was extended, his mind settling on a primary reason. President Blaylock did not want Drew, or any candidate visiting the White House. A popular candidate boldly striding into the White House was hardly an image an incumbent President wanted in the public consciousness in the middle of an amazingly close campaign. The only reason the administration approved of this call, Brian thought, was polling information must have been analyzed, the conclusion being Drew coming to the White House for aid bolstered Blaylock's image. Brian considered asking for a meeting at a neutral location, but he knew Drew would be outraged that a discussion concerning Erin's situation became a staring contest, the first to blink losing the privilege to name the site.

"Politicians worry so much about how their actions play in the media they often forget to act," was one of Drew's favorite sayings. The S.D.P understood the moment they placed Drew at the top of their ticket that the pursuit of victory would take place entirely on Drew McClure's terms. Brian always honored this policy, even at the expense of his own intuition. Erin's kidnapping, however, compromised Drew's normally keen political sense. Anxiety, fear and fatigue took their toll, the time was right for Brian to interject his discretion. If things go well Drew would never know.

"There is no way this meeting will be unreported, you do realize this." Brian foresaw both conservative and liberal press agents playing Drew's visit to the White House as a sign of frailty, perhaps even subservience to the Republican Party. Drew would not care, especially not now, but Brian knew every misstep until November could doom more than the election, the very existence of the Self Determination Party hung in the balance. The meeting should happen, but not at the White House.

"Could you meet elsewhere? I could give you the address to my apartment."

"Don't want to give up home court?" Maxwell said, half jokingly. "I understand your misgivings, no one wants their candidate appearing to be a mongrel begging for scraps from the big table. Of course, my coming to your home would send a different message, wouldn't it?"

"That it does. Are we at an impasse? Any neutral site you can think of?" Brian asked, not expecting an affirmative answer.

"Sometimes I like a midnight snack in front of the Lincoln Memorial. I think I'll have one tonight."

"Drew may be out walking at that hour."

"Excellent," Maxwell Grahm declared as he hung up the phone.

Brian's cell phone was barely back in his pocket when he turned to watch Drew taking the last question of the morning. Inside of five minutes, Drew was free from the table and by Brian's side, walking towards their car.

"Went well," Drew declared, pleased with both the mood of the conference and having concluded the first post-kidnapping media event without incident. Brian nodded in agreement as Drew continued. "What's next on our agenda?"

"We meet the NEA tomorrow. Maybe we will make a positive impression."

"That's right. The NEA," Dew said with little enthusiasm. "Maybe we'll make a good impression, but I doubt it. My remarks about the teaching profession do not exactly mirror the opinions held by their union."

"True, but four million people don't all think alike. You don't need their endorsement, you just need their attention."

"That I can do. Nothing more today?"

"Actually, I just scheduled a last minute appointment, something that wasn't even in the works."

"A surprise destination," Drew smiled. "Where are we headed?"

"The Lincoln Memorial... at midnight...to meet with Maxwell Grahm."

Drew looked quizzically at Brian who was opening the car's back door.

"Just get in," Brian said. "I'll explain the details on our way to Bethesda. I promise."

Brian closed the door forcefully as Drew settled in to the back seat. "At least the detail you need to know," Brian muttered as he circled to the other side of the car. When Drew asked him later what he mumbled after closing the door he claimed to be repeating lines to one of his favorite songs. It wasn't the worst lie he had ever told.

Chapter 20
Hellish Progress

The road Rasputin traveled reeked of fear and anticipation. The systematic herding of the defeated souls of Mashada into three makeshift containment centers was well under way. The humorless eyes of Himmler and Mengele oversaw the procession of frightened souls. Mengele was particularly attentive, as he hand selected certain individuals for his field experiments, conducted in what had served as the town's reception hall. A majority of the captives looked despondently at the ground, unwilling to look upon their captors as even the impulse to muster the slightest act of defiance had long been stripped away. Even the most terrified spirit, however, invested a second to observe the arrival of Rasputin, for the Russian made a spectacular entrance.

As Nazi's and Vikings drove their human cattle, Rasputin slithered by on the back of a fifty-foot anaconda. The serpent was equipped with a saddle and bridle, although it moved with the rhythms of Rasputin's own unfathomable imagination. The creature appeared to smile as it raised its head fifteen feet into the air, reflecting the superiority Rasputin felt as he stared into the terrified masses. Flanking the mythological snake were twenty Mongolian riders, some on horses, others on the backs of large, pre-historic lizards, creations of the snake rider's bizarre mind. The chilling entourage made their way to Himmler, stopping their parade in front of the Nazi. Rasputin addressed Himmler, but did not step down from his mount, or will the creature to lower its head.

"I bring news from Stalin for Hitler. Where can I find your supreme commander?"

"He waits in our field command center, which was once the towns museum. It is a mere three hundred yards in that direction," Himmler answered coldly, pointing to his right.

"I thought Stalin frowned upon such indulgent displays," Mengele noted as he motioned at Rasputin and his bodyguards. The hisses that Mengele spoke with could well have come from Rasputin's serpent.

"You are correct, butcher of souls," Rasputin answered with self-importance. "But that cheerless man is not watching me now and I would use the powers this land grants me as I wish. My actions bring harm to none and I do not force my will on my subordinates, although some freely requested similar transportation. Do you mean to tell me you follow your Fuhrer's every whim?"

"Not whims, commands issued with precision and purpose," was Himmler's agitated response. "We have important business to attend. Preening and posturing is not on our agenda today."

Himmler marched to oversee the transfer of prisoners as Mengele retired to his lab, eager to conduct another series of experiments on a hapless soul. Rasputin smiled sardonically at the two high-ranking officers as he guided his reptilian steed towards Hitler's command center.

Six Vandals halted the frightful procession one hundred yards from its destination. Rasputin dismounted and walked the final distance, three vandals on either side. Soldiers created a corridor from the point Rasputin dismounted to the front door. Flags and tapestry displaying the swastika adorned the small homes and hamlets to the left and right of the human walkway. As Rasputin proceeded, the troops fell into ranks behind him, keeping his bodyguards away from the rendezvous.

A soldier positioned at the door pulled the entrance open so Rasputin and his escorts did not have to break stride. The desecrators of Rome led the manipulator of men into the main foyer of the gallery. A museum once dedicated to the work of artists making their way to Heaven was rapidly becoming a shrine to the new Reich. A monstrous portrait of Hitler's victory over Andrew Jackson dominated the atrium. To Rasputin's left was a single door, the twisted cross blazing on it. Above the door was a painting that mirrored Raphael's *School of Athens*, but instead of great thinkers converging in an acropolis, it honored the Nazis. Fully uniformed men, including Himmler and Mengele, toured the nightmare that was Auschwitz. The Vandals led Rasputin through an arched doorway underneath the artistic portrait of Jackson's defeat. The Vandals stopped at the arch, gesturing Rasputin through. Hitler stood alone, intensely staring at a map on the table before him.

"Planning more triumphs, oh Scourge of Limbo?"

"Spare me your compliments, Rasputin. Your tongue could be more twisted than Lucifer's. Pawns should know their place."

As Rasputin walked to the table, he noticed the sculptures and paintings throughout the room. Each depicted a tyrant of history.

Stalin, Caligula, Pol Pott and Thutmuse III were but a sampling of the figures present in the Hall.

"I sought not to offend, I merely pointed out the truth. You have stormed through the whole of Troothgnase and have made your way to the Dagduada Forest. Your efforts should be commended. Stalin himself is impressed, hence my visit."

Hitler's ego swelled, despite his wishes, at the thought of Stalin growing envious of his exploits. He quickly regained his thoughts and demanded the details of Rasputin's message.

"I would not waste your time, for you have achieved much and have much to achieve. More than Stalin would dare attempt. The cold spirit of Stalin wishes to lend some aid to you. Your battles stretch you thin and your subordinates in Galiktus grow apprehensive, fearful of an invasion from Valdor. Heydrich rules in your stead, but he lacks your daunting presence."

"Heydrich is an excellent and trusted leader. You would do well to be respectful of him," Hitler's anger caused a thin mist to form in the room, for despite thirty years in Limbo his spirit creations were still directly influenced by his moods, a trait most souls control after a decade.

"We in Nafarhel do not doubt his skills, merely his resources. Also remember many battles in Limbo are decided by the force of will, not the force of arms. And Andrew Jackson can attest to the formidable will you posses. No, we ask permission to reinforce Galiktus, creating a force of numbers that will dissuade attack."

"You may reinforce Galiktus if it is attacked," was Hitler's gruff reply. "I trust Heydrich, he will not fail me, or fail to maintain Stalin's precious buffer. Besides, Columbus informs me that there has been little troop movement in Valdar. The city of Tylferling braces for our assault and well they should, for we shall splinter her walls and enslave the entire populace."

"This brings me to my next offer. You are gathering prisoners at an impressive rate. Stalin would open his gulags in Nafarhel to the fallen....heroes.... you have imprisoned. Send as many as you wish, for you do not need to weaken your attack force by leaving guards behind to protect your rear."

"This is an excellent proposal and I am thankful to Stalin for his generosity. Inform him that he may send a force into Troothgnase to collect five hundred prisoners. I will also deport the casualties at Tylferling to him."

"How many casualties can we expect?"

"If the new weapon Mengele is perfecting is complete, less than you would think."

"And, pray tell, what weapon would that be?"

"You know enough and I have little to tell, for Mengele has been tight lipped about his experiments, merely promising to find an alternative to some of our current methods of warfare. If any man can find ways to disfigure a soul it will be Joseph. He so loves his work." As Hitler spoke, the rolling mist generated an unearthly heat, mirroring the smoldering embers of his soul. Rasputin grew uncomfortable, turning to his favorite weapon, his words, to exert his will into the room.

"He is a renowned member of your reborn Reich, second only to your self in importance. Please accept my sincere wish for a successful raid of Tylferling. I believe if you claim authority over the Dagduada Forest you will stir Stalin to action, for seeing one third of Limbo controlled by Hitler would inspire him to abandon his own slow moving plans and embrace yours. You could well become ruler of all, just as you planned."

"Stalin's active participation would be welcome, for the force he commands is fearsome. I do not doubt our twin sickle would easily cut the chafe of Limbo. Limbo then the Earth. Power over all, for all eternity. Who would not desire that?"

"Who indeed," Rasputin quietly agreed. "And what leader better suited to guide us to that victory. I will take my leave of you now, for I have taken enough time from your planning."

"Tell Stalin all goes well. I look forward to the day he joins me in combat. I will also inform my underlings they are not to tell him of your chosen style of transportation. I am sure Stalin did not authorize such a vulgar display."

"Horses and chariots only in Nafarhel—but then we are in your realm now, and it appreciates such displays. Why should the powerful restrain themselves?"

The question echoed in Hitler's mind as Rasputin departed. Hitler already knew the answer, but found himself fascinated by the man who asked it. If Stalin did not join him after the victory at Tylferling he could at least allow Rasputin to follow his desire to join the Reich, a use could always be found for such a being.

Chapter 21
At the Foot of a Giant

Maxwell Grahm stood at the top of the steps looking into the sanctuary that housed the huge statue of the seated Lincoln. Grahm was more serious than he let on when he informed Brian Murphy that he occasionally ate midnight snacks in front of the memorial, for while food was optional Grahm tried to find time, often late at night to view the various monuments that decorated Washington D.C. The Lincoln memorial was among his favorite.

As he stared at the sixteenth president, set at the back of the temple, he pondered how often Lincoln felt such isolation during his life. The Civil War was a terrible burden to bear and it dominated Lincoln's presidency, the president himself being the last casualty of the conflict. Grahm's mind wandered to his own feelings of isolation in the White House. President Blaylock was growing increasingly secretive as the fall approached. Grahm recognized this as one of Blaylock's personality traits, for he often distanced himself from others during their first run at the White House. This was different, though. Grahm could not pinpoint the cause of his unease, deciding the tension caused by the Erin McClure situation could well be the culprit, while simultaneously dreading the possibility the kidnapping was merely an obvious, but incorrect choice.

"Are you daydreaming about the President we deserve to have?"

"Daydreaming anyway," was Maxwell's only response as he shook hands with Drew McClure. "I am glad you could make it. Sorry about the unusual setting, but appearances matter."

"A condition created by you and your Democratic counterparts. Don't attempt to credit me for the inauspicious manner Washington D.C. operates."

"You are not as far above the fray as you think, Mr. McClure," Maxwell responded, remaining amiable. "We don't need to have that conversation, but your own man did suggest a neutral site."

"Did he?" Drew replied. Brian had conveniently omitted that detail when explaining why the meeting would take place in front of the memorial at midnight. Drew attempted, unsuccessfully, to conceal his surprise.

"Did I let some information slip? So, Brian Murphy told you the pushy Republicans demanded this time and place? You might want to ask him about his role in the conversation."

"I guess I will. While I am at it I will work on my poker face as well."

"You might want to, especially if you pull through this election."

Drew nodded and turned his head to glance up at Lincoln's countenance. Both men stood uncomfortably in silence for a few moments.

"What the hell am I doing?" Drew asked no one in particular, his voice agitated and shaking. "We are not here to match barbs with each other. Tell me what you know." He turned back to Maxwell, his eyes darting uncontrollably yet communicating volumes.

"No, we are not here for small talk," Maxwell stated flatly. "I have information for you about Erin."

Drew looked down at the shorter man, not wanting to get his hopes up, but desperately wanting some news to bolster his fading spirit. "I assume if you had her I would know already and, conversely, you would have been more direct if she were dead."

"Correct on both counts. The C.I.A. has noticed an increase in activity in three training camps run by the Fist of Allah. One in particular, located in Northern Iran near the Anatolian Plateau, could be where she is. The Saudis and Iraqis are being helpful gathering information from the ground. The other two bases are also located in Iran. The Iranian government has proclaimed their steadfast belief that Erin is not in their country and any U.S. activity in its borders would constitute an act of war."

"Three locations? You could clean out all of them in minutes with your new Theve Technology. Can't you just go in and get her back?"

"No, actually we can't. If she is not in any of those camps and we burst in, the Iranians will use the attack for recruiting purposes, infidels of the west violating their sovereign land. We will not provide them opportunities for fresh anti-American propaganda. Those flames still spread far too easily."

"Flames that were near extinguished until President Blaylock pulled his sophomoric prank at this month's summit." The shortness of Drew's statement relayed his anger. Maxwell collected his thoughts quickly, not wanting to offend the worried parent, but also not wishing to exhibit weakness to a rival.

"Don't be naïve. If what you say were true there would be no Fist of Allah, Desert Scorpions or Holy Blade doing business over the past two decades. Iraq's democracy is still tenuous, but alive. Our relations with Saudi Arabia are at an all time high. Even Israel and Palestine have lobbed nothing but angry words for three years. These successes are what spread anti-American feelings in zealots. Radicals don't think like you and me. They definitely don't think like democrats and liberals think they should. There is a lot more to being in the White House than making personal appearance, there are tough decisions. I am sorry that some of them involve your daughter."

"As am I," Drew stated the obvious while exhaling heavily. His mind searched desperately for the words that could initiate a rescue attempt, all the while knowing they did not exist.

"Based on the information we have, extraction scenarios have been investigated for all three locales. General Christopher Stilwell of the joint chiefs is closely involved in the formulation of all three plans. In a situation like this, I would want few other people on my side. His attention to detail is stunning...."

"That's great," Drew exclaimed, frustration swelling. "I am sure he is eminently qualified! Just get her out! Get her the..."

Maxwell stood unfazed as Drew regained some composure. Head bowed he whispered, "Just get her out." His head rose again, eyes locking onto Maxwell's. "Get her home safe."

Maxwell nodded, torn between speaking as one father to another or as one opponent to a respected rival.

"Know this. Let it reassure you in some way. The knowledge and experience Stilwell possesses are without equal. He planned the multiple missions that crippled the Eternal Jihad's entire organization, and he did that without the Theve Technology. He's the man to trust to get your daughter back alive. There is no one better to accomplish this. No one."

Drew listened intently and found he had no more words to say, at least not here. He slowly extended his hand, which Maxwell quickly pumped with a firm handshake. "Thanks for meeting me. I feel, somehow, better than I thought I would when Brian informed me he set this up. I can't help but feel a little guilty, however. You would not meet with me one-on-one if I were an average citizen."

"True," Max conceded, "but you are not an average citizen. Average citizens don't travel overseas to meet with the heads of state. You may have the man of the people angle working for you, but that doesn't make you one of the people."

"How can you be so sure?" Drew asked as he walked down the marbled steps of the monument.

Max stood quietly for a moment and called down, "How's the shopping at Wal-Mart these days?"

"What?" Drew's query was born from confusion, not a failure to hear the question. Maxwell repeated his inquiry and supplied the answer.

"The shopping at Wal-Mart. How is it? The average citizen knows."

With that Maxwell Grahm walked into the memorial to read the quotes inscribed on the wall. The thoughts of Abraham Lincoln were always inspirational to White House Chief of Staff, but he wished Lincoln's Second Inaugural and the Gettysburg Address were still chiseled on the monument. Alas, the two monumental speeches which both invoked God and other unfavorable words like hallowed and consecrate, were casualties of recent Supreme Court decisions.

Drew continued down the stairs and made his way to his car. Erin would be fine, she had to be. He also knew it would be a shame when Maxwell Grahm lost his job because he chose to back the wrong party.

Chapter 22
Final Preparations

Sundiata raced from Mylganst for the military encampment that was Tylferling. The travelers, other than Jon, accepted Danielle's new position in stride. Leonidas, being from ancient Sparta, saw no need to have any woman at the forefront of a battle. Lincoln and Seamus understood and respected Niccolo's reasoning. Danielle spent a career in education without forming meaningful ties with any students, now she would be the guardian of a region dominated by young souls. Despite the fact he had almost no relationship with Danielle, Jon did not embrace this change readily. He viewed Danielle's action as desertion, not a promotion. None of the others felt a need to discuss the differences with the young man, time would teach him this lesson more readily than words.

Jon's presence on this mission was weighing heavily on Niccolo's mind as he guided his craft from the plains to the Dagduada Forest. The only comfort he took, the only fact that prevented him from cursing himself a fool for bringing the neophyte to a war zone, was the powerful bond forged between Jon and Seamus. Seamus assured Niccolo he would watch over Jon and keep him as safe as possible. For his part, Niccolo trusted the information his intuition brought to him, Jon and Seamus needed each other and would follow their now connected road regardless of where it led.

Niccolo stood on the platform where he often set himself when pushing *Sundiata* to top speed. He realized the location from which he chose to will the ship was inconsequential, but standing thusly reminded him of sailing the open seas of Earth and any action that stirred those happy memories was most welcome. As Niccolo's thought drifted to the South Atlantic Seamus' voice brought him back.

"Sorry to disturb yuir mental vacation, Cap'n, but we seem to have a lit'l news."

Niccolo looked at his friend and smiled. "Is it good? Hitler's decided to return to Hell voluntarily?"

"I said 'lit'l, Cap'n. Not mindblowin'. Abraham gotta message."

"I am afraid my presence has caused a little stir," Lincoln said as he stepped to Niccolo and handed him a shimmering note. "I just received this."

Honored sir,
   We have been unable to keep your arrival a secret. When the Americans stationed in Tylferling discovered you were among the souls on board they asked for permission to greet you upon your arrival. I approved their request, for it seemed to raise their morale exponentially. I hope this decision is acceptable to you as they only seek the honor of treating you with the respect you have earned.
                                                    Sincerely,
                                                    Marshall Zhukov

"It appears some American soldiers feel a need to honor a fallen president," Lincoln said in subdued tones.

Niccolo smiled wistfully. He had met many politicians in his five hundred years and none seemed as effortlessly authentic as Lincoln. The loyalty he inspired in men he had never met never surprised Niccolo.

"Who did you receive word from, Abraham? Zhukov?"

"Yes. Marshall Zhukov."

"Send him word, Niccolo. Tell him *Air Force One* will be landin' soon," Seamus chimed in.

"Very well, Seamus," Niccolo said as he stepped down to the main deck. He saluted Lincoln as he walked by, "Mr. President."

Lincoln returned the salute with a wry smile, "Regardless you are still the pilot, please don't crash us into any of the trees below."

As *Sundiata* sped onward, sadness crept into Niccolo's consciousness. The Dagduada Forest had served as home to many great poets, including Walt Whitmen, Henry David Thoreau, Emily Dickenson and William Butler Yeats. These creative minds gained serenity and peace in the dense woods that surrounded Tylferling. As Niccolo looked down, he could see small clearings, hamlets inhabited by small groups seeking Heaven. Legend held that the tranquility of life in these communities actually prolonged the stay in Limbo of the inhabitants, for how much better could life be than to live peacefully, touring the woods and entertained by the yarns of visiting storytellers like Mark Twain or George Bernard Shaw? The skies above the forest mirrored the tranquility below, the normal gray peppered with faint blues and crimson. It was little wonder that, after his release from captivity centuries earlier, Niccolo spent seventy years touring the woods of Dagduada.

Niccolo's mood did not improve as Tylferling came into view. Hundreds of stumps stood where trees once did. The lumber had been used to build the wall now surrounding Tylferling. The wall was fifteen feet high and built doubly thick, reinforced by rocks and stoned hastily quarried in the Skadistie Mountains. Soldiers patrolled the ramparts looking Northwest, towards Mashada and their enemies. The main gate looked to be the weakest point, for it was not reinforced by stone or a second row of timbers as some parts of the wall were. Three hundred feet behind the first wall stood a second, this being the last barrier between the forces of Hell and Tylferling itself. Two gates allowed passage through the second wall. These doors were located around the bend in the circular wall, forcing any who crossed the main threshold to circle far to the left or right to reach the secondary entry.

Niccolo guided *Sundiata* towards a clearing behind the second partition. The chessboard patterns of the ground could have been the result of tilling or, perhaps, overly structured Zen gardening. As *Sundiata* was slowly willed to the ground it became clear the ground was not patterned by hands but occupied by people. Five hundred soldiers stood in formation. They formed twenty squares awaiting their landing.

By the time the ship gently touched down all could plainly see the assembled men were American veterans, their uniforms ranging from World War I to Operation Windstorm, the code name given to the series of excursions that ended the existence of al Qaeda. Five hundred arms saluted in unison as Lincoln disembarked. Lincoln, slightly embarrassed, leaned down to whisper in Niccolo's ear.

"I am sorry my presence has generated such a fuss. I did not int-"

"Do not worry my friend. You earned this long ago. Besides, the road ahead could be rough and such enthusiasm may smooth out many rugged edges."

Lincoln stood erect, towering over the five foot seven Italian. He saluted and shouted at ease, an order that brought an instant response. From the center of the men strode a lone individual.

"President Lincoln, I am…"

"I am afraid you are mistaken. Firstly, I have not been President for over two hundred years. Call me Abraham. Secondly, my companion, Niccolo Bontecelli is who you ought to address."

"Very well, sir," the man dressed in the simple garb of an enlisted soldier responded courteously. "Niccolo Bontecelli, my name is Alvin York. I have been asked to bring you and your companions to town hall. We have a lot to discuss."

"And likely not enough time to do so," Niccolo responded as the group began to walk between the assembled soldiers. Alvin shook his head, agreeing wholeheartedly with Niccolo's words.

Small huts and cabins stood side by side, creating the streets of Tylferling. The entire city spoke of humility and simplicity, no structure rising above three stories and the statues positioned on the corners of some streets were carved of wood, not marble and stone.

"Two more streets and a left at the statue of ole Jim," Alvin stated in an off hand manner, not caring if anyone heard or answered.

"Just Jim?" Jon asked, more than a little confused. "No last name or anything? Guy sounds a little lame."

Seamus rolled his eyes, "Jim is the name of a character in the book *The Adventures of Huckleberry Finn*. He was, to many discerning readers, the most heroic character in that fine tale. Be careful openin' yuir gob, Jon-boy. Ye may lead others to believe yuir a right eejit. Literature is greatly respected here. Maybe while we fight ye can catch up on yuir readin'"

Alvin did not notice the exchange between Jon and Seamus, for he was intent on his destination. The group approached town hall, a long rectangular building, which seemed more suited as a cafeteria than the seat of government. Statues of King Arthur and Atticus Finch welcomed visitors to the entrance of the building. A look from Seamus prevented Jon from speaking.

Alvin directed the group down the main corridor and through a rectangular opening to his left. The opening led to a small, nearly empty room. Seated around a table were Grigori Zhukov, Saigo Takamori, Henning von Tresckow and Chief Joseph. Illuminated on the table before them was a three- dimensional schematic of Tylferling and the Dagduada Forest as it stretched towards Mashada. Four empty chairs were placed on all sides of the table, enough for everyone but Jon. Niccolo summoned a seat to appear in the angular passageway and glanced at Jon, then the chair and back to Jon. Jon understood and plopped down with a disgruntled look.

"Greetings comrades," Marshall Zhukov said happily. "I am glad you have arrived. Hopefully the ceremony our American contingent deemed necessary did not cause you any discomfort."

"None," Niccolo answered. "I am glad our arrival filled them with such spirit."

"As am I. Any light one can bring to a battleground is greatly appreciated. Do you all know each other?"

"If we do not I am sure we will grow acquainted as this conference proceeds," Lincoln answered while successfully focusing all on the matters at hand.

"True words, Mr. Lincoln. As all can see the walls of Tylferling, while not formidable, create a perplexing barrier for an invading force. Breeching the main gate leads one only to the gap before the second wall. The intruders would then have to circle the walls to gain access to the town itself. Archers placed on the ramparts of both walls will have easy pickings."

"Aye, they would. But what would prevent the invading force from tearing the first wall down completely, giving them a morale victory and increased space to operate?"

"Seamus, correct?" Saigo Takamori asked. As Seamus nodded Takamori continued, "The main gate is designed to collapse much quicker than the rest of the walls—and our archers intend to protect the stronger sections much more readily. We desire the gate be torn asunder and the invading force to pour through."

"We desire that do we?" The Irishman's body language and tone conveyed his lack of enthusiasm.

"Yes, for when the main gate breaks Alvin will fire a bolt of light into the air, singling the Americans waiting before the gates to begin their charge. Two hundred fifty cavalry units will enclose the enemy from both sides, supported from above by our archers." Every word Takamori said created images moving about the hologram, illustrating in light the plan for defeating Hitler. "I will ensure the forces of evil do not retreat the slaughter."

"And ye will accomplish this alone?"

"My methods include some military tactics only the best warriors of Limbo have perfected."

Leonidas noticed a small pouch on Takamori's belt, much like the one he carried. Leonidas placed a hand on Seamus' shoulder and locked eyes with the samurai.

"Relax my Irish companion. I see in Takamori's possession a weapon that fills me with faith. He will cover the retreat, provided he times his arrival precisely."

The samurai saw the pouch on Leonidas' person and replied, "True, for if I leap too early the forces of Hitler may be divided by my attack, some in the trap and some still in the woods. We must keep as many here as possible, allowing Mr. Lincoln to confront Hitler in psychic and spiritual battle in the streets of Mashada without undue interruption."

Niccolo stared grimly at the unfolding drama of the battle in the hologram. As he spoke, three thousand Vikings, Nazis and vandals joined the assault, pushing violently through the second wall. "If we are to look at this, let's be honest. By all accounts, the military forces Hitler gathers are far greater than you have depicted. He decimated Troothgnase, Ang Lu and Mashada with relative ease. Moreover, you plan to invite him in? His men will strike viciously, possibly capturing us all and claiming victory. How badly are we outnumbered? Three to one? Four?"

Henning von Treskow watched as Niccolo forced his images onto the plan, destroying Tylferling. He spoke with confidence as he rearranged the images, creating a hard fought scene of victory for the defenders.

"Five to one, actually. And you are correct, the attack will be brutal. We are counting on this. Hitler still believes he can blitzkrieg his way to victory. His greatest weakness on Earth was his own ego, his security that his decisions were always correct. His conduct thus far reflects the same self-importance. He has summoned no great military minds to his side, relying only on himself. In fact, his arrogance has driven Columbus from his side. While patrolling the woods, Chief Joseph watched Columbus sail west, towards Nafarhel. Columbus has defected to Stalin's ranks, taking his ability to spy from above with him.

Hitler will empty much of his holdings to overwhelm us by force of arms, but we will hold, and by doing so he will enable Joseph to infiltrate his command post with Abraham Lincoln. Remember the key to victory lies not on this field, but in the singular defeat of Hitler himself. The longer we detain his army here the greater the chances of Lincoln's triumph."

"Besides," Alvin began. "I was present at Ang Lu when we evacuated that town. I witnessed the bravery of Hitler's men firsthand. They do attack fiercely, but only as long as they are winning. We managed a small counter offensive as we retreated and saw some of our foes run. You see, they know if they lose its back to Hell. They have no loyalty to each other. The Vandals in particular seem…uninspired by the thought of risking everything for Hitler. I saw a Vandal clearly push one of those Nazi fellows in the path of my attack to save himself. The first sign we may be victorious will send a number of Vikings and Vandals headed towards the mountains in Hodvold, where they can hide in Limbo indefinitely rather than be forced back to Hell. We will be outnumbered, but our resolve is stronger than theirs."

As Alvin spoke the walls on the schematic rose again and the frightened hordes of Hitler ran before the might of the defenders. "I think the biggest challenge will be keeping the enemy from retreating to the Skadistie Mountains, not back to Mashada."

"Let us assume," Lincoln declared, "this plan works as expected. Hitler invades with a majority of his force and we trap them between the walls of Tylferling. How am I to fulfill my role in this scheme?"

"It is my privilege to lead you into the lair of our enemy," spoke Chief Joseph in a calm and confident voice. "When the next criers voice is heard we, along with Leonidas, will head into the forest. We will head due west, turning slightly north in order to gain access to our foe. We will watch as the armies of hate defile the woods approaching the defenses of hope. When enough depart the true battle will begin."

"A battle without my Spartan blade?" Leonidas roared. "Am I to be a nurse maid this entire conflict? It is not my way to slink in shadows whilst others risk their souls."

"You will have time to test your mettle, general. I have no doubts Hitler will keep a small force near him, to protect him if needs be. You will be needed to clear a path to the villain."

"Gladly would I, but spiritual power matters greatly on this plane and the might this Hitler wields alone may cause him to disregard the need for body guards."

"General Leonidas," Grigori Zhukov began in a tone Leonidas was unaccustomed to being addressed in. "Chief Joseph is likely correct that Hitler will maintain a security force, if only for appearances. Hitler likes to feel he lords over all he surveys, but what good is being such if there are none around to lord over?"

The pause following Marshal Zhukov's statement was broken by the noble voice of Chief Joseph.

"Don't forget the infinite gap which runs between Mashada and the Dagduada Forest. If any of the invaders retreat successfully, evading Takamori's grasp, they must cross the gap to return home."

Leonidas did not follow Joseph's thought, but Niccolo understood instantly. "I had forgotten the great and mysterious fissures which run like a river from the peaks of the Skadistie Mountains. We all are aware that small fissures exist throughout Limbo that souls must enter to touch Earth. For reasons unknown these great rivers of nothingness cannot be bridged by light manipulation, only wooded bridges cross the chasm. Moreover, souls who enter that vast gap cannot make their way out. The bridge that spans the gap can only carry two rows of men moving shoulder to shoulder. Retreating forces would have to cross the bridge to return to Mashada. One man standing on the bridge could ..."

"Could hold off as many foes as his courage allowed!" Leonidas shouted triumphantly. "Let these beasts evade Takamori. None will cross this bridge if it be my charge to hold it!"

"And if Hitler has bodyguards and the bridge carries reinforcements back to him?" Lincoln asked.

"That is why you have a Spartan companion, Mr. Lincoln," Takamori stated with great conviction, enough to dissuade Abraham from asking more, for the confidence the samurai infused was undeniable.

"I bend to your superior knowledge in the ways of the sword, Master Takamori," Lincoln said.

Marshall Zhukov cleared the table of all holograms before speaking. "So, we are agreed. When the next cry is heard, Mr. Lincoln, Chief Joseph and General Leonidas will disappear into the woods and make haste to Mashada. You will stay in hiding until you see the movement of our enemies toward our defenses. The defenders of Tylferling will bend, but not break before our foes, ensnaring them in a trap, leaving Hitler alone to face his fate."

Leonidas picked up the plan from this point, "And if he is not alone we will clear a path to him. Lincoln will have his day, I promise this."

Niccolo rose form his chair, "I have but one request. The young soul at the entrance is our companion. He aspires to be a hunter, a protector of souls on Earth. I would have him stand with Seamus and I on the parapet of the first wall."

"While I see no need to send a callow youth to battle, I believe you are more than capable of judging the youths capability to withstand battle. If you want him at the forefront, so be it," Marshall Zhukov replied.

"Perhaps we could alter the plan slightly," Henning von Tresckow spoke hurriedly. "In life I failed to stop Hitler from desecrating my beloved Germany and the Earth itself. I would accompany the small contingent to Mashada and succeed in Limbo where I faltered in life."

Marshall Zhukov sent an agitated look towards von Tresckow. The two men had discussed this matter privately, agreeing the German who attempted to assassinate Hitler in life would not confront him on this plane. Henning's plea was an attempt to gain support from the consortium, thereby pressuring the Russian to change his view. Takamori also flinched at von Tresckow's sudden request, for his words settled the matter originally. To have this resolution challenged now smacked of disloyalty and the samurai stood to speak. Fortunately, Chief Joseph, who felt Takamori's temper rise the moment von Tresckow began, calmly interceded.

"It is your past which makes you a poor choice for this mission, my friend. Your desire for vengeance may well jeopardize our mission. The mere sight of our quarry could well drive you to rash action, attacking when the way is not clear. If Tylferling and Hitler both stand at the day's end we can be assured, he will return, twice as determined. He will have called up more forces from Hell, and the knowledge of his near defeat will make him more cautious and difficult to defeat. No, defeating him now, while he clings to his invincibility, is a necessity. Don't forget Stalin, watching this drama unfold from the safety of Nafarhel. Every move Hitler makes undoubtedly teaches him much. Your moment of glory could well be when Stalin's ambitions are revealed. Patience must rule you for the present. You served the light proudly on Earth, would you do less in Limbo?"

The words of Chief Joseph not only soothed von Tresckow, but they reverberated in Niccolo's mind and soul. The Italian recognized his own desire to confront Columbus in battle and force him back to the tortures of Hell. When the news of Columbus' defection hit his ears, Niccolo felt an inexplicable disappointment, but now he understood. Much like von Tresckow, Niccolo had, perhaps subconsciously, placed a personal vendetta above the actual mission. Worse, Niccolo realized his desires could have easily led him to leave the battle in mindless pursuit of vengeance. Such rash action would only place others in harms way.

So lost in thought was Niccolo that he did not hear Marshall Zhukov conclude the meeting. He became aware of his surroundings again only when a voice whispered, inside his ear, "Time to wake up, Niccolo, yuir wonderin' again."

Niccolo looked over at Seamus, who was still seated across the table. Marshall Zhukov was already walking from the room, followed by Leonidas and Takamori, who were engaged in a spirited conversation. Von Tresckow was thanking Chief Joseph for his council, although it was obvious from the Native American's composed expression he did not need to hear the words as much as von Tresckow needed to say them.

Lincoln also approached Joseph, wanting to acquaint himself with the man who would lead him to his clash with Hitler. As Lincoln made his way he waved to Niccolo, communicating he should leave when he wanted. Niccolo returned the gesture as Seamus walked to his side. The two men headed towards the door and Jon, who sat impatiently awaiting them.

"Voice bubble in my ear? How long ago did you plant that?"

"Oh, Niccolo, yuir words sting. Why would I plant such a message in the ear of a man who is always focused on the here and now? To be honest, I made it when I saw ye driftin' away. I have become quite good at creatin' those littl' buggers."

"So I see. Did it occur that, I may prefer my mental vacations above spending time with you."

"I did not call ye back because I missed ye, laddie. I was merely afraid the others may see yuir blank expression and start wonderin' why I am friends with a Cap'n who does nae have a full shilling. I 'ave a reputation to protect after all."

"Indeed," Niccolo stated flatly as the two friends gathered up Jon and walked into the streets of Tylferling. Jon was anxious about the coming battle but Niccolo recommended patience and the conservation of energy.

"Don't wish for the hurricane to come and level homes, it will arrive on its own accord. The best we can do is prepare for it's coming and have faith that our preparations guarantee survival."

As was often the case, Jon was not one hundred percent sure what Niccolo was talking about, but he was sure he meant well.

Chapter 23
Operation Nighthawk

"Mr. Grahm, President Blaylock requests your presence in the oval office."

Maxwell Grahm looked up from the speech he was reading with surprise. He was scheduled to meet President Blaylock in twenty minutes; only important news that could not wait would prompt an early summons. He put down the speech; one the president was to deliver later that week to veterans in Virginia. Susan rolled her eyes and sighed, for she knew the chief of staff did not normally preview speeches at small venues, but the tight race filled Maxwell with tension and he was coping by micro managing the senior staff. This behavior only increased the stress in the most anxiety-ridden work place in America.

"Thank you, Susan," Maxwell said in what he hoped was a cheerful voice.

"No problem, sir," Susan replied in a tone that caused Maxwell to grimace. Susan had worked for Maxwell for years and she often spoke in a tone that directly mirrored his own. Susan's tenor this morning clearly conveyed Maxwell was speaking in a less than genuine manner. If his secretary was tired of him, the senior staff was surely over the edge. He would have to schedule a brief meeting during the day, if just to appease some egos.

"Good morning, Mr. President," Maxwell stated as he entered the oval office. "What news do you have?"

"The best kind, Maxwell. Erin has been located. She is being held in the base at the foot of the Anatolian Plateau. We're headed to the situation room now. General Stilwell will present the extraction scenario, one I am sure I will readily approve, and we should have Erin McClure back soon."

Without another word, the president and his chief of staff proceeded to the situation room in the basement of the White House. The conversation in the room ceased when the duo entered.

"Mr. President. Maxwell," General Christopher Stilwell stated respectfully as the other staffers took their seats.

"What are we looking at on the screen, General?"

"What we see there, Maxwell, are live satellite pictures of our target. You see some movement, but 1 A.M. is not their busiest time. To the right are sleeping quarters. At the northern most extremity of this location is a small hut, where little activity takes place. Some of our men on the ground, working with Saudi and Iraqi agents, have pinpointed that as the holding tank for Erin McClure."

"Are we ready to go get her?"

"Operation Nighthawk can be launched in two hours. We will employ Theve Technology to drop four agents into Erin's room. One of the men will carry a disk for her. When he pins it to her and activates it a light will flash on the workstation corresponding with the disk. By the fifth time that light flashes she'll be in our embassy in England."

"So this will be a quick rescue mission?" President Blaylock asked, simmering anger flowing beneath his words. "They violently kidnap a little girl and we just take her back? What are we doing here? Playing catch or something?"

"No sir," the unflappable General Stilwell answered. "We have a little punishment in mind as well. Seventy-five marines will be dropped off by teleportation instead of boats. Five seconds after Erin's disk is online we will drop in twenty-five marines. They will appear fully armed and facing targets. They will have five seconds of fire time before we pull them back. As they are brought home, the next wave will appear with the same five seconds, and finally the last wave. The confusion each wave generates leads us to anticipate suffering zero casualties while inflicting massive damage in a short time. We estimate three hundred terrorists at the site, we may well get them all."

"You said Nighthawk will be ready for launch in two hours?"

"It will take two hours to prep the operation, which means we will strike the compound at three in the morning, Iranian time."

President Blaylock stood up and looked at his watch, "Launch Nighthawk when ready General. I will be back at 11 A.M. Happy hunting."

President Blaylock turned quickly and exited the room, closely followed by Maxwell Grahm. The door had not closed behind them before the President addressed his Chief of Staff.

"Any qualms about Nighthawk, Max?"

"None in particular, sir. It sends a strong message, the days of kidnapping Americans is over. Besides, most people thought our response to the Fist of Allah's bombing of the U.S. embassy in France was soft. This could well renew some confidence."

"I thought our response to the Fist was appropriate after that bombing," President Blaylock offered, "although, we could have been tougher on the French."

"Very good, sir," Maxwell said, smirking despite himself. The gulf between an excellent plan and excellent execution can be quite wide. Maxwell glanced over his shoulder for a second assuring himself that General Stilwell did not hear their banter. Sufficiently calmed he refocused on the already speaking President.

"I am going to contact Gene Grant and Alexander Schipp. I am sure Thomas talked to them already, but I just want to be sure we all are on the same page right now."

"Of course. I will gather the senior staff. We need to plan our message to the nation proclaiming Erin's safe return."

"Be sure to mention the Iraqis and Saudis, everyone who deserves credit for this should receive it. I will see you in the situation room in two hours."

"You couldn't keep me away," Maxwell stated proudly. It was, potentially, a very good day to work in the White House.

Chapter 24
Improved Fortunes

"Michael, we've got her!" Maxwell Grahm exclaimed as he dashed into Michael Sinko's office. It was twenty past noon and Erin McClure was at the American embassy in London, England. The exuberant Chief of Staff continued his report to the White Hose press secretary.

"She's been cleaned up, given a preliminary exam and resting quietly in the safety of the complex."

"How is she? How did our troops do?" Michael's mind was racing, attempting to anticipate the questions he would soon be hearing in the White House pressroom.

"She seems fine. They will want to perform a psyche evaluation at some point, but she shows no signs of rough treatment. Our boys cleaned out the compound, while suffering only one casualty, and we did that to ourselves. One troop was teleported into another's line of fire. He suffered a shoulder wound, he'll be fine."

Michael nodded as he read the brief Maxwell dropped on his desk.

"The President will be interrupting mid-day programming to make the triumphant announcement. Before he does we will contact Drew McClure, he should find out before the rest of America."

"That seems proper. Who'll make the call?"

"I will. The President already approved. He will talk to Drew later today," Maxwell said. "If the media asks how Drew found out you can tell them, I don't see it causing any harm."

"How is Erin getting home? Will she be teleported to Washington?"

"No. We are not sure how much teleportation a body can take in a day. Our troops are fine teleporting twice in a twenty-four hour span, but they are trained for this. We have never tested the technology on kids and we don't need to end this story by scattering her atoms. A plane will do fine."

"Sounds good. The President going on soon?"

"Yes, he is. He is broadcasting from the Oval Office if you want to watch. I am going to make my call now."

Maxwell strode purposefully to his office, intent on sharing the good news then hurrying to the Oval Office to witness the broadcast, a broadcast sure to raise the spirits of Republicans and Democrats alike. Maxwell could not recall the last time an announcement was able to cut partisan lines. He wanted to savor the moment the best he could. Who knew when such a moment would occur again?

As he entered his office, Susan handed Maxwell a message, a note he quickly folded and put into his pocket. Whatever it was could wait. Brian Murphy's cell phone seemed to be the best number to call and, as expected, Drew's top confidant answered quickly.

"Hello, Brian. Maxwell Grahm here."

"Hello Mr. Grahm. Do we need another midnight meeting?"

"No, sir. Is Drew available?"

"He is talking to farmers today. I can see him standing on a tractor. Do you have news for us?"

"Only the news he's been waiting for—Erin is safe! She is in our Embassy in England."

"Good God," Brian exhaled heavily. "That's fantastic! I have… I'm not sure what…"

"Stay on the line Brian. My secretary, Susan will be on in a second to give you flight details and answer your questions."

Brian composed himself enough to stammer out some words. "Thank you. And Drew thanks you. This has been quite an ordeal. I… thank you."

"It's what we do, Brian. Sometimes this place isn't so bad. Here's Susan."

Maxwell left Brian in Susan's professional care and leaned back in his chair, relishing the moment alone. Later he was sure to be shaking hands and accepting praise from all comers. That was all well and good, and appreciated, but Maxwell Grahm had learned long ago there were few better feelings than sitting alone and enjoying the company, to feel sincere pride in a job well done. If Heaven took this feeling and stretched it to eternity, that would be worth the price of admission.

Unfortunately, this was Earth and duty called. Max stood up and moved towards the Oval Office. The President was due to speak in ten minutes and Maxwell rarely missed a televised broadcast from that illustrious room.

The Oval Office was clamoring with activity. It was a small miracle, or perhaps a large one, that anyone ever looked calm on television considering the calamity behind the scenes. Maxwell caught the President's eyes and pumped his fist in the air. President Blaylock smiled broadly in response, even as hands clipped microphones to his suit and fussed over his hair. Max stepped back, knowing the best course of action he could take was to stay out of everyone's way. He reached into his pocket to check the message, hoping it was a minor problem, one easily pushed down the chain of command. He was surprised to read the American consulate in Klobazkha was attempting to contact him. The name on the message was Brett Ramos, someone Maxwell did not know, but with whom he was eager to speak.

Chapter 25
Surprise Visitor

The stranger who casually strolled the streets of Koba was well aware of the attention his presence garnered, while all together disinterested in the souls that trembled in his wake. The foreigner, despite his impact, would be a difficult topic to discuss at a later hour, for every soul viewed Lucifer differently. Some saw a man exuding incalculable confidence, emitting an aura they wished to possess. Others observed a woman of power, free from the expectation societies would place on her. Some would ask if anyone else witnessed the seductress strutting the streets or the elderly man of wealth and means. Some felt an inexplicable desire to talk to the wandering artist whose opinionated perspective was so different from theirs, yet his disposition hauntingly similar; for many men used the words open-minded as a euphemism for disagreeable. Abandon all thought and agree with me, for I am complex and you are not.

A teenager dashed through the streets, seeking guidance, but also leading all who extended their hands into an endless spiral of anxiety and depression. A rare few stared in horror at the winged demon glaring at all who crossed its path with eyes of blackest night. Regardless of the visage used to tempt the residents of Koba, the entire populace recoiled in terror, for they had long ago learned the rewards for succumbing to Lucifer's manipulations.

The fallen angel sauntered to the entrance of the immense structure that now dominated Koba. Rising above the small buildings and huts, which were strewn throughout the city, was a new Kremlin. The walls surrounding the compound stood sixty feet high and measured thirty feet thick. From outside the wall towers could be seen stretching towards the gray skies of Limbo. The distance from one tower to the next, coupled with their placement suggested a minimum of four buildings within.

Lucifer eyed the monstrous project with approval, for it befitted a soul who had achieved so much to live in such a place. When Stalin first came to Limbo thirty years ago he was content to live in a simple cottage nestled into the rocky cliffs at the Northern edge of Nafarhel. As Koba grew Stalin moved to a small hut in the center of town, a domicile he still occupied occasionally, even with the Kremlin available.

Deciding he had engaged in enough sight seeing, Lucifer entered the Kremlin, walking through the walls as if the only barrier was empty space. He continued in this manner until he reached a vast throne room in the compounds third, and largest, building. Fifty- foot columns supported the ceiling above. Nooks carved into the columns contained the busts of individuals Stalin had long requested released from Hell to join his neo-politburo in Limbo. To this point, Lucifer had sent none of them to Stalin, wanting to see some successes before honoring a subordinate's appeal.

Stalin sat on a throne at the rear of the room, eyes closed and face tense. He was obviously not resting, but focusing his considerable energies on a difficult task. Lucifer stared for a moment at the soul most responsible for lengthening his existence. He almost felt a tinge of gratitude as he spoke.

"I bring you good tidings, Iosif Vissarionovich Dzhugashvili."

Stalin's eyes shot open, but he saw no one in the room. The very air seemed chilled, however, and he felt a perverse presence.

"Show yourself, Gentlemen Jack, or are you Yaga Baba today?"

"All your townspeople saw me in one form or another, why can't you, their magnanimous leader see me?"

"They saw that which tempted or terrified them. You do neither to me. Choose your form, I will not stand and speak to the air."

"Where are your manners, Georgian? I grant you freedom from the pit and enable you to gain a small kingdom in Limbo. Some gratitude would be in order." As Lucifer spoke, he took the guise of a well-muscled athlete. He also allowed his angelic origins to be viewed, as inspiring white wings unfolded from his back. Stalin stood unimpressed.

"You granted me freedom to extend your life, not as an act of kindness. Your selflessness was selfishness in disguise. I would know what brings you here after a twenty five year absence."

"Far be it for me to argue with the lord of the manor. By the way, you have been most helpful to me. Your ability to touch Earth without leaving Limbo is most impressive, as was your manipulation of the U.S. Supreme Court, God removed almost completely from public discourse. And with Him some of the greatest speeches in the history of mankind. Brilliant."

"Appropriate, I think," Stalin stated brusquely. "Stalin is the bad guy. I created the cult of personality, nothing to be honored more than the state, and its leader. Intellectuals and free thinkers were eliminated before they could disrupt my plans. Now America celebrates its victory in the cold war, victory over the godless Russians. What are they now, if not the cult of personalities? They honor celebrities, actors, athletes and anyone willing to be the fool on television above all. Any intellectual who attempts to combat these forces is attacked in their media and silenced by unthinking, reactionary buffoons. They even lacked the conviction to stand up for one of their heroes, this Martin Luther King, as his words were silenced and his visage erased from public view. Who is winning the cold war now?"

"Your accomplishments are legion," Lucifer said with a calculating grin. "It is the actions of your contemporary, Hitler, that brings me to you now."

"How does his action concern you? What fear brings you from Hell to Limbo?"

"Not fear, I merely wish to guarantee all that has been gained is not lost. Hitler's aggressiveness has granted us control of one-third of Limbo. Should he fall, our enemies may feel inclined to reclaim lost territories. I do not want this... and neither do you."

"On that fact we are agreed. I want no enemies on my borders."

"And I would live forever," Lucifer stated deliriously. "Control of three regions grants enough influence on Earth to secure that. A fourth section is desirable, however."

"If you desire a fourth section why not aid Hitler or force me to do so?"

"Conquering a region and holding it are two different matters. At the peak of his power, Hitler owned one of the largest empires on Earth, but it lasted in the space between breaths. I would see a fourth region added to your holdings, Stalin. For you know how to hold that which you acquire."

Stalin stood and paced the floor in front of Lucifer, hands clasped behind his back. A fourth realm would increase the buffer zone between Koba and the multitude of enemies Stalin faced in Limbo. It also would divert attention to the periphery of his surreal empire, not the heart of it. A fourth region not only made Lucifer never-ending, but Stalin realized he too could become eternal, but as premier of Limbo rather than captive in Hell.

"I see you comprehend the benefits of a slight expansion in your holdings. Trusting me may be a bit of a stretch, but every victory you have aids me. Double- crossing you would be akin to stabbing myself in the back, and I never enjoyed the point of a blade piercing my body."

"You may be forth coming," Stalin said somberly, not trusting Lucifer anymore than he had ever trusted anyone. "Of course your reputation does precede you." Lucifer smiled and bowed.

"Then I would say part of that reputation is built on self-preservation."

Stalin stared, unflinchingly, into the eyes of Lucifer. The Morning Star was surprised how long the Russian held his gaze, for most withered when in the eyes of Satan.

"What say you, Lord of the Manor?" Lucifer asked graciously.

"I would need more men. The men I have requested in the past. You realize in order to maintain four I will invade a fifth, making it the battleground. The number of souls with which I would invade this fifth territory with would be vast and many of the men would be sent back to you by the defenders of the Light."

"And to waste souls in a battle you do not even want to win does not bother you, Iosif?"

"No more than it offends you. Our desire for this land must appear immense, forcing the defense to be formidable—too fearsome to allow attacks on other sections. I would wage this pointless war for all eternity, for it would mean my survival."

"Our survival, Iosif. However, what of Hitler? The army he prepares for the razing of Tylferling is alarming in its own right. The weak willed cowards who broke rank when he took Mashada have been exiled to Hell, replaced by scores of Nazis, Vandals and Visigoths. His demented sidekick, Mengele, has created a weapon the likes of which I have never seen in all the battles between augmenters and hunters. He lacks the force of will to create many of these weapons, but they will be devastating to the guardians of Tylferling. The Fuhrer could well annihilate his foes."

"I already know of this weapon. Mengele has forced some captured scientists to dedicate their minds to weapons of woe. There are few secrets in this realm hidden from my eyes. As for victory, I would welcome it. The longer Hitler is the enemy to confront, the longer I live undisturbed."

"But should he fall, the men I send you will continue your reign untouched by your foes," Lucifer stated quickly. "I will even discuss the terms of their release before they reach you, lessening the amount of time you will need to invest teaching them who makes the law in Limbo."

Stalin stood in silence. For the first time he considered sending aid directly to Hitler. Allowing the Nazi to handle the bulk of the war mongering in Limbo would free time to manipulate Earth from the safety of Koba. There was one inescapable problem with this thought; it involved trusting Hitler, the man who betrayed him on Earth. If Hitler gained control of one third of Limbo, would he turn and attack Nafarhel before continuing his rampage on the other regions? He could not be sure, but the self-serving Lucifer offered unilateral control of Limbo, no Hitler to meet with and all the twisted souls of Hell at his disposal. As long as his fate was tied to Lucifer's he had some leverage in the relationship. The fact Lucifer only periodically checked on Limbo only made the idea of sole proprietorship more appealing.

"When can I expect the first round of new arrivals?" Stalin asked without emotion.

"As soon as their… education, is complete," Lucifer said with a smile. "After all I aim to please."

A black hole opened under Lucifer's feet and he sank calmly into the nothingness beyond. Stalin stood alone; eager to greet the promised souls.

Chapter 26
Concealed Plans

Maxwell Grahm hesitated as he prepared to pick up the phone. Susan had Brett Ramos of the American consulate in Klobazkha on the line. Maxwell was not sure what news to expect from the volatile and unstable country.

"Mr. Ramos, I understand you have some news for me."

"I do, Mr. Grahm. Please call me Brett. I have admired your work for years. The integrity you bring to the White House is why I felt a need to contact you first. If anyone would know how to handle this you would."

Maxwell rubbed his temple and reflexively bit his lip. Compliments are given for a number of reasons, not all of them welcome. "Has Alexander Karensky made more threats in his rhetorical speeches? We know he sees himself as the next great man in Russian history. He wants a return to Lenin and Stalin, with himself as premier."

"Karensky is part of the story, his rhetoric more intense and his voice more confident. Somewhere along the line, he went from trying to convince himself of his greatness to actually believing it. It was this shift in his attitude that made a lot of ears perk up and a lot of rumors swirl."

"Klobazkha is a hot bed of rumors and unfounded speculation." Maxwell Grahm hoped stating the obvious would, somehow, make the unknown disappear. "If we jumped for every story that country generated we would never have our feet on the ground. Brett, I am not trying to sound off putting, but calling me with a rumor from Klobazkha is like calling to tell me you discovered there is sand in the Sahara."

"I am aware of that, sir, but I still need to tell you what I've heard...and to let you know we are almost positive someone from the consulate has already contacted the Democratic leadership with this."

Maxwell felt his heart drop for a second. The Republicans were sure to build on their lead with the successful rescue of Erin McClure. The Democrats could use, even an unfounded rumor, to muddy the water, create doubt and cast dispersions disguised as facts gathered from reputable, anonymous sources. Maxwell drew a deep breath as he spoke.

"Let me have it, Brett."

"As you wish, sir...I hope you're sitting."

* * *

Howard Halsworth knocked solidly on the door of John Tensler's office. It had been two days since the party whip had shared his secret with John and he was a little surprised the media had not started circling the water yet.

"Enter," John shouted from behind the closed door.

Howard pushed the door open, entering the room with confidence. "How are we doing today, John?" The question was spoken in a friendly tone and John Tensler replied in kind.

"We are alright," John said as he stood to greet Howard. John's eyes whisked over the door even as Howard gently closed it. "Still behind, but gaining momentum."

Howard, following John's lead, sat at the desk and whispered, "We may have more momentum if you leaked the information I gave you. I didn't tell you so we could just sit on it."

"We also don't want to use the information if it doesn't help us. If Blaylock was the only obstacle I would have sunk him by now, but Drew McClure's presence in this race makes thing more complex. We don't want to play our ace too soon."

"If you have a plan I would love to hear it," Howard said edgily.

"Think about it, Howard. You let this slip now all we do is ruin Blaylock, he's out of the race, Hell his political career is done and the entire Republican party is raked across the coals."

"So why not do it?"

"Because," John Tesler said with exasperation, "releasing this information sinks Blaylock and catapults McClure. He'll be untouchable, win the election and proclaim from this day forward the irreversible arrival of the S.D.P. How many more independents will rise up and forever alter the political landscape?"

"A situation we don't need," Howard stated, starting to see the direction John was headed.

John smiled as he continued, "Your battles in the House have given you a little tunnel vision, Howard. We can't just bring down the Republicans, not when we can end all this third party nonsense as well."

"You have a strategy for the S.D.P as well," Howard stated. There was no question in his voice.

"We have to end their upstart reign. I hate them as much as I hate any republican. That arrogant bastard McClure turned down our best efforts to recruit him. Hell, he would be running for President for us right now instead of William Casey."

"William can't win, can he?"

John looked down at his desk and then out his window. With a glance he communicated to the Party Whip a negative answer. "I can't answer that question and you didn't ask it, understand?"

An obliging look from Howard was answer enough.

"Good," John continued. "McClure winning the White House changes everything. He loses, the S.D.P never recovers, and all those underdog parties out there go back under their rocks where they belong. Blaylock wins, which it seems he will right now, and we approach him sometime in December with the evidence in our possession. Either he agrees to be very supportive of Democratic legislation or we go public. Think of it, a Republican president in our back pocket. Four years running over the White House and the Republicans will be at a loss. They will be in such disarray they will never win in 2076 and, with the S.D.P crippled, the Democrats control the executive and, if all goes well, the legislative branch. If Blaylock refuses our offer, we go public, he gets impeached and the Democrats control the White House anyway. With just a little patience we win."

"What about William Casey?" Howard asked, legitimately concerned about the candidate's future.

"What about him?" John looked shocked to even hear the question. "It is not as if he was winning and our plan sinks his election chances. He's out of this race and has been for some time. Before you passed on this information, the party was going down with him. He may be done, but the party lives on and that's the way it should be."

"You're right, John. Absolutely right. Losing this election is only a small step back in the larger scheme of things. We just need to make sure the story doesn't leak."

"Other than you and me, and your contact in Klobazkha, who else could leak the story?"

"No one I know of. If there was ever a time for secrecy this is it," Howard said as he turned to leave the room. He still felt a twinge of remorse for William Casey, but he knew John was right. Casey wasn't going to win anyway and there was the party to consider. Institutions must matter more than individuals.

The Eternal Struggle

Maxwell Grahm haphazardly hung up the phone in his office, failing in his fumbled first attempt. He may have said goodbye to Brett Ramos, but was not sure he did, or that such politeness mattered at this point. The knot in his stomach made it impossible to breathe. As he struggled to gather his wits and maintain his equilibrium, all he could envision was the darkest of futures. There were no easy roads ahead, only the quiet footfalls of dead men walking.

Chapter 27
Stalking the Enemy

Jon stood atop the outer wall of Tylferling, wondering how far into the thick woods Lincoln, Joseph and Leonidas had ventured. Seamus stood along side his young protégé, smoking one of his summoned pipes. Jon's face lay bare his confusion as he was losing all concept of time under the perpetually gray skies above. He struggled, without success, to ascertain how long ago the trio departed; was it five minutes, five hours, or five days?

"Starin' into the wood won't bring 'em to view, laddie. They go to perform their duty, what more would ye know?"

"When they left," Jon answered, in a more aggravated tone than he intended. He looked sheepishly away from Seamus as he continued, "I just get frustrated with not knowing the time, just when I get used to it something happens…"

"…like friends rushin' off to risk their souls…"

"…that you think you should be able to keep track of." John's demeanor reflected a deep sense of helplessness, one Seamus was not sure he could easily dispel.

"Do nae feel banjaxed by yuir confusion, Jon-boy. You come from a place, Earth, where timetables were of utmost importance. Everyone runnin' here an' there, with little concern fer each other. Thousands of nameless faces are encountered. A thousand stories never told— and neither the potential listener nor storyteller notices in the moment. They only take heed later, when they wonder why friendships become strained and family becomes more a burden than blessing. Anyway, in Limbo hours, minutes and days have no meaning; we are eternal lad, unencumbered by the restraints o' time. All souls struggle with this."

"I can see why, but I learned light manipulation pretty quickly, why not adjust to time, or the lack of time, or whatever it is a little better."

"Yuir life experiences make a difference laddie, as does imagination. You loved animals on Earth and long to see them here. Plus, on some level, I am sure ye envisioned workin' with animals. Yuir light manipulation merely gives substance to yuir dreams, and dreams are easily tapped into."

Jon smiled, amused by his thoughts even before he uttered them, "I guess I never dreamed of carpentry, at least not making chairs."

Seamus chuckled at Jon's self-deprecating joke. "Aye, laddie. That you did nae. Neither did ye spend much effort envisionin' a timeless world, hence yuir difficulty adjustin'. Time schedules are often that last bit o'Earth souls cling to. Yuir in good company on that count."

Seamus and Jon stood in silence as they looked over the preparations for battle. Alvin York walked the inner wall, shouting instructions to the soldiers below. In the quad between the defensive walls, Niccolo practiced shooting with forty other men. Niccolo continued using his self-loading crossbow pistol as a marine demonstrated a tactic calling upon his experience with automatic weapons. The man touched his index fingers together and pulled them apart, creating a levitating string of marbles across his chest. In rapid succession, he flicked each agate towards a target, his hands moving at blinding speed.

Two hundred feet to Niccolo's left stood Takamori, extending his arm towards a target, arrows flying from his outstretched hands. A group of men watched him intently, trying to match the speed with which the samurai unleashed his volley. The best any compatriot could muster was one arrow for every four Takamori summoned.

"What will it be like?" Jon asked as he watched Takamori humble another challenger in friendly competition.

Seamus looked down at Takamori and answered, "I would wager nae a soul will come close to matchin' him."

"Not that," Jon stated. "I mean...."

"Hold on a second, Jon boy," Seamus said, obviously distracted. "Things are about to get interestin'."

Following the slant of Seamus' eyes Jon watched as Takamori, with unnerving speed, sent four more arrows hurtling at their respective targets. The arrows never struck true, however, as a small bolt fired from Niccolo's crossbow pistol intercepted each shaft. Moreover, three additional bolts screamed past the arrows, racing at Takomori and the crowd gathered near him. Takamori hastily dispatched more arrows, defusing the weapons that sought his head and the chest of a fireman ten feet to his left. A third shaft, however, missed its mark and Niccolo's bolt froze inches away from a marine's skull. As a slight grin stretched across Niccolo's face the bolt faded from view.

The marine, agitated by Niccolo's display, started to step forward. He stopped when Takamori's hand pushed against his chest. The samurai locked eyes with the sailor and, with great effort, hurtled six arrows. Niccolo appeared unfazed by this assault as he again used his crossbow to completely negate the attack. Once again three additional bolts were not used for defense and Takamori swiftly summoned a shield and a facemask, the mempo, to protect himself. The shield successfully absorbed two bolts but the third bore through it and struck the mempo, shattering it completely. Takamoi was unharmed and undaunted. A katana appeared in his hand and he settled into a horse stance, perfectly still but poised for combat. His eyes locked on Niccolo, who formed his own katana and rushed forward to test his sword skills. Only highly trained eyes could discern the slight edge Takamori held in this art.

"What the hell was that all about?" Jon asked in slow and quiet tones.

"Don' worry," Seamus smiled. "They cannae hear ye. As fer what their doin'…jus' two old war dogs sayin' hello."

"But Niccolo is just a sailor. Where did he…?"

"Aye," Seamus crooned. "Jus' a sailor."

Seamus looked back at the woods, no longer interested in the greetings being shared below. Jon was still interested, but a question gnawed at him. He watched Niccolo and Takamori a few seconds longer until his query demanded an answer.

"Seamus?"

"Aye?"

"War. A major battle. What will it be like? I mean…look at those two down there. I don't even know how to create a weapon."

"The animals ye manifest are yuir weapons. Create them and will them at yuir enemies. Yuir faith in the power of yuir weapon matters much more than the weapon choice. As fer the battle, I guarantee ye will witness three things."

"What will that be?"

"When yuir weapons cause an enemy to fall he will be sent back to Hell. The sight can be distractin' so do nae allow yuirself time to gawk or ye could fall next. When a resident of Limbo is felled by a damned soul, they glow fer a minute an' blink away—reappearin' at the site chosen by the soul who felled him. So ye will see black portals bringin' the damned back to Hell and souls of Limbo blinking away to locations unknown."

"And the third thing I'll see?"

"Me standin' beside ye, laddie," Seamus said with a proud smile as he descended the stairs to the courtyard below.

Jon watched Seamus for a moment before turning to look over the forest again. The one sight he wanted to view, the progress that Lincoln and the others made, was, as expected, hidden from his eyes.

* * *

Abraham Lincoln was amazed at the pace Joseph set for the adventurers as he cut through the woods. The trees and bushes bent out of Joseph's path, not hindering him in the least. Only after Leonidas and Lincoln passed by did the branches and brush close ranks. The assistance offered by the woods was not limited to the clearing of a path. From high above tree limbs conspired to maintain the anonymity of the trio. The branches reached for each other as if saving a drowning man, creating a sheath of leaf and branch preventing detection from prying eyes that could be stationed on the surrounding hills. The shrubs and bushes swelled all around them, confounding any eyes that would spy upon them or seek to hinder their progress.

Lincoln had never witnessed such a miracle and he called ahead to Joseph as they dashed tenaciously through the woodland.

"The woods themselves seem to be aiding us, Joseph. Have you ever seen the like?"

"I have Abraham." Joseph stopped moving as he spoke, allowing Lincoln to close the distance between them before continuing. He did not want to shout words that could expose them while nature provided coverage. "In my time in Limbo I have learned the woods often endow what is needed without asking, provided a soul knows how to open oneself to be understood by nature."

"Fascinating," Lincoln whispered, more to himself than anyone. "How long does it take to develop this skill?"

"Almost as long as it takes some to learn when it is time to speak and when it is time to make haste," Leonidas snapped with acrimony, perturbed that their progress was slowed by the sudden need for conversation.

Joseph quickly turned and resumed the race to Mashada; secure that Lincoln had learned the need for silence from Leonidas. The Spartans delivery was impertinent, not a tone Joseph would have used, but the effectiveness of his reprimand was unquestioned.

Lincoln was embarrassed to be chastised, but was also, despite being commander in chief every day of his presidency, well aware of his shortcomings as a warrior. To not recognize the necessity of silence when his comrades understood it without a word only reminded him of his own lack of experience in the field of battle. The defeat of Hitler, according to all with whom he spoke, resided in his hands; and he did not have the common sense not to shout a question while on a mission dependent on secrecy. The sixteenth president thought an unspoken prayer, hoping a back-up plan was in place should he foolishly ruin the original.

The three guardians of Limbo reached the edge of the Dagduada Forest and gazed upon the infinite gap, which separated the woodland from the occupied town of Mashada. The trees and underbrush stretched themselves to their limits in order to conceal them from sight.

Lincoln lay prone on the ground, taking his cue from his more practiced companions. He slowly inched his way to Joseph's side and spoke in a soft whisper.

"What do we wait for?"

"Mashada has not been emptied, therefore we must wait until Hitler's venomous host cross the bridge and enter the wood. When they reach the first wall of Tylferling we will precede to Mashada ourselves."

"How will we know when they reach the walls of the city?"

"The vine and leaf will inform us. They know full well who their allies are and who would defile them. We will wait, secure in the grasp of nature, until the moment is ripe for your attack."

"Your attack? Do you not mean our?"

"My duty has been to bring you and Leonidas here. Long ago, exhausted by battle and pursuit, I foreswore the raising of arms in conflict. I aid Limbo's defense the best I may without breaking my solemn pledge to myself."

"And you fulfilled your duty well. Leonidas and I would not have made such time without your skillful guidance. The ground itself seemed to carry us faster than mere legs could. Now we must hope I can perform as admirably."

Joseph nodded, not wanting to voice any words that may reveal the doubts he harbored. Lincoln, he was sure, was a strong willed man, but the flora whispered their awe at the raw power Hitler wielded without remorse. Nature itself seemed frightened by Hitler's willingness to flaunt his ability and lay waste to his enemies. The manner in which Lincoln carried himself paled in comparison to the brazen dictator. The spirits of nature feared this gangly defender, for all his good intentions, would be found wanting when the great battle began.

Chapter 28
Bitter Fruit

President Blaylock sat alone in the Oval Office, furious over the headlines that dominated the news for the past week. Alexander Karensky's rhetoric had grown increasingly inflammatory, promising a return to a powerful, independent Russia. Alexander had gone so far as violating Russia's border by sending a small force twenty miles into Russian territory, a precursor to future action and a major world event with enormous implications.

There was still time to resolve the situation peacefully, but it would be a massive undertaking convincing two diametrically opposed parties to find common ground. The word, Russia, called to mind a powerful nation, but in reality it was little more than a crippled, old bear. Any awe generated was the fragment of what had been, not what existed now. The Russians clung to alliances with France, Germany and, most recently, Spain—other nations whose past was more glorious than their present, but whose stable economy and society were far superior to the disorder most Russians were accustomed to.

Alexander Karensky was ashamed of the never-ending downward spiral of his homeland. So resigned were they to their impoverishment they saw the alliance formed with other weak nations as a triumph. Twelve years after treaties bound Russia to France and Germany, Alexander had built enough support and strength of arms to break away from Russia and create the nation of Klobazkha. He now vowed to bring his leadership to the rest of his countrymen, freeing them from the groveling bureaucrats who desecrated Moscow.

The idea that Alexander Karensky had designs for Russia was hardly shocking; his invasion would be reported as little more than an indiscretion in the United States if not for one piece of information that accompanied the attack. The media was reporting the United States had secretly provided weapons to Karensky, enabling him to equip his men with superior technology. Some reports implied a covert operation was planned to assist, not only the toppling of Russia, but the rebuilding of her economy as well. Newspapers implicated President

Blaylock as being intimately involved in these maneuverings, causing the good will generated by the rescue of Erin McClure to dissipate at a most rapid rate.

Maxwell Grahm inhaled deeply as he prepared to enter the Oval Office for the morning briefing. The air outside was cool, as it tended to be at six a.m. in mid-September. Maxwell thought, for just a second, he would much rather be walking the woods of New Hampshire or the fields of Gettysburg than walking to meet President Blaylock. Truly, he would rather be walking barefooted on hot metal than entering the Oval Office, but duty called so he entered the room.

Unrelenting was the first word President Blaylock shouted when Maxwell crossed the doorway. No pleasantries or small talk, merely the desire to leap into a fire that was impossible to contain.

"The media has not let up!" Blaylock continued. "Non stop coverage of the Russian crisis and linking the White House to Klobazkha's aggression! No evidence has been presented, mind you, only rumor and intrigue. Life is not a damn spy novel—sometimes revolutionaries just revolt—without secret alliances and double agents!"

"I understand Mr. President, unfortunately you don't have to convince me of that and we can't just shout it at the press corps. Give it a little time, when no evidence is found the press will have to let the story go—conjecture only goes so far."

"It may well go far enough to get Drew McClure elected. My double-digit lead has shrunk to four; even William Casey is gaining. Why can't we slow this thing?"

The question was, for the most part, rhetorical. The President knew there was little the administration could do to curtail the media's doggedness. To protest too loudly conveyed guilt; to do so weakly resembled an act of contrition. His staff was, in fact, handling the crisis admirably, which was why the President still held a slight lead. Maxwell knew the President understood this, but offered some additional reassurance.

"We are holding our own, Mr. President. The damage is not as bad as it could have been. Inevitably..."

President Blaylock exhaled as he interrupted Maxwell, "I know, Max, but these battles wear on me sometimes. No proof, no evidence. Only the word of some unknown instigator and we are under siege, just when things started turning our way."

"Well, Mr. President, I guess this just proves there is more truth in the adage 'no good deed goes unpunished' than either of us thought."

"Maybe," Blaylock said with little emotion, "but I will not be felled by some nameless jackal who covets all we have built. This fight will go the distance, that I promise."

"I never doubted that for a moment," Maxwell stated as he handed a folder with the day's schedule to the President, wondering if his actions had created any positive results.

The swirling controversy that threatened to engulf the White House did little to raise Brian Murphy's spirits. Drew was not cutting into the President's lead as much as the President was returning to the pack. A week before the Russian rumors hit the media 33% of voters leaned toward voting for the S.D.P candidate. Now, after a week of speculation and gossip, which whittled the President's support from 44% to 35%, Drew had gained a mere percentage point, raising up to 34%. The big winner was William Casey, who had leapt from 23% to 28%.

Brian could pinpoint exactly why this had happened, Casey was campaigning furiously, undaunted by his looming third place finish and determined to make progress. His determination and unwillingness to relent, but redouble his effort was winning voters, many of whom had deserted the President Blaylock bandwagon, but did not find themselves attracted to Drew McClure's camp, for what Brian saw as obvious reasons.

Drew had cut back his campaign appearances by nearly a third. Erin's return, lifted his spirits, but also sent Drew into guilt driven depressions when she wasn't with him, or he with her. Every speech, every public appearance weighed on Drew's mind as an example of a neglectful father, work being more important than his child. While Drew's devotion made him sympathetic, his inactivity, especially when compared to the intensity William Casey had suddenly found, created a great deal of doubts about his desire to win the election and devote himself to the presidency. Brian knew what Drew was experiencing was probably normal, but when one is attempting to become president normal is not part of the experience. Drew had been slumping politically since Erin's return and Brian had been reluctant to ask tough, but needed, questions.

Drew was sitting in his office looking at a newspaper, it could not be said he was reading for his eyes had not moved from the first sentence on the page. Brian walked resolutely into the lion's den desiring an interrogation, not a conversation.

"I would hand you a copy of our itinerary, but it is so short we can probably work from memory," Brian said dispassionately to the figure slumped in the chair once occupied by the energetic Drew McClure.

"We are doing enough, Brian, there is no need…"

"I disagree, we have a serious need." Brian Murphy spared no energy hiding his discontent. The entire staff was tiptoeing around Drew and the time for decisiveness had arrived. "We need to know if we should just withdraw from the election."

"I never said that was my desire," Drew responded in a most unconvincing manner.

"Said it, no you never said it. You just live it everyday. No conviction. No drive. No desire to articulate your message. I will not continue to watch you pretend to be a candidate."

"You're right, I should just pretend to be a parent instead." Drew stood as he spoke, his eyes glaring an unforgiving intensity.

"Seeing Erin once every two weeks, usually including a photo op in that time like she's some kind of political prop. I finally convince my ex-wife to let me have her for two weeks. Let her spend time with me. Travel with me. Meet people. It will be a good experience and educational."

As Drew said the words that persuaded his former spouse to send Erin to his side his tone grew increasingly sarcastic, his face a mask of controlled rage.

"It was educational alright. She learned people will hurt you just for being who you are. She learned the Pollyanna bullshit her teachers spew is nothing but lies. 'Treat others nicely and they will be nice to you,'" Drew said with a condescending sneer. "Not really, teach!"

He yelled at the imaginary figure he saw in the corner of the room. "Be a good person and you become a target for those who hate. Reaching out to others doesn't do anything but make you a victim, a weakling easily taken advantage of. She was drugged the entire time she was held captive! Did you know that Brian? Some barbarians took my little girl, bound and terrified to the desert, but that wasn't enough. To guarantee she wouldn't cause problems they kept her in a drug induced stupor half the time. And you are, what? Pissed at me for not campaigning harder? For not saying I have answers to our nations problems? I have no answers for my daughter! What else is there?!"

Drew turned quickly on his heel, arms flailing as if striking an invisible foe. He had no more to say but anger and frustration still to release. He grabbed a paperweight from his desk and hurled it against the wall. The sound of the marble bust striking the wall was swallowed by the expletives Drew unleashed.

Brian watched the scene for what it was, waiting for Drew to sit before speaking.

"What happened to Erin was horrible. I can't imagine the fear and anger you have felt this past month, but I know this... she's back. Physically fine and surrounded by supportive people. She doesn't blame you. You need not blame yourself."

Through his guilt, pain and sorrow Drew looked up at Brian and in a hushed tone admitted, "I can't. I have been trying, but I can't."

"Well," Brian said listlessly, "there is one thing to do, completely pull out of this thing. You already have mentally and emotionally. Don't drag it out. Everyone will understand why."

Drew met Brian's words with complete resignation, "You are probably right. No sense making others work hard when I don't want to. It would be the proper thing to do."

"Proper thing? No, the proper thing is to get up and fight for everything you've believed in for the past twenty years!"

"Maybe my beliefs have changed," Drew said coldly.

"Maybe," Brian said with an increasing lack of sympathy. With what calm he could muster he picked up the phone and started to dial. "I'll dial, but you should make the announcement."

Drew nodded, "Who will I be talking to?"

"I am calling your ex-wife. Erin should hear this first. Call her and tell her why you're dropping out. Explain so she'll understand how the kidnappers couldn't hold her but they stole Daddy's convictions and we haven't recovered them yet. She's a bright girl, she'll understand."

"God damn you!" Drew snapped as he snatched the phone from Brian and sent it crashing against a window. It was more than an emotional outburst. Drew said it with the desperation of a man wishing he could order the almighty to condemn another man to eternal suffering.

"I don't think He will," Brian said sincerely. "He won't damn you either, you're doing a good job of that yourself."

Drew fell into his chair, which rolled back with the impact. There were no more words to say, only the shedding of tears to cleanse the sins of the past.

Chapter 29
A Plot Revealed

William Casey walked briskly from the podium located at the center of the make shift stage assembled for his visit to the Detroit Industrial Park. His speech focused on the skill and imagination of America's workers and the need to reverse the never-ending exodus of jobs overseas. The speech was received warmly, but without authentic enthusiasm. This was to be expected for Democrats and Republicans alike had been promising aid to workers only to find their pledges were meaningless before the irresistible global economy. The workers had heard it all before and seemed reconciled that the best politicians could offer were handshakes and hollow proclamations, at least they still showed up to offer those caveats.

Michelle Bele accompanied William Casey as he sat in the back seat of the Sedan that would whisk him to the airport and San Antonio. The pace Casey set for himself was becoming manic, but the recent problems President Blaylock encountered and the inactivity of Drew McClure filled him with renewed hopes and he would not allow himself to be seen as an aged animal knowing it was time to die.

The fact John Tenslar did not share his enthusiasm, even as polling data supported the progress Casey intuitively knew he was making, was disconcerting if not shocking. William maintained John was being cautiously optimistic, tempering his enthusiasm with the cold reality that Casey was still running third. As one week became two, Michelle grew worried that John was a little too dour, seemingly unwilling to entertain the possibility of victory. While such a disposition could provide motivation it could also deplete the enthusiasm of the campaign team.

"Not a bad showing," said Michelle, hoping she sounded upbeat.

William snorted as he smiled humorlessly, "Honesty check, Michelle. You are the last person I expect to pull punches."

"Alright, it went as well as anybody else's speeches to America's workers has gone in the past thirty years."

"And that is not altogether a good thing. It's a wonder those people haven't completely lost faith in the system yet."

"They almost have. The S.D.P appeals strongly to them, no recent history of perceived double crossing and neglect. However, with McClure's recent hibernation the tree was ready to be picked, your timing here was immaculate."

"I am glad you said so. I felt the same way, but John was lukewarm about my coming here. I don't know…he seems very controlled lately. I thought he was just attempting to stay on an even keel, but I believe it could be more than that. Of course my judgment could be impaired by fatigue, any thoughts?"

The mood in the car shifted instantly with the utterance of William Casey's question. It was obvious that a topic had been broached that Michelle wanted to investigate, but was uneasy pursuing. The three seconds of silence between William's question and her response felt like three hours.

"You understand with all that has been said about President Blaylock of late rumors are ubiquitous, making the truth very difficult to find."

"Of course. I am not looking for universal clarity here, merely an inkling why his behavior has changed."

"Fair enough," Michelle said. She looked down at the floor as she weighed the words she was about to speak.

"Once again, rumors are everywhere, but this one I heard from a trusted source, Eric Petrowski…"

William's stunned expression gave Michelle pause. "Eric Petrowski? From the Washington Post?" Michelle looked as if to ask how many Eric Petrowski's do you know in the media, but wisely refrained. "Eric is a thirty year veteran. His reputation is as spotless as one can have in the press. He rarely…"

"If ever, engages in the spreading of idle chatter."

"Exactly," the attentive candidate stated. William's jaw tightened and he rubbed his hands together as Michelle continued.

"Eric came to me four days ago, saying he had heard a bizarre tale, one he couldn't believe or forget. He hunted the story down and was comfortable enough in its legitimacy to approach me with it. He felt the story was of such importance I should hear it before he went public. He even promised to sit on it for a week before printing anything."

"What do you have, Michelle?"

"Evidently John and Howard Halsworth have met more in the past three weeks than they have in their careers. The accepted reason for these meetings has been that John was looking to the next big name to help make a run for office. Howard could easily be groomed into a fine candidate and, no offense meant, we haven't been doing very well."

"I've come to grips with that, Michelle, but thanks for trying to ease the blow. So John is withdrawn because he has concluded this fight is over?"

"That's what many people thought, but Eric just couldn't buy into it. He snooped around and called in twenty year old favors and found out Howard had received disturbing information from Klobazkha."

"Klobazkha? Was Howard tipped off that Karensky was planning his incursion?"

The darkness that crept into Michelle's countenance was answer enough.

"Worse," she said grimly, "the rumors that the President has granted at least tacit approval to Karensky…"

"That's true?" Casey asked, legitimately startled.

"Actually," Michelle proceeded nervously, as if the secret service, or worse, was nearby. "Those stories are understating the President's involvement. It seems he gave ten chips, the controls for the Theve Technology, to Karensky in exchange for his aid in his re-election."

"Karensky's recent actions haven't exactly helped the president, unless Blaylock steps in, negotiates a cease fire, an action worthy of the Nobel Peace Prize. That would be difficult to overcome."

"That it would," Michelle concurred. "However, that was not the plan. Evidently Karensky's recent actions have been undertaken on his own. What he and Blaylock did orchestrate was the manipulation of our political process by kidnapping Erin McClure. Eric discovered Blaylock gave Karensky some Theve Technology to kidnap Erin. The trip to the Middle East made it easy to blame the abduction on terrorists. When Erin was "found" they coordinated her teleportation to the training camp to occur seconds before the rescue team arrived. The special ops scoop her up, eliminate the terrorists, bring her home safe and make a hero of President Blaylock, who rides the patriotic wave back to re-election."

William Casey sat, bewildered. He mumbled, "People died in this scheme. People were hurt. A child was placed in harm's way and drugged - "

Michelle sat for a moment, waiting to see if William had more to say, but his voice trailed off as he labored to comprehend what he heard.

"Michelle," Casey's voice was more forceful than he planned. He restrained himself as he continued. "What you say, the allegations made. How much proof does Eric have? Is it substantial?"

"William," Michelle said in a confident tone. "Eric would not print something of this magnitude without a mountain of evidence, he has not built his reputation by being careless. He also would not risk his legacy by suddenly acting like a reckless, headline grabbing hack. Eric Petrowski has enough money, influence, respect and even fame to last the rest of his life and his grandkids' lives. He doesn't need to pull some sensational stunt, there would be nothing for him to gain."

Satisfied by this answer, William Casey sat in silence for a moment. He started thinking aloud, voicing a question he knew had no real bearing on the situation, "I wonder who is involved?"

"Eric wasn't sure who was involved in the cover up, but he thinks it was a small number. The less people who know about something like this the better. The Russians, or Klobazkians, provided the man-power, Blaylock the plan and technology. Eric's not even sure who leaked the story, incomplete as it was."

"Does he think John and Howard leaked it?"

"He can't be sure, but he does believe they have known about this for some time. If they did leak it, why not share the information with you first or at least leak the entire story and completely ruin President Blaylock? I am not convinced Eric didn't leak a little of the story himself, just to get the ball rolling."

"Good point," William said in a disorientated tone, as he still searched for his equilibrium.

"Regardless," he said with increased vigor, "it would look as if I have things to discuss with John."

"And some decisions to make," Michelle said caustically, "because you have information about the illegal undertakings of our President."

William leaned back in his seat, quietly and quickly weighing his options.

"Get John Tensler on the phone," he said sharply to Michelle. "He needs to meet us in San Antonio. Contact Eric as well, tell him you talked to me and he should be at my first campaign stop in Texas, it would only be proper."

Chapter 30
The Battle of Tylferling

For the first time since he had adjusted to Limbo, Abraham Lincoln was growing impatient. The destructive multitudes loyal to Hitler had crossed the infinite gap by what felt to be days ago. Leonidas estimated the army to be fifteen thousand strong, leading to speculation that Niccolo's concerns may have been prophetic. Joseph remained quiet, sitting in a trance like state while Lincoln fretted for his friends at Tylferling and prayed they could prove victorious before the hateful gathering. Leonidas stood watch, if for no other reason than the comfort it brought him. Joseph's eyes opened as he tilted his head upwards, a subtle breeze blew unnoticed by his companions.

"Tylferling is under siege. It is time for us to play our part."

Without another word, or a backward glance, Chief Joseph darted across the bridge, closely followed by Lincoln and Leonidas. The trio raced up the small hill, which began its slow roll some twenty yards beyond the gap. Mashada rested on the other side, as did their greatest trial.

* * *

The howling of wolves announced the arrival of Hitler's army of annihilation at Tylferling. Niccolo stood alongside Seamus and Jon on the first defensive wall. All eyes stared into the Dagduada Forest, waiting to see that which their ears had already heard. The howling intensified, growing louder as the enemy approached, tree tops shook, trembling as if fearful of what was passing beneath them. Jon felt a tight knot form in his stomach and wondered why he was there, for no matter how much strength he borrowed from Niccolo and Seamus, he needed more. His eyes revealed his fear.

"It's all right to be afraid, Jon," Niccolo said bluntly.

"Aye, jus' do nae freeze, laddie," Seamus added with a smile.

Soldiers from various backgrounds and eras stood shoulder to shoulder along the battlements. Native Americans who fell at

Wounded Knee stood besides veterans who charged into Armageddon on the beaches of Normandy. Western lawman and eastern archers occupied the same space, guided by the same principle; evil would not win the day.

Niccolo looked around and smiled, his mind drifting to Danielle, who undoubtedly would find the menagerie of faces a testimony to the wonders of diversity. The concept smacked of divisiveness to Niccolo, people searching desperately for differences, usually superficial ones at that, to exalt. Having encountered many modern souls he found that those who screamed loudest for others to respect diversity usually granted little authentic respect themselves. Diversity did not live on those walls and no sacred cow could possibly bring victory. Only common humanity and spirit could.

The time for reflection ended as the enemy burst from the wood like blood pouring from a gaping wound. Battle cries bellowed with incoherent rage filled the air as the maniacal horde charged the walls of Tylferling. Field commanders ordered their men to fire at will and the area became a festival of light and the macabre.

A firefighter standing near Niccolo sent a blast of light speeding towards his foes, the beam pouring from his hands like the water he used on Earth. The cascading shaft of light engulfed a Viking and a black circle opened, transporting the fallen warrior to the underworld. The firefighter turned his attention to another Viking while Niccolo summoned his crossbow pistol and let loose his fury on the enemy.

Niccolo fired a single crossbow shaft that ripped through seven Nazis. All seven men were pulled into Hell in the space between heartbeats. The first two disappeared before the bolt even struck, as if the mere thought of being touched by it caused them to flee to Hell. Niccolo, not content to stand on the rampart, willed himself to levitate above his comrades, making himself an unmistakable target.

A Viking's axe flew with unerring precision at Niccolo, who casually called up a shield, which deflected the attack and promptly disappeared, allowing Niccolo to fire two more deadly bolts. Fifteen men disappeared from the field as the tentacles of Hell seemed to struggle to keep pace with the ancient sailor's assault. Six more weapons, a combination of axes and spears, hurtled at Niccolo, who willed his crossbow pistol to fade from sight. With palms facing up he allowed the weapons to strike him, his eyes smoldering with an unholy intensity. His body absorbed the wicked potential, which he returned to the senders in the form of dark beams fired directly from his eyes before he rejoined his comrades along the wall. Jon, who was crouching below the wall and behind Seamus, drew courage from his veteran mentor.

The teenager looked to the sky and a dozen birds of prey swooped into the fray. Hawks and owls tore at the faces of Vandals as they approached the gates of Tylferling. The attackers were not without their own powers and their counter attack deadened the bird's assault while shaking Jon's confidence.

"Yuir doin' fine, laddie," Seamus shouted. "Send another flock down and allow me to lend a hand!"

Five imposing bald eagles swooped from the sky while Seamus tossed two sparkling orbs of light. Seamus' "light grenades" exploded into a haphazard spray of light, banishing three Vikings closest to the blast and weakening six Vandals who were nearby. Two of these drained barbarians fell victim to the Jon's aerial assault. Seamus winked at Jon as two more glowing orbs formed in his hands. The screeching of hawks and an understanding smile was Jon's only answer.

All the efforts from above, however, could not stop the wolves pounding into the walls of Tylferling, some of them standing fifteen feet at the shoulder. The spears thrown by the Visigoths struck true, skewering the defenders on the walls and transporting them to the Gulags of Stalin. Jon tasted terror for the first time when an axe struck a firefighter, who had come to add to Seamus' attack, in the skull. The man dropped instantly and was snatched to the hideous halls of Koba. As shock settled into Jon a glowing light surrounded him, deflecting to beams that sought to ensnare him.

"Ye can thank me later, laddie," Seamus said quickly. "This is na the place fer daydreamin'!"

Jon refocused himself as Himmler led a wild charge of mounted Nazis at the main gate. The riders dismounted, willing their lycanthropes to batter the entrance. The force of the blow splintered the door and the forces of iniquity rushed headlong into the opening, slowed only by the remnants of the barrier and their own inhumane traffic.

The enemy crossed the breach only to find themselves running into the courtyard, not Tylferling. Alvin York stood atop the second wall leading a collection of World War I veterans and Hungarian freedom fighters that had resisted the Communist occupation of their homeland in life. The men summoned miniature glowing spheres and peppered the invaders with them, causing the pits of darkness to open wide. The U.S. troops waiting beyond the curl of the wall rushed forth, adding to the desperation gripping the souls seeking the eternal corruption of Limbo.

Niccolo looked down from his post in astonishment at the unrelenting torrent coming from the woods. Even with the enemy paused between the gates their sheer numbers could well overwhelm them. Three aggressive vandals replaced every fallen enemy; the volume of their weapons filled the sky with a deadly torrent. Niccolo caught the eye of Marshall Zhukov and sped to the Russian's side. Zhukov fired beams of light with tremendous force, the rays penetrating up to four foes at a time. He saw Niccolo approach and summoned a circular shield to contain them as they exchanged words. Niccolo added his will to the shield, making it all the mightier.

"The enemy is legion, Marshall. We will not be able to hold them all between the walls!" Niccolo shouted to be heard, for the shield did nothing to muffle the sounds of battle. "Their numbers alone could lead to the capture of every soul present!"

"I agree," Zhukov said glancing below. "Takamori was to come from behind the enemy, not leap into the middle of them. I doubt even he would last long surrounded by that throng."

Niccolo shouted his concurrence as he opened a small hole in the shield; dispatching five attackers, for maintaining his shield hindered his ability to strike with his usual force.

"We will let them in further!" Zhukov shouted. "Allow them to enter the city itself! The only people here are warriors, there are no civilians at risk."

Niccolo considered this for a micro -second, his mind picturing the brutal urban warfare Zhukov had described to him in a previous, much more comfortable, conversation. Visions of the decimated cities of Russia danced in his head. In the end, however, there was little alternative. Unknown to Niccolo, or any of his comrades, Zhukov had held a contingent of three thousand White Russians at the outskirts of Tylferling, a surprise for Hitler's troops should they enter the city. Now these men who valiantly resisted the Communist takeover of their homeland would be the last line of defense against the forces of Hell and wickedness.

"To save Limbo let structures of Tylferling be forfeited!" Niccolo shouted. "Your orders, sir?"

"You return to your post, Niccolo. Hit the enemy with all your ferocity. I will send word to Alvin and order the opening of the city itself."

Niccolo grabbed Zhukov's shoulder, silently communicating wishes of luck and loyalty. Marshall Zhukov created a small slip of paper and quickly carved his orders on them. When he snapped his fingers, the shimmering square disappeared, appearing almost instantly in Alvin York's hand. The soldier was surprised by what he read, but knew this was no time to question the order. He created a row of thirty bullets and blasted them into the amorphous horde, which was already starting to overpower the Americans.

"Fall back!" He yelled. "All men cover the retreat! Cover their retreat!"

Niccolo echoed Alvin's orders, demanding the marksman standing along the outer wall turn their attention to covering the retreating Americans. A cascade of light and weapons poured onto the invaders, giving them a moment of pause and testing their conviction. While the combined ranged assault hindered their pursuers, the withdrawing forces hastened into the city, preparing a second stand, awaiting as the grand numbers of the enemy would again be funneled through a small opening.

Seamus stood on the wall, deflecting the missiles of the enemy instead of covering the retreat. He was not alone in doing so, for every fifth man performed this deed for his comrades, freeing them to fight without fear. An unexpectedly heavy barrage forced Seamus to raise his shield higher than he wanted. Himmler saw the opening and pulled a small, spiked sphere from his jacket. He fired the globe towards Seamus, concentrating all his energy on the weapon, just as Mengele had instructed. Jon, standing near Seamus saw the sphere coming, and grabbed the Irishman's arm. Instinctively, Seamus pulled Jon to his side, shielding him with his own body while maintaining the protective screen he stretched before Niccolo and two Native Americans.

Himmler's weapon shattered Seamus' protective field and struck him in the back. The spikes became imbedded in him, an unprecedented occurrence in the warfare of Limbo as weapons always faded from view upon the halting of their flight. Seamus had expected to absorb the blow, but continue fighting, trusting his constitution could withstand the damage. Now he had an object clinging to him, black lights trickling down his back like blood.

"Niccolo...," Seamus groaned as he tumbled down the stairs, coming to rest on the first platform. "...I think we found...somethin' new."

"Seamus!" Jon cried as he leapt to Seamus' side. Niccolo joined them, silently dedicating the entirety of his energy to a protective shield that engulfed the threesome in a circular globe of yellow and white light.

"This is… most… alarmin'," Seamus said while staring at a distant point, as if his soul was suffering a mortal death.

"What's happening, Niccolo? Help him!" Jon yelled, his demeanor and voice hysterical.

"I…can't," Niccolo said, stunned by his own words. He rolled Seamus over and looked at the weapon imbedded in his back. "I don't even know what it is."

"Whate'er it is…ye do nae want one," Seamus said as he struggled, and failed, to rise to his knees.

Without warning, a circular portal to Hell opened below Seamus, talons and tentacles grabbing him, pulling him to Lucifer's domain. One tentacle lashed violently at Niccolo's shield, effortlessly shattering it.

"No! He is not of your realm!" Niccolo bellowed, blasting the claws of Hell with his bolts. Jon summoned tigers to rip at the tentacles, but their efforts availed them little. The tentacles of Hell paused momentarily, snapping like a whip at Niccolo before engulfing Seamus. Niccolo's summoned a katana and slashed violently at the beastly form before him. Almost instantly he found himself lifted by a single tentacle and callously tossed aside.

The tentacles receded into the black portal and Seamus was gone, but not to a prison located somewhere in Limbo. For the first time in eternity, a soul destined for Heaven had been dragged into Hell itself.

"What…," was all Jon could mutter through his shock.

"Hell," Niccolo whispered to himself and Jon. "They took Seamus to Hell."

Jon's shock turned to grief as he mourned the fall of Seamus. Jonathan Styles never knew his father, who impregnated a sixteen-year-old girl and left town, perhaps not even knowing, or caring, he had a son. A seventeen-year life was filled with self-loathing and hate. Every man became his father, the man who deserted him—and Jon found hating them all easier than trusting them. Niccolo was the first adult he ever felt a need not to despise, but Seamus may have been the first man he ever admired, respected, perhaps even loved. As he stared at the deck where Seamus recently lay he bit his lip and shook, mourning the death of his spiritual father. Souls cannot cry, but Jon's hawks and eagles screeched a haunting lament.

Grief quickly twisted into a primordial rage as Jon remembered where he was and what he could do. He ascended to the top of the wall, allowing his anger to mix with his imagination. Jon released his anger in an inarticulate scream to the gray skies above, a scream matched by an otherworldly roar. The trees of Dagduada Forest bent before the nameless beasts Jon called forth.

Rage blurred the lines between fantasy and reality as a herd of Triceratops stormed from the woods. Their heads, however, resembled the horrible visage of a Tyrannosaurus, their teeth longing to rend the bodies of its prey. Accompanying the amalgamation were raptors and fierce gorillas standing twenty feet tall.

The forces of darkness fled before the rampaging beasts, unsure how to respond. Jon's anger made the monsters impervious to attack and they tore through the ranks of Hitler's army as a child may destroy a tower of blocks.

Niccolo stood by Jon watching the bedlam unfold. He hurriedly snapped off a note card as he made his way to Jon's side. Saigo Takamori also examined the chaos and knew he had to act, but could not, not while Jon's creations ran amok. The panicking forces were fleeing in all directions, including back towards the infinite gap. While no one could be sure what transpired in Mashada it was irrefutable that Chief Joseph and his company did not need five hundred extra foes to deal with.

Niccolo saw Takamori's frustration and grabbed Jon.

"Stop, Jon! This is not the way to help!"

Jon's creations slowly faded like a mist, not because of Niccolo's words but because of the sheer exhaustion maintaining such monstrosities caused. Jon was barely coherent as his eyes strained to focus on Niccolo.

"I just wanted to strike back," he whispered.

"And so you did and you still can. Takamori needs to be transported to the field of battle. Help him there and he will continue what you started."

Jon's head lulled to his right, spying Takamori standing atop the ramparts. He attempted and failed to create a winged lizard to carry Takamori forth.

"I am too tired," Jon mumbled.

Niccolo looked at the boy, who lay completely spent by his rage. "Anger won't serve you now, Jon. Think of Seamus and aid Takamori."

Jon lay for a moment, unsure what to do. He had no energy or emotions left, anger, grief and the thirst for vengeance had depleted him. But one energy source was still untapped, his love for the man he would call friend and mentor. As the most ancient power of all filled Jon's being a winged horse appeared before Saigo Takamori. The samurai sprung nimbly upon its back, perfectly balanced for the unusual ride. Jon commanded the majestic steed bring the warrior to the battlefield and it leapt into the air before plummeting towards the fray with impossible speed. As the mythological beast skimmed over the combatants, Takamori prepared to dismount. The horse slowed enough for the warrior to leap to the ground and roll to his feet, ripping the pouch from his belt.

Tearing the pouch open also caused a tear in the very fabric of space and samurai from various phases of Japanese history emerged and formed ranks. Three thousand samurai flooded the arena, their discipline perfectly contrasted by the chaos all around them. Hitler's forces, still rushing through the rupture in the main gate, turned to face a new, unexpected enemy.

Takamori shouted orders and the group dove into the battle. Their precision displayed a deep commitment to their duty. Archer and swordsman alike knew their mission: contain the enemy and prevent retreat. Support would come from the soldiers occupying the wall. The tight quarters favored the defenders and they would crush their foe between them, samurai on one side combining their might with twentieth century soldiers battling in the city itself. None of the enemy must escape.

Marshal Zhukov viewed the battlefield from Tylferling's wall and turned for word from Alvin. The soldier expressed concern as the U.S. forces at the threshold of the city were beginning to give way. Many men would be captured before the samurai cleared the field.

Zhukov smiled scornfully, creating a message card. As he snapped his fingers he calmly said, "Then it is time to lend them aid."

Victor Malinowski stood at the head of the White Russians, awaiting the summons to battle. A card appeared in his hand and he turned to his troops. Malinowski led the charge of the Russians who had failed to protect their homeland from communism, now they joined forces with a communist marshal to protect an even greater prize. The forces of Tylferling would take no more backward steps for the trap was successfully sprung. Only the uncertainty of the outcome in Mashada remained.

Chapter 31
Lincoln's Battle

The town of Mashada appeared tranquil from the surrounding hills. Leonidas glared at the settlement with ferocious intent, his eagerness for the coming conflict frightening the lanky former President.

"The time is come, Abraham," he said. "Follow me into our enemy's lair. We will cause him despair in his own home."

"We are just going to walk in?" Lincoln asked. "The two of us?"

Leonidas tapped his pouch and smiled, "Three hundred and two. Be well, Joseph, your guidance was most appreciated."

"I will view the conflict from above and warn you if more enemies approach from behind."

"Well met," Leonidas said as he marched down the hill.

Abraham Lincoln felt growing unease as they approached Mashada. He had entered an opponent's capital once in his life, touring Richmond the day after it was liberated. His advisors wished him to delay his visit, for the area was far from secure. Lincoln disregarded their protests; feeling destiny dictated he set foot in the Confederate capital as soon as possible. Where were the advisors to protest this action? Walking into an enemy's base knowing it was completely inhabited by the enemy smacked of recklessness and false bravado.

As the duo approached Mashada, Leonidas demanded Lincoln announce their arrival. Lincoln yelled at the top of his voice, hoping to sound as confident as his companion, "Adolf Hitler, justice and judgment comes for you! Show yourself, desecrator of Limbo!"

Hitler, hearing these words, came forward from his makeshift headquarters where he and Josef Mengele were planning their next battle.

"You have come all this way to bring me to justice? You enter my sphere of control, two men, and expect me to cower, to submit. You must not know whom it is you seek. You also must be much braver than intelligent."

Josef Mengele, standing behind Hitler and to his left, slapped his hands together, causing eight buildings surrounding the central square of Mashada to melt away. In the mists of the fading structures stood two hundred members of the Gestapo, Hitler's bodyguard and the enforcers of his will. They assumed a protective ring around the Fuhrer, awaiting his order to descend on the intruders.

"Five hundred more occupy the town, they will be here in minutes. Your cause is already lost," Mengele hissed. His venomous voice caused chills to run the length of Lincoln's spine. Leonidas' reaction was completely different.

"How little you know who you face, breeder of hate and malice."

With those words, Leonidas opened the pouch he carried near his sword. From the bag emerged the three hundred Spartans who held the Persian armies at bay before the hot gates of Thermopylae. The greatest warriors ever to walk the Earth intuitively formed ranks, emotionlessly awaiting their commands from Leonidas.

"Spartans, brothers—long have I waited to enter battle with you again! We have but one mission; cut a swathe through our foes! Teach them the true nature of war!"

Without hesitation, the Spartans surged forward, forcing the Gestapo to part before them. Reinforcement arrived, but the Spartans gave no ground for the anvil has no defense against the blows administered by the hammer. A space in the middle of the din opened and Hitler and Lincoln locked eyes, each measuring the others spirit.

"So it shall be," Hitler snarled as he unleashed the hot flames of his rage.

Lincoln stepped back and formed a thick wall. The flames licked at the barrier, their heat insufficient to cause any cracks. From the wall itself, Lincoln sent a thin beam of light hurtling towards Hitler. A wave of his hand was enough to protect Hitler from the beam's force.

"You will surely be found in need of greater energy to defeat me," Hitler sneered, four rays of blackest night accompanying his words. Lincoln's thin beams intercepted three of them, nullifying their potential. The fourth struck his shoulder, causing him to recoil in pain. The depths of Hitler's hate slowly filled Lincoln with dread. His counter strikes were brushed aside by the nefarious being before him. Doubts seeped into Lincoln's mind, causing him to hesitate and allowing Hitler to press the advantage. Four more black rays sought to damage Lincoln, but he responded with eight thin beams, dissipating the attack and striking Hitler's knee, causing him to stumble, grimacing as the light tore through his wickedness.

"Enough preliminaries," Hitler declared, wiping his hand along the ground. A hole appeared and thugs from the pit crawled out rushing to attack the president. The souls were former Klansman, neo-Nazis, and gang members. On Earth, these groups would have readily destroyed each other, but in death, they were united by a common trait, their hate and their complete unwillingness to allow their minds to be opened, to allow their souls to grow. Their views, their hate for their fellow man, which they used as an excuse to perpetrate violence and murder, now fused them into a lethal fighting force. They attacked Lincoln with all the brutality that once consumed their souls.

The bewildered Lincoln threw up an array of barriers, hindering the brutes approach. Some of the would be attackers returned to Hell upon coming in contact with the shield, but the sturdier souls battered the barrier, seeking to shatter it. Hitler unleashed more of his spiteful beams, which Lincoln failed to block. Struck in the chest and stomach, Lincoln fell to the ground. He managed to crawl onto his knees before surrounding himself with a collection of shields and obstructions. He fought for all existence and those beings that sensed the spiritual conflict held their breath, hoping beyond reason for Lincoln's renaissance.

Leonidas witnessed Lincoln fall and longed to rush to his aid. His men were holding the Gestapo at bay, but what would be gained if Hitler did not fall? Leonidas' duty was clear, or so he thought. A card appeared in his hand, a grave message from Niccolo.

Four hundred villains have escaped the chaos outside of Tylferling. If they cross the gaps you could be overwhelmed.

Leonidas turned quickly, racing for the infinite gap. Lincoln must face his fate alone.

Hitler stalked Lincoln, weary of a possible ambush. The closer he crept, however, the more obvious it became his query lacked the resolve to strike back, his energy completely dedicated to protecting his integrity from his assailants. Hitler concentrated for a few precious moments, preparing to focus the horrors of the holocaust into a single beam of repugnant power. The attack that claimed Andrew Jackson would be equally effective here.

Lincoln continued to struggle, but made no progress. The summoning of these base thugs was unexpected and kept him incapable of mounting an attack. Equally imperative, his energy slowly drained. His legs were beginning to glow, the first sign of a hunters impending capture. To see this possibility, but to lack the means to prevent it eroded his conviction.

Suddenly, a cry came from behind Lincoln. It was a simple phrase, but one that rekindled the dying embers of hope.

"Forward 54!" shouted Lieutenant Colonel Robert Shaw; leading the gallant 54th Massachusetts into battle once more. The soldiers tossed the rabid criminals from Lincoln's presence and rushed to engage the multitudes that still crawled from the ground.

Hitler was taken aback by the 54th's arrival, but quickly focused on his enemy. "Too late," was all he said as he unleashed his wrath.

Lincoln screamed in horror and agony as the incomparable pain of the Holocaust entered his consciousness. He felt the pangs of hunger and the anguish of witnessing the suffering of loved ones. The absence of dignity and the supreme wickedness men were capable of tore through him. Worst of all, as he fell writhing to the ground, he experienced the death of hope.

* * *

Leonidas knew nothing of Lincoln's demise as he made haste towards the infinite gap. He passed the vigilant Joseph, still standing watch on the hills of Mashada. Joseph spied Leonidas' approach just as the ground was relaying the events of Tylferling to him. Leonidas spared no words for Joseph when he passed for this was not a time for talk.

Legend held that the bridge, which spanned the gorge, was itself eternal, existing from the moment of Limbo's creation. One would be less challenged to move a mountain with a shovel and pail than to rend the overpass. Leonidas hoped these myths were false, for severing the bridge would be the simplest of solutions.

As Leonidas drew near his goal, he saw the first of the retreating souls leaving the Dagduada Forest. He summoned his great sword and brought it swiftly down on the ropes before him. Sparks flew and the target was unscathed. Leonidas did not waste his efforts on another blow, proceeding to the center of the suspended passage.

The retreating rogues caught sight of Leonidas and summoned their weapons, charging manically at their lone enemy.

"Come, servants of evil! This road is closed to you!" Leonidas shouted joyfully.

The first seven soldiers to reach Leonidas were brushed aside as if they were crippled old men merely seeking defeat. The next ten, then twenty also fell before the Spartan's strength. The relentless rush of bodies, and their growing determination, forced Leonidas back. He formed a second sword and swung mightily, gaining a brief refrain from the relentless column of Visigoths and Vandals. A heavy sphere avoided Leonidas defenses and he lurched to his left, his head turned over his shoulder. His body's position enabled Leonidas to spot Joseph on the hills beyond the battle. The proud Native formed ten arrows, which hovered above his head. To save existence, Joseph decided, was of greater importance than a silent oath made to oneself. Joseph raised his hand, preparing to unleash the arrows' awesome potential.

"Stop!" Leonidas snarled through his clenched jaw. He snapped his head back to his foes and sent a beam of light bulldozing forward, pushing his foes back. Such a display was as draining as it was impressive and Leonidas knew he could not sustain the shield for long. The shelter provided by his efforts enabled Leonidas to encapsulate the arrows of Joseph in a cocoon of light, preventing their use. Joseph stared at his ally, who returned the look with one of admiration.

Leonidas took a deep breath as he willed his barrier to fade away. The shields departure coincided with a twisted smile spreading across Leonidas' face. He reinforced his armor with his spiritual force causing it to glisten despite the absence of sunlight. Twin swords reappeared in his hands as he charged boldly at the gathering before him.

That day the trees of the Dagduada Forest learned of a new tale to whisper to travelers who understood their language. They spoke of the man who stood alone before many and whose valiant stand sent four hundred corrupt souls back to Hell. He stood alone, not allowing aid from the one ally he had, for honor is not only won on the field of battle, but it exists in the nobility of the spirit as well. Four hundred souls returned to Hell that day; and handpicked tormentors ruthlessly abuse them. When the bringers of woe are asked why these souls are whipped with such disdain they only say one stood before them and would not fall.

* * *

The beleaguered Abraham Lincoln knew nothing of Leonidas' heroics, he was only aware of his own misery. He lay prone on the ground, vile images of the Nazi regime becoming part of his own experience. Hitler knew Lincoln was finished; it was only a matter of time before he succumbed and was transported to the prisons in Koba. The Fuhrer turned to engage other foes, unleashing his strength on the 54th.

As Lincoln quietly yielded to the frightful images Hitler forced into his being a voice from nowhere and everywhere caught his attention.

"This is not your way, Abraham. The time is come for you to rise up."

"Who?" Lincoln asked. "How could..."

"I am here as I always have been in your hours of trial." A hand swept aside a vision of Nazis burning a pile of bodies. The hand belonged to the one voice Abraham Lincoln could never ignore during his presidency; Frederick Douglass' majestic presence replaced the frightful images that tortured Lincoln.

"You are more than this, Abraham. Stand and make a full accounting of yourself."

"He is too powerful, Frederick. This soul..."

"This soul only wields a most familiar weapon. Hate, rage, bigotry. You have seen these, and overcome them, before."

"But never like this; never so focused. The depth of his depravity is much greater than that of Jefferson Davis."

"Perhaps," Douglass conceded. "But once you found resolve, you swept Jefferson Davis as if he were a sparrow battling the hurricane. Hitler is a greater foe, but forget not your own greatness."

Suddenly Lincoln's mind was flooded with the jubilee slaves exhibited when they learned of their freedom. The black soldiers who joined the Union and fought valiantly despite the discrimination they faced. The determination that led to the emancipation proclamation and the great speeches of his life called out from his core. The moments of weakness he always overcame as he steered his shattered country towards reunification and the legendary "new birth of freedom."

Lincoln witnessed Martin Luther King proclaiming his vision for America at the steps of the monument constructed in his honor, forever linking the civil rights movement and the great emancipator, for the threads of freedom run long from one great leader to the next. He saw a nation still struggling with ancient foes, longing for the resolve the sixteenth president personified And lastly, perhaps most importantly, he learned every man who died for his cause had long ago forgiven him, and wished he would forgive himself. Their voices called from everywhere, assuring him he had suffered enough. He had suffered enough, from the images he carried in his own mind, the guilt he could not dissipate and at the hand of this tyrant of Hell. No more, they shouted to him. No more!

"It is time to throw down the shackles of your mind, Abraham. Be the man of our redemption one last time."

With these words Douglass and the pain brought on by Hitler's assault faded to nothingness. Lincoln still lay on the ground, but felt unencumbered and indomitable. The marble and concrete used to construct the multitude of statues in Lincoln's honor were nothing but castles of sand compared to the conviction that coursed through his being.

Hitler witnessed Lincoln pull himself to his feet and fired a beam of flowing hate at him. "Back on your belly, bringer of justice," Hitler mocked as the bolt split the air.

Lincoln turned and caught the beam in his hand, rolling it into a small ball before dropping it to the ground.

"Your hour has come," Lincoln declared.

He wasted no more words on Hitler. Lincoln gathered his energies, his body glowed as the very air cracked around him. Bolt of lightning flew from his fingers descending upon the man who would wrap Limbo and Earth in an eternal nightmare. The bolts struck Hitler from all sides and he found all his viciousness availed him little before the strength of the man who stood before him.

"Let this end," Lincoln whispered as terror gripped the very core of Hitler's demented being. The ground opened and the minions of Hell called Hitler home. In his panicked mind, Hitler did not see tentacles and talons. He witnessed Russian soldiers coming for him, but no bunker in which to hide. No suicide to escape the vengeance of the people whose homeland he ravaged. A horrific scream split the air as the Red Army dragged him to a Russian peasant village. Final judgment, long delayed but impossible to deny, had come to Hitler.

Chapter 32
Cleansing a Party

John Tensler rode the elevator to the top floor of the Marriott in downtown San Antonio. The Democratic campaign team occupied the entire floor and William Casey had requested, demanded, five minutes with John before meeting the press that afternoon. Casey would leave the conference and head for Dallas as he traveled and campaigned for the huge state's electoral votes.

The hallway leading to Casey's room was flanked by security and buzzing with aides who scurried from room to room carrying reports and seeking clarification on every minute detail. The bustling atmosphere was commonplace to John Tensler, but still he felt uneasy. He was scheduled to meet Casey in Houston and was troubled with the abrupt, and very formal, summons.

Michelle Bele stood outside William Casey's room and greeted John politely.

John returned the salutation and raised his fist to knock on the door.

"Hold on, John," Michelle said. "William wanted five minutes before meeting with anyone. I will bring you in when the time is up."

John's anxiety increased, he could not recall the last occasion he had to wait for an audience with William. The elevator had felt less cramped than the hallway did at that moment. Michelle's disinterested silence only added to the uncomfortable mood.

Michelle checked her watch and announced William would see them now. She entered the room before John and sat in a cushioned chair in the corner of the room.

"Hello, William. Still trying to steal Texas?" John approached Casey a little too fast as he shook the candidate's hand.

"And here I thought I was trying to win the state," William replied. "I am meeting the press in five minutes. I have a few things to get off my chest before Eric Petrowski's exclusive goes live tomorrow."

"Eric? What's that wily veteran going to reveal—the secret to maintaining one's integrity while being an effective journalist."

"That is quite a feat," William said. "Almost as good as maintaining integrity while in politics."

John laughed nervously, but the tension in the room was not eased. William did not speak further, allowing the silence to augment his press secretary's anxiety. John spoke, seeking an answer to the question that had haunted him for the past twenty-four hours.

"Why am I here, William?"

"To be honest, I was going to ask you to resign. But a resignation often leads to speculation and the rumor mill has been running overtime long enough. I plan on meeting the press and informing them I fired you today because of your failure to report a crime."

"Crime? What are you…"

"Reckless endangerment. Kidnapping. These things ring a bell? Conspiracy. Don't worry I won't let you go down alone. I will mention Howard Halsworth's role and Eric will provide a much more detailed analysis in his piece."

"You can't do this!" John shouted. "If we go down you will come with us. Do you think anyone will believe I knew and you didn't?! We could make this work. You could still become President."

"I could still be President, you have that part right at least," William snarled. "As for my downfall being linked to you—I will take my chances. The bottom line is the only thing I could do wrong would be to willfully sit on this information. To choose to do nothing; to ignore the President's and your wrongdoing."

"Well, aren't you noble?" John sneered condescendingly. Michelle started to stand but William motioned her to remain calm. Michelle sat, taking out her cell phone.

"That's right, keep her in her place. You are just as power hungry as the rest of us! You think if you were in first place you would be doing this—no! You would be kissing my ass! I'm sorry we are pulling up the rear, William, but don't take out your frustrations by firing me. It's not my fault you are a weak candidate."

"Maybe I have been." William's calm tone was the polar opposite of John's angry rant. "Maybe I am a weak candidate, but I won't be a weak man or a mindless party guy on this one. We resent good cops who cover for bad ones. We long for good teachers to call out bad ones. And yet, we cover up our own for every indiscretion. Reassign people. Let them resign so their future in politics remains safe. Maybe we need to be stronger. To be the example we are looking for. To be the example for a nation to follow rather than a punch line. We've disgraced ourselves enough. Time to begin a new journey to freedom. I hope someday you join us."

Michelle put down the phone. Four armed guards entered the room, surrounding the still defiant John Tensler.

"You wouldn't do this if you were winning, William. It is easy to be carefree when you have nothing to loose. This is bigger than me! You are hurting the entire party!"

Those were the last words William would deign to hear from his former press secretary. John was escorted from the room by a security team. He was whisked into the hall and out to a car in the back of the building.

William sighed as the room emptied. In the quiet following the storm William wondered aloud, "Was he right? Would I have maintained my silence if I were leading this campaign? Maybe he was more right than I care to admit."

Michelle walked to the door, which was slightly ajar, and closed it.

"From my seat William, not just today, but throughout this campaign, I would say you should not let the ranting of a man seduced by power allow you to doubt the qualities of your heart. You're personal integrity would not change regardless of your position in the campaign."

"I don't know," William said, falling into a chair rather than sitting in it. "I just don't know."

Michelle's eyes gazed at some distant point, beyond the room and the space surrounding them. In an instant she was back, words flowing without fear.

"I have always been amazed by Robert Frost's poem 'The Road Not Taken'," she said thoughtfully. William looked up at her, but chose not to speak.

"In the poem the character sighs and we are never told why. I wonder, was it the sigh of a man who chose a difficult path and was sighing out his frustration, or the sigh of a man who has accomplished some great feat and was recalling, with some joy, the accomplishment? Can we ever know for sure, in our own lives, when the one replaces the other?"

William listened carefully to Michelle's words of encouragement, hoping, over time, they would replace the spiteful words of John Tensler, which were still ringing in his ears.

"John was right about one thing," Michelle added. "This problem was bigger than him. You may be the man we need to cleanse the party of like minded individuals."

"I doubt I could perform that task alone. Surrounded by the right people…who knows what we could accomplish?" William said with a smile as he stood and followed Michelle out of the room towards the historic press conference.

Chapter 33
Loss of Power, Claiming Pride

Eric Petrowski's exposé in the *Washington Post* turned the political world, and President Blaylock's entire life, upside down. The commander-in-chief willfully placed a young child in a dire situation, needlessly risked the lives of American soldiers and offered aid to a revolutionary leader all for the single purpose of maintaining his office. Prominent members of the rival party, upon hearing of the scheme, voluntarily hid the information. These men showed no concern for the lives disrupted, taken and threatened by the malicious actions of the President. They only set their eyes on what they could gain from the fallout. They may as well have arranged some abhorrent plot themselves.

President Blaylock stood in the Oval Office, for what he knew would be his last day as the head of state. There was no ship that would enable him to ride out the savagery of this storm. He stared blankly out the window behind him, not turning to greet Maxwell as he entered the office to present him with resignation papers.

"This is the only way, sir."

"Is it, Max? Is there no other path? No one was hurt, no one…"

"Mr. President," Maxwell said strongly, not wanting to hear any rationalizing or justifications. "Many people were hurt. And five of the Self-Determination Party's security team were killed. This office was hurt. People's dwindling faith in government was reinforced. Believe what you like, but don't tell me no one was hurt. We are surrounded by pain. And you will take the first step to make it right."

"This is why you were never involved in this Max. You lack foresight. You would have spilled this the moment you found out, but we hid it from you, for the nations own good."

"So you were helping the nation?" Maxwell asked despite himself.

"Yes! Yes, God damn it! You think the S.D.P or Democrats can help this country? We need a Republican in here. We need a strong Russia to do that which this nation, inhabited and run by cowards are afraid to do. That's right, Max. Don't pretend you do not agree. Terrorists keep coming and we chase them like a child trying to catch sunbeams. A strong Russia, run by a man like Karensky can do things to hunt down terrorists that we could never do. Hide on holy ground? Respect the sovereignty of a nation harboring their enemies? You know none of those thing would stop Karensky. Terrorists would understand terror and Russia would become the only ally we needed. Their resources combined with our technology and wealth would enable the creation of a terror free world. Europe doesn't agree? The U.N. doesn't approve? Fuck 'em both. We need power and progress not anachronisms, outdated allegiance and useless institutions. And now, I am disgraced because a throw back journalist would not stop searching for his Pulitzer Prize!?"

Maxwell listened the best he could, but all he heard were the words of a madman. He would never know when this scheme was conceived and put in motion, nor did he care to. All he wanted was President Blaylock out of the White House and into whatever court tried criminals of this magnitude.

"Don't blame Eric too much, Mr. President. He may have lost the story's scent had I not leaked information to the press."

President Blaylock looked ready to lunge over his desk. The presence of uniformed soldiers were all that kept him at bay.

"Bastard!" He snapped. "You've done this!"

"No, sir! You've done this. I merely condemn it. You were right, the moment I heard about this I let some information out, hoping fear would cause you to rethink your position. But you have been sending aid to Karensky anyway, how else would he be making such progress in Russia? You would not take a backward step. If William Casey had not come forward with Eric Petrowski I was going to do so. This is not how things are supposed to be."

"And you know how they are meant to be? Idealistic fool. You will be no hero, every staff member will be guilty by association, and your career is over. Your reputation destroyed. You have nothing."

Maxwell weighed the President's words carefully and handed the resignation papers to a soldier. "No, Kevin. You have nothing and I will find my way, as will this nation. The papers you need to sign are in his possession. The signing will be televised at ten A.M. Until then, these men are to keep you constantly in sight. After the signing they will take you, somewhere. I do not even know where. Nor do I care, so long as you are no longer desecrating this room."

Maxwell exited the Oval Office for the last time as Kevin Blaylock's Chief of Staff. He would stay on when Vice-President Ward took office, although he knew the Republicans could not possibly win in November now. He also decided he would not watch President Blaylock's telecast from the Oval Office. The conclusion he needed had already occurred; signing papers to make it official seemed trite.

Chapter 34
Post War Activity

Niccolo and Marshal Zhukov walked the streets of Tylferling, assessing the damage to the huts and homes of the city. The structures would be rebuilt easily as most of the damage was superficial. Niccolo was still amazed, as was Zhukov, at the neatness that followed a battle in Limbo, as all fallen combatants are transported elsewhere, leaving no bodies to clean up or count. The lack of visible carnage did not alter the need to estimate the number of P.O.W's they would have to rescue from Nafarhel, and the one they would have to rescue from Hell.

"This victory has not brought us rest," Zhukov stated. "Thirty five hundred captives are in need of rescue. Not counting your friend in Hell."

"My friend in Hell," Niccolo repeated, the sadness of his voice failing to mute his determination. "How does one descend to Hell and bring back a soul?"

"I do not know, comrade. But I do know if I were held captive in the pit I would be comforted knowing you were the one searching for me."

"Shouldn't I aid in the liberating of those souls held in Limbo first?"

"Your heart would not be in such an adventure. Go and tend to your friend. We have resources without you. Go to the city of Heliotrus in the heart of Valdar. You will find aid there."

Niccolo thought for a second, then his face portrayed his understanding. "Provided he has not ascended"

Zhukov looked skeptically at Niccolo. "Do you think he has ascended?"

"No," Niccolo said through a small laugh. "He is here, talking so much to some soul as to make the fool wish he chose reincarnation."

"Your battle plan was impeccable, Marshal Zhukov. None could have defended Tylferling better."

"And your skills were awesome to behold," Zhukov responded with great sincerity. His admiration was tampered as he voiced a grim warning. "Be careful. The adventure you embark on will surly test you to your very limits."

Niccolo shook hands with the Russian and went to sit with Jon. He would take the boy with him to Heliotrus, with the intent of leaving him there. Of course convincing Jon not to join him in the rescuing of Seamus could well be more difficult than the mission itself.

* * *

Abraham Lincoln stood alone in the center of Mashada, having thanked Robert Shaw and his men for their service yet again. The Spartans faded like an illusion the moment the last foe fell. Leonidas was nowhere to be seen, but Lincoln assumed he joined the rest of his men in Heaven. Joseph waved from the hilltop and disappeared over its crest, no doubt returning to Tylferling. Lincoln decided he too should journey back, if only to see how Niccolo and Seamus fared. He also wondered if Jon had fought or, as Niccolo wished, was sent to the safety of Mylganst.

Before he could begin his solo expedition, Lincoln witnessed a portal open in the sky above him. The tranquility of Heaven washed over him, causing the town and hills to fade from awareness. He instantly recognized the figure striding towards him.

"Frederick, my friend."

"Abraham," the great civil rights leader said with a smile. "I am glad you are well."

"I would not be without your assistance….and that of Colonel Shaw."

"Gould Shaw did indeed come to your side, for he had volunteered for the duty when trouble first began. But I was not present. Battles are not my forte"

Lincoln gawked unintelligibly at his friend. He thought to pursue the matter but, standing in the radiance of Heaven, he concluded sometimes logic can't explain everything. Some piece of Frederick Douglass was on the battlefield, that was all Lincoln needed to know.

"Are you here to guide me to Heaven?"

"Indeed, but you cannot bring your burdens."

"I know this, Frederick. And I know the men who died on my orders and have passed to Heaven bear me no ill will."

"Few of them did, Abraham. The rage you saw in them was your own angst, misplaced and conspiring against you."

"I am done now, I know I am forgiven, by myself and by those whom I assumed held malice for me. Let us be off."

"Not yet, you have one more weight to unload."

Lincoln stood in stunned silence before allowing his greatest grief to come forth.

"Mary?" Lincoln said sadly. "Does she forgive as well?"

"Much quicker and more readily than you ever did yourself," Frederick said in comforting tones.

"But she suffered so much because of me. The Civil War always took precedence over her, even when she was in pain. Her name was always connected to some outlandish scandal, some labeled her a spy, others a country tramp. Then Willie died in the middle of the war. I tried to comfort her, but the war always pulled me away. A mother grieves for her twelve-year old son and her husband is only good for part time comfort. There is much more, and still you say she forgives."

"Indeed she has, just as you absolve her for her faults. Do you think you are capable of exonerating another, yet they cannot do the same? Such arrogance, Mr. President. It does not become you."

Lincoln listened intently, but still felt doubt. "Even when the war ended and we were free of its shadow we had no time. She sat beside me as I was shot. The war that divided us took our future, our chance for reconciliation. How much should one woman endure? Neglect. Death. Tragedy."

"These things separated you on Earth, but eternity's timetable, as you are well aware, moves differently. She forgives you. Lay down your burden and follow me to her. Let the past wash away and your spiritual lives together begin."

Lincoln, as was his custom, considered these words carefully. As he did so he noticed something was lacking. The venom with which he poisoned himself could not be found anywhere within his being. Smiling broadly he laughed at the spectacle of his own foibles. Eyes glistening he spoke for the last time as a resident of Limbo.

"Take me to her, Frederick,".

"I shall, my good friend. You have earned your rest."

Mashada was now a ghost town, although souls that would settle the area after the great upheaval swore a peace radiated from the land, bringing serenity to the residents in a manner unlike any other place in Limbo.

* * *

The conclusion of the raging battles in Tylferling and Mashada did not bring peace to Troothgnase and Galiktus. Hitler's defeat in Mashada sent shockwaves of uncertainty throughout the new Reich. Himmler had escaped Tylferling and fled with fifty Nazis into the Kadistie Mountains. The small band returned to Troothgnase, vowing to regroup and attack again. Hell could provide an unlimited supply of desperadoes to refill their ranks. Success in a single battle does not make for victory in wars.

Any hope these beasts felt was dashed as they entered Troothgnase. They were met by the intimidating visage of Ivan the Terrible, recently freed from Hell to perform the bidding of Stalin. Ivan's elite guard descended wordlessly on the vagabonds, for a lion would not mix words with a zebra.

Stalin's military also overran Galiktus. Reinhard Heydrich and his small force were focused on preventing the anticipated invasion from the sentinels of Limbo stationed in Valdor. They were ill prepared for the brutality Attila the Hun brought to them. The warlord descended on Galiktus with the anger only a soul that resided in Hell for two thousand years could hold. His newfound liberty was bound to his ability to carry out Stalin's instructions, and Attila would do much to remain free.

As Hitler's influence in Limbo waned, Stalin's wicked star rose unabated into the Heavens. He knew the forces of Limbo would not let the captives Hitler provided languish indefinitely in his Gulags. They would come to liberate them, expanding their forces and weakening their resistance. Stalin needed only to wait. Unlike Hitler, he did not need to charge at the enemy, the enemy would come to him, bringing the keys to two worlds with them.

Chapter 35
Like Nothing We've Ever Experienced

Drew McClure stood on the steps in front of the Self Determination Party's headquarters preparing to answer another wave of questions. He anxiously looked at his watch and considered the litany of places he would rather be at the moment. Eric Petrowski's investigative article and President Blaylock's resignation made it impossible for either candidate to move without being lost in an avalanche of media.

"Hello again, everyone," he called from his slightly elevated position. Twelve concrete steps led to the building's main entrance and Drew stood on the eighth stair. "I cannot be late for my eight o'clock phone call to Erin, so let's get started.

"How does it feel to be the front runner yet again?"

"Fine, but as I have said all along—it matters much more to be first in November, not mid-October."

"Are you at all surprised William Casey is a mere three percentage points behind you?"

"Why would I be? William has proven to be a man of great integrity and resilience, exactly what this country needs. The fact his actions have garnered him support does not shock me at all."

"Mr. McClure, do you realize your words almost sound like an endorsement of William Casey?"

"So I should lie and not state what I admire about his character?"

Brian Murphy sensed trouble and pointed to the next questioner. "Mr. La…"

"You hold on," Drew stated angrily. "My question hasn't been answered. Do you want me to lie?"

No response was forthcoming.

"Do you want more lies coming from your politicians?" Drew demanded. "I can tell by your sheepish expression you don't. Then why castigate me for honesty? How did you get in the front row? Brian get his name. Next!"

Brian Murphy stood placidly behind his friend and candidate; pleased he was back and wishing he weren't.

"You have yet to speak out against the Republicans for their role in bringing such misery to you and your family. What would you say now?"

"It would be very easy for me to lambaste the entire Republican Party. Blame them all for the actions of Kevin Blaylock, but that would not be fair. I will admit there are times when I want to categorize them all as charlatans and manipulators. Whenever I feel that way, I think of Maxwell Grahm. He was nothing but supportive in his role as liaison between the White House and my family throughout our trials. He represents the best that party has to offer, so I cannot condemn the party as whole, for I will not condemn Maxwell and the other Republicans like him."

"With three weeks before election day, and no clear favorite in sight, are you at all nervous about the recently scheduled debate?"

"I am worried that President Ward may surge into the lead." Drew looked at his feet, wondering why he felt the desire to kick a good man placed in an impossible situation.

"Sorry. That was a cheap shot. President Ward deserves much better than that. He deserves me shutting-up for the rest of the day so, you will excuse me, I have to go make my phone call. As for nervousness about the debates—when have I ever given you the impression I didn't look forward to the exchange of ideas? Goodnight all!"

Drew waved to the press and trotted up the remaining stairs, Brian Murphy on his hip.

"Had to chastise a reporter from the *Post*. Couldn't just answer the guy's question. Sometimes your bullshit wears thin, you know."

Drew looked at his campaign manager and smiled, "Yea, but it has been weeks since I did that. You were getting bored without my outbursts. I don't want the campaign to get boring for you."

"Thanks for looking out for me," Brian said through a humorless smile. "As always, I appreciate it. The last question raised a good point. Three weeks, no clear-cut leader. No favorite. What does the future hold?" Brian pulled the heavy glass door open and ushered Drew inside. As Drew crossed the threshold, he paused to answer Brian's question.

"I'm not sure, but it will be like nothing either of us has ever experienced."

About the Author

James Rourke teaches history and psychology at the Norwich Free Academy in Norwich, Connecticut. *The Eternal Struggle: Two Worlds, One War* is his first work of fiction and the first book of The Eternal Struggle trilogy. He is the author of two non-fiction titles, *From my Classroom to Yours* and *The Comic Book Curriculum*.

James lives in Connecticut with his wife, Shannon and their four children; Juliana, Logan, Alice-Ann and Ray. Two dogs, two cats, two guinea pigs and a degu also find space to live in their home.

Rourke is online at both www.jamesrourke.com and Facebook. Messages can be sent to James through his website and he monitors and posts on the James Rourke—writer Facebook page. He is very happy to discuss his books and writing with readers and fans so feel free to visit his sites.

Visit James at www.jamesrourke.com.
And on Facebook under James Rourke-writer
http://www.facebook.com/pages/James-Rourke-Writer/177519105613268?v=wall

CPSIA information can be obtained at www.ICGtesting.com

234258LV00002B/60/P